Every woman looks better on a Mediterranean island. . . .

In a Victorian novel I'd be the plain sister, but there's no such thing as a plain woman anymore. It's too bad really; there must have been a certain comfort in not being beautiful, a sort of restful anonymity that gave you the space to develop your mind, like the Brontë sisters, or Jane Austen. Today if you don't look good it's your own fault, for not exercising or making more of yourself, all of which I do sedulously. I am trim and athletic and even chic in a nonthreatening American way. Why, then, did it take me so long to find a boyfriend? Based on the mating behavior I have observed around me, I've come to the conclusion that it's more an indictment of my character than of my looks.

"An absolutely enchanting and delectable read. The sisters in Megan McAndrew's tale are delightful creatures who bare their inner hopes and desires, and sometimes more."

—Clive Cussler,
New York Times bestselling author

"If Jane Austen and Jacques Tati collaborated, they may have produced a novel as lively, insightful and lavishly entertaining as Megan McAndrew's *Going Topless.*"

—Avodah K. Offit, M.D.,
author of *Virtual Love*

Going Topless

Megan McAndrew

doWn tOwn press

New York   London   Toronto   Sydney

An *Original* Publication of POCKET BOOKS

A Downtown Press Book published by
POCKET BOOKS, a division of Simon & Schuster, Inc.
1230 Avenue of the Americas, New York, NY 10020

Library of Congress Cataloging-in-Publication Data

McAndrew, Megan.
   Going topless / Megan McAndrew.—1st Downtown Press trade pbk. ed."
    p. cm.
   ISBN 0-7434-7724-3
    1. Americans—France—Fiction. 2. Family reunions—Fiction. 3. Women—
   France—Fiction.
   4. Stepfamilies—Fiction. 5. Islands—Fiction. 6. Sisters—Fiction. 7. France—
   Fiction. I. Title.

   PS3613.C2655G65 2004
   813'.6—dc22

                     2004044286

First Downtown Press trade paperback edition June 2004

10 9 8 7 6 5 4 3 2 1

DOWNTOWN PRESS and colophon are
trademarks of Simon & Schuster, Inc.

Manufactured in the United States of America

Designed by Jaime Putorti

For information regarding special discounts for bulk purchases,
please contact Simon & Schuster Special Sales at 1-800-456-6798
or business@simonandschuster.com.

For Bill

CHAPTER *one*

We're here on vacation, though leisure was the last thing on the minds of the Genoese warlords who settled Santerre, hewing their towns and villages out of the mountainside into the flinty strongholds that I point out to Jim as we hurtle along the coastal road that hugs the *cap*. I've made the trip from the airport so often that I've come to enjoy the hairpin turns, the vertiginous drops into the winking sea, the sharp intake of breath as an insane native comes careening around the bend in a beat-up Peugeot, honking too late in warning. The same can't be said for Jim, who stares fixedly ahead, missing all the scenery. By the time we reach the town of Orzo, he has grown unnaturally quiet, his unease betrayed by the overly casual tone in which he asks, "Why are all the road signs painted over?"

"Nationalists," I cheerfully reply.

"Pardon me?"

I swerve to avoid the mournful cow that appears in the middle of the road after the next turn. "They drive around at night with paintbrushes."

"I don't get it."

Sometimes I forget that what passes for local color on Santerre would be viewed by most people as criminal behavior, just as I don't notice anymore the lurid slashes that deface the island's road signs. "Resistance to French cultural imperialism. They blow stuff up too."

"Yeah, right," Jim says wanly.

"Honest," I say, motioning to the charred hulk that once housed the administration of Orzo's defunct asbestos mine, though no one knows for sure how the building reached its present state. Jim, however, is by now entirely focused on not throwing up. Watching him stagger out of the rental car, I can't help but feel a little guilty. Poor Jim: I doubt this was what he had in mind when I proposed a French holiday.

At first sight, the village of Borgolano presents none of the standard Mediterranean charms, especially at dusk, when it takes on a frankly lugubrious aspect, with its tall shuttered houses deep in gloom. Like all Santerran villages, it is carved out of the rock that surrounds it, its four levels connected by a maze of alleys and steep stone stairs patrolled by feral cats, a mangy specimen of which slinks by as we unload our bags. "Where's the beach?" Jim asks, having regained his equilibrium, and I point down, far, far below, to the rocky inlet where sea urchins and jellyfish lie in wait.

Our wheeled cases bumping behind us, we set off down the path, past the Benoîts' and the Paolis', the Perettis' gated compound, and the old Albertoni place, its crumbling stucco baring the stacked stone slabs beneath, until we reach the last bend before the cliff. And there, in the gloaming, awash in purple shadows, rises my family's summer house, the great black oak door flung open to reveal Odette waving in the embrasure.

"*Alors,* did you have a nice trip?"

Odette used to be a stewardess, and she has retained from those days a brisk social efficiency that I've always found disconcerting but seems to put men at ease. It works on Jim; having ushered us in and installed him in the comfortable chair, she sets about plying him with *apéritifs* and solicitous chatter, all the while dutifully showcasing me with questions about my exciting life in New York City and my terribly *glamorous* and *important* job, the unglamorous nature of which Jim is well acquainted with, since he works with me. I suppose Odette sees this kind of thing as a maternal duty, even though by the time Ross married her I was too old to require a stepmother.

She's done some decorating since I was last here: Lace curtains hang in the windows and a flowered slipcover has been thrown over the couch. Still, the *salon,* as Odette wishfully calls the big common area on the ground floor, with its refectory table and the picture of General Marconi—the only local figure ever to have achieved international celebrity, in the eighteenth century— betrays the fact that Ross was already broke when they moved in.

"*Tiens,*" she now says, "do you know that we had a *cambrio-lage?*"

"The house was broken into?"

"Yes, but it is very strange: They took nothing."

"It was probably just kids," I say, "looking for a place to party."

Odette frowns. "I had the lock changed nonetheless."

"They'll just find another way in," I say, glancing at the windows. In daylight they look out on the Mediterranean, but now all you can see is an inky black void.

"So," Odette says when we have finished our drinks, "what room will you take?"

I've been waiting for this.

"The yellow room," I drop casually, as if it were the most natural thing in the world—which it isn't, because the yellow room is the best in the house after Isabelle's, with the firmest mattress and a sea view, and mine to grab since I got here first (before Lucy, that is, who regards it as her birthright). Odette raises an eyebrow but says nothing. With a profound feeling of triumph, I lead the way up, cautioning Jim about the hole in the stairs and showing him the (only) bathroom on the landing. I tell him the house is three hundred years old and used to belong to a pirate, and he says, "Cool."

While we are unpacking—Jim now rather giddy after two glasses of wine and, I can tell from the way he brushes against me, planning on sex tonight—I hear voices downstairs, strange since no one else is due until tomorrow. I assume it's Madame Benoît, with whom Odette is friendly in the way the French are, which means that after five years they've moved beyond stiff *bonjours* on the road to discussions of the weather and finally, last summer, joint outrage at the cacophonous renovation of the Paoli's house, undertaken in July! When I go back down, though, I find not Madame Benoît but a slim, dark-haired Frenchman whom Odette introduces as Yves. An old friend, she explains. He is staying in the attic room, the one no one ever uses because it gets too hot. This Yves, it turns out, on top of being a nervous smoker, speaks good English—he's some kind of schoolteacher in Paris—so that when Jim comes down to join us, they shake hands and embark on a conversation about the World Cup. For lack of anything better to do, I follow Odette into the kitchen.

Here, too, improvements have been made: A red and white checked curtain blocks the view of the ruin across the way—one of Borgolano's many abandoned properties—and a new light illuminates the stone sink. It's been Odette's long-standing dream to put in new appliances, but for now she's still making do with the original fixtures. Odette takes great pride in her adaptability: As she has often pointed out, if you can cook in a galley you can cook anywhere. Since there are men in the house, she is making a sybaritic feast of lamb in a wine and garlic sauce and even, I notice on the sideboard, cheese and a peach tart.

"*Eh bien,*" she says conspiratorially, "he seems very nice this Jeem, very *présentable.*" She lifts the lid off the stew and gives it a brisk stir, then adds a pinch of salt. It's always amazed me how Odette can cook entirely by smell, undoubtedly the reason she remains a size two despite being nearly fifty.

"Well," I say, chewing on an olive, "he's an investment banker: He *has* to be presentable."

"*Ah, bon,*" murmurs Odette, who has a healthy respect for power and position and, I can see, is wondering how I managed with my meager charms to snare this prime piece of eligible manhood. I should mention that Jim is good-looking in the square-jawed Brooks Brothers way that appears to be a requisite for a career in corporate finance. Meanwhile, I am wondering exactly what kind of old friend this Yves is. Ross died less than a year ago and Yves seems a bit young for her, not to mention slightly prissy in his ironed jeans and navy blue polo shirt. An odd choice, you would think, after having been married to a dead ringer for Lee

Marvin. But Odette doesn't want to talk about Yves, or me, or even her late husband, my father. Now that she's acquitted herself of her stepmotherly duties, her eyes take on the haunted cast that heralds a discussion of what really interests her: the dissolution of my sister Isabelle's marriage to the famous Czech dissident poet and philanderer Jiri Orlik.

"Alors . . . how does she seem?" she asks, for I am the last one to have seen Isabelle, my former job as an analyst in the emerging markets division of Grohman Brothers having taken me twice to Prague this year.

"The same. It'll take more than a divorce to knock Isabelle down," I reply, helping myself to a gooey wedge of Camembert. Odette, who subscribes to the French canon that cheese is strictly *après*-dinner, winces. If she could get you into a corner, she would tell you that I am *difficile,* that she sometimes even finds it hard to believe that Isabelle and I are related.

"Ah, Constance, you don't know what divorce does to a woman," she says, making me wonder how she's so sure since, as far as I know, she's only been married to my father. "And to have to endure it in public!" she adds, for the whole debacle about Jiri abandoning his wife and two daughters for an eighteen-year-old starlet was played out in all the tabloids, since the Czechs take a far greater interest in intellectuals than we do in America. Isabelle even sent me one paper, called *Halo,* with a picture of Isabelle in a bikini on the cover under the caption, ORLIK DUMPS AMERICAN WIFE!

"If you want my opinion," I offer, chomping on another olive, "Jiri is a jerk and she's well rid of him."

She shoots me one of her *How can you be so heartless?* looks. Poor Odette: I can't say she hasn't tried hard. It's not her fault that, unlike Isabelle, I didn't need her ministrations. To placate her, I throw her a bone. "So, when are Lucy and Jane arriving?"

It always works: Her preternaturally smooth (collagen injections) brow relaxes as the one bond we share takes hold. Lucy, she informs me with the faintest moue, is arriving from London tomorrow.

CHAPTER *two*

Jim and I did fuck last night, and again this morning, and when I fling open the shutters, the Mediterranean glitters in the early light and he finally gets why we've come all this way. At this time of day, the mountains beyond the Gulf of Flore are dark blue. Jim wonders if we can go hiking. I tell him better not, we might get shot at, to which he replies, "You're so weird, Connie."

Jim is from Kansas. He is universally considered to be a good guy, the kind of person who is friends with everybody and never seeks out conflict. Don't think I haven't wondered what he sees in me, though it's not like he's proposed marriage or anything. I have a theory that most relationships arise out of convenience. Well, I have all sorts of theories, but the fact is, I finally have a boyfriend, and you might be forgiven for thinking I've hauled him all the way over here to show him off.

Yves has been out already for the flaccid bread and croissants that are delivered daily by truck to Madame Peretti's shop. Though technically in France, Santerre is no gourmet paradise. The biggest specialties are a kind of sheep's cheese called *ortu* and various rock-hard cured meats that all taste like beef jerky, all of which are vigorously marketed to tourists as *produits locaux*. It seems amazing that neither French nor Italian cuisine has rubbed off, considering the island's geographical position, but Santerrans have never set much store by pleasant bourgeois sensibilities, so why should they make an exception for food? The deficient local products are a pet peeve, incidentally, of my dear stepsister Lucy, who, on top of being an expert on Italian baroque painting, is also a gourmet cook.

We're just finishing breakfast, throughout which Yves holds forth in great detail on the geological features of Santerre (layers of schist), making me wonder if he's perhaps a geography teacher, when something makes me look over my shoulder. Standing in the kitchen doorway is a gigantic little girl of about four, with that stunned look all fat kids seem to have, as if they couldn't figure out why it had to be them.

"Hi there," Jim says.

She stares wordlessly back. She's wearing a sprigged dress that makes her look even huger and clutching a bedraggled toy rabbit by the ear. Hurried footsteps sound in the pathway, followed by a familiar voice, of the defiantly *Upstairs Downstairs* variety that English people get when they've lived in America for too long, except that it's yelling, which kind of ruins the *Masterpiece Theater* effect: "Electra! How many times have I told you not to wander off!"

No wonder the kid looks familiar. Lucy comes flying through the door and grabs her by the arm with a murderous expression I know well. She looks like she's about to smack her until she remembers she has an audience: us, all watching the scene bemusedly—especially me and Odette, who I know is thinking the same thing I am: *When did Electra put on all that weight?*

"She does this all the time!" Lucy exclaims in exasperation, letting go.

More bumping luggage and voices. "Have you found her?" Richard, Lucy's husband, appears, followed by Jane, whom I run up to and hug. Remembering my manners, I peck Lucy and Richard on the cheek and even lean down and pat Electra on the head. I'm not very good with children unless they have a personality, which most don't seem to. Odette clicks around on her little heels and dispenses air kisses while marveling in the artificial voice she always adopts with my stepsisters at the earliness of their arrival: They must have gotten in at five in the morning!

Jane drops into a chair and pours herself a cup of coffee. "Mmm, heaven: real French coffee! They served us some kind of swill on the plane, little plastic cups with toss-away filters." Jane has a way of putting people at ease; all of a sudden we're all laughing and chattering, until little Electra reaches for an abandoned *pain au chocolat* on the table. Like a hawk, Lucy swoops down and snatches it from her, setting off a bloodcurdling shriek.

"For God's sake, Lucy," Jane says. "She hasn't had any breakfast."

Dagger look from Lucy, who snaps, "She's on a diet." Then, turning to the still-howling Electra, "Mummy will make you some Weetabix, darling. Richard, where is my blue bag?"

A frantic search ensues while Electra continues to howl. Her face has turned bright red and bubbles of snot pop out of her nostrils. She looks like she's going to have a seizure. "Lucy, just let her have it," Jane coaxes. "One croissant isn't going to hurt her."

Defeated, Lucy hands the now squished-up mess back to Electra, but it's too late: She just goes on screaming. Richard says through clenched teeth, "I'm going to take her outside." Nobody objects. He picks her up and drags her off as she flails and sobs with rage, and we all sit there, stunned, until Odette says briskly, *"Eh bien,* shall I make another pot of coffee?"

We can still hear Electra's howls, coming from outside. Lucy has collapsed in a chair and is wearing an expression of profound martyrdom that doesn't really go with her sleek bourgeois-bohemian Kensington look—one that relies heavily, I find, on composure. Jim and Yves are appraising her with the fearful admiration that five-foot-ten blondes with cantilevered cheekbones tend to inspire in mere mortals. Perhaps this is why she presently gathers herself together and announces, "Well, then, I think I'll take my bag upstairs." Jim and Yves leap up to help (highly uncharacteristic gallantry on Jim's part: He may be a nice guy but he's not exactly Prince Charles) and have gathered up the luggage when Odette lets drop, with childlike innocence, "Jeem and Constance are in the yellow room, but the whole third floor is free."

Lucy turns majestically around. One eyebrow rises—a neat trick, I've always found. "I beg your pardon?"

All of a sudden I feel like a cretin. But then, Lucy has always made me feel like a cretin, so I have to wonder why I'm even surprised.

CHAPTER *three*

Jane heads up to the third floor, which, until I upset the apple cart, was where the mateless dwelled. There's no bathroom up there and the mattresses are lumpy. The walls are thinner, too, and a mere curtain separates the connecting rooms that Jane and I usually occupy. I feel a twinge of regret now as I realize that, by my defection downstairs, I am relinquishing the pleasure of late-night chats with her. Not that I'm planning to budge.

I've always been close to Jane, closer in a way than I am to Isabelle, if for no other reason than that we both know what it's like to live in the shadow of a beautiful sister. She and Lucy moved in with us when I was six, after Ross married their mother, Daphne. Our own mother, Vera, had died of cancer two years earlier. We'd lived in Paris until then, where she had a ballet studio on the Rue Vavin. After her death, Ross couldn't bear the memories, so he moved us back to the States. Two years later he met Daphne at an art auction in London.

I didn't mind Daphne. I was too young when Vera died to have anything but the haziest memories of her, but Isabelle, who was fourteen, was bereft. In New York she papered her walls with stills from Vera's days as a ballerina, losing no opportunity to reminisce about her, especially when Daphne was in the room. I used to think she got away with it because she was Ross's favorite, but in fact, I'm not sure he even cared. Ross was never in love with Daphne: He'd married her in a moment of weakness, still reeling from the loss of Vera. I think that Lucy sensed this and that this is why she set out to seduce him, as if she could somehow get him to love her mother by proxy.

In her zeal, though, she tried to unseat Isabelle. Jane and I watched bemusedly from the sidelines as the two of them went at each other, knowing all the while that Lucy was doomed to failure, for my sister has something that Lucy never will: a combination of wacky charm and restive pheromones that appear to make her irresistible. Why will be a matter for the history books: Like Josephine with her rotten teeth, Isabelle is more than the sum of her parts. She's not that smart—she barely got into Bennington, and then only by sleeping with her high school drama teacher—nor clever; and while she unquestionably has a spectacular pair of knockers, her nose is crooked and her butt is too big. But none of these defects have mattered a bit to the droves of men who have grown besotted with her, our father included. Poor Lucy, it must have driven her crazy: There she was, blondly perfect, top of her class at Brearley, admitted early to both Yale and Harvard and, in due course, winner of the Rome Prize, and who got the attention? Lazy, slatternly Isabelle, who got thrown out of Saint Anne's for smoking dope.

And who everyone said was the spitting image of our mother.

Daphne never had a chance. From the beginning, Ross seemed more in awe of her than anything else. My father didn't come from money—I'm not sure he even finished high school—and all his life he was dazzled by the world of art and culture that Daphne represented. Not only was she a Sotheby's expert on French Impressionism, she was (extremely remotely) related to Vita Sackville-West. But Ross was a commodities trader at heart. Daphne couldn't handle his cowboy side, and in the end she bored him.

The sad thing is, she never stopped loving him. I'm afraid Ross had that effect on women: They disconnected common sense in his presence. So they hobbled along for five years—a happy time for Jane and me, who were under the care of a nice Irish housekeeper called Bridie, but a Calvary for Lucy, who took it all personally. When Ross and Daphne finally split up, she was devastated, all the more so as the rest of us barely noticed. It wasn't until a good two years later that he met Odette, on an airplane, but the way Lucy carried on, you'd think she had lured him straight out of Daphne's bed.

And so, here we are—or most of us, at least. I follow Jane up under the pretext of helping with her bags but really to apologize for deserting her and gloat a bit about my incursion into the blessed regions below—which, naturally, she picks right up on.

"Making mischief, little sister?"

Through the wall we hear Lucy snapping at Richard to open the window. Thumping sounds follow.

"There goes *their* sex life for the next month," I remark. It's a long-standing joke that no one but a crass exhibitionist would attempt sexual intercourse on the third floor, Isabelle being the only one to have ever tried.

"Whereas yours, I gather, will be flourishing," Jane says with amusement.

"So, what do you think of him?" I say. I don't really care about anyone else's opinion but Jane has a sixth sense, which probably explains why she became an artist, and an awfully successful one too. She paints gorgeous, voluptuous pictures of naked ladies that people actually buy—I own one myself—and shows at one of the top galleries in London.

"Nice. Very *sportif.*"

I sit on the floor, my back against the wall, and watch her unpack. Jane doesn't look at all like her sister. While Lucy is all angles, Jane is big and soft and messy, her hair perpetually escaping from the various ineffectual clips with which she tries to hold it back. I was the first to figure out that she was gay. Jane isn't the kind of person who comes out to people, but the clues were obvious if you were paying attention, which no one else was. Daphne thought all those girls with crew cuts and hairy legs that Jane hung out with in college were female athletes, even though Jane has never shown the slightest interest in sports, and both Lucy and Isabelle were too self-involved to see anything beyond the tips of their noses. As for Ross, I think the concept was just too foreign.

"He's obviously boosted your standing with Odette," Jane adds, and I feel a surge of love for her, because she at least is not going to make a big deal about my finally landing a man. Jane never makes a big deal out of anything—not even Odette, who is single-handedly responsible for one of the more tragicomical crises in our family history, the one that resulted in Jane's girlfriend Marge refusing to ever set foot in Borgolano again. On her first and only visit, Marge did not take well to being relegated to the third floor while all the straight couples got the good rooms downstairs. Her dark mutterings about the heterocracy, however, were completely lost on Odette, who finally cooked her goose by exclaiming at the dinner table, in response to Marge's accusation that she didn't consider gay people to be normal, *"Mais enfin,* you are not normal! Normal is a man and a woman!"* Jane has come alone ever since, compromising by only staying for ten days.

Next door, a wrenching sound followed by a furious "You bloody idiot!" suggests that Richard has succeeded in opening the window, and breaking it. Jane and I glance at each other.

"What's going on with Electra?" I ask in an offhand way. Last summer, the Delicate Topic was the fact that Electra, then age three, hadn't started speaking yet. Lucy put her in some kind of special therapy but, based on the scene in the kitchen, it doesn't seem to be working too well. You have to wonder if it was such a great idea to saddle the child with a pretentious ancient Greek name, especially considering this latest development.

"What do you mean?" Jane says.

"I've never seen a four-year-old pitch a fit like that."

Jane, who is piling up T-shirts in the cupboard, shakes her head with irritation. "She was hungry. You'd be raving, too, if you were starved."

We are, I see, going to tiptoe around the fact that Electra looks like a blimp. Jane doesn't have many hot buttons but this is a big one, eating disorders being something of a *spécialité de la maison.* The fact is, you can't look like Daphne or Lucy without interfering with your bodily functions, and no one knows this better than Jane, who's always struggled with her weight. I am saved from the temptation of further commentary, though—on, for instance, the exquisite irony of Lucy's having a fat daughter—by the appearance of Lucy herself, who can't possibly have heard us since we were whispering and, I can tell from the look in her eyes, is not about to forget my little *coup d'état*. I'm going to have to watch my back.

"I don't know about you," she announces, "but I can't believe that less than a year after Dad's death, Odette is disporting herself with some revolting little Frenchman."

Jane looks at her quizzically. "Really, Lucy, you have the most lurid imagination."

"I see. So you've actually been taken in by this 'old friend' nonsense?"

"To tell you the truth, I hadn't really thought about it," replies Jane, calmly closing her suitcase.

"He's very nice, actually," I say. "He knows a lot about schist layers."

A look of withering contempt travels in my direction. I often wonder if Lucy is aware that she acts like a caricature of herself.

"Well," I announce, "I'm going down to make Isabelle's bed. She's arriving this afternoon," I add gratuitously.

It has escaped no one's notice, I am sure, that Isabelle's room was available all along for the taking, but that not even Lucy would go that far.

CHAPTER *four*

Why are we all here? Because it's what Ross wanted. In his will, a document that turned out to be a spectacular exercise in wishful thinking, the only practicable request that he made— gifts to various museums and the New York City Ballet, which to my knowledge he never attended, having been rendered moot by the state of his finances at his death—was that we meet in Santerre to scatter his ashes at sunset over the Mediterranean. Most people don't realize this, but under all the testosterone, Ross was a romantic fool. This goes some way toward explaining why he thought that once he was no longer around to keep us in line we would want to get together at all. It also elucidates another seemingly inexplicable trait, the one that got him into trouble in the first place: my father's lifelong allegiance to gold. For Ross was what is known in the financial world as a goldbug, an unwavering adherent to the belief that gold and only gold is money. This means that in the late seventies he got very rich. Then the price of gold tumbled and, undeterred, he went on a shopping spree. Gold was going to go back up again. It had to. After the big crash, all the fools who had been seduced by the fairy dust of high-tech stocks would rush back to the one true store of value, that radiant yellow metal that, as Ross liked to remind people, has held humanity in its sway for three thousand years.

Still, even I, who am supposed to understand these things, did not realize the full and glorious extent of his monomania, as revealed by the state of his affairs after he crashed his two-seater plane into a New Hampshire mountain, making us the outright owners of two gold mines, and shareholders in every prospecting concern on the planet. Our empire spanned the globe from Canada to Zaire, ranged from soaring mountains to African jungles, and was worth nothing. The New York apartment and the East Hampton cottage—even the plane in which he met his demise—were mortgaged to the hilt. All that was left was the house in Santerre

And Odette, his final folly. Even Isabelle, who likes her, never understood why Ross had to marry her. After he and Daphne got divorced, we thought he'd learned his lesson. No woman could ever supplant Vera, who everyone knew was his one true love. As the legend goes, he saw her dancing one night at the Kirov in Leningrad and became so obsessed that he risked his life to smuggle her out of Soviet Russia. It all sounds rather cloak-and-daggerish today but this much I know is true: As a rising ballet star, Vera was not the kind of person the authorities were eager to see decamping to the West. On the other hand, Ross was buying a lot of Siberian gold in those days and had all sorts of official and not-so-official connections in Moscow, so he could conceivably have just bribed her way out. Either way, their marriage had a mythopoetic quality that was going to be hard to beat, as Daphne and Odette both discovered, along with every other woman Ross became involved with.

If you're getting the impression that my father was some kind of pathetic philanderer, that's not entirely the case. He was a thrilling man and women flocked to him, and I'm convinced that each time he truly believed he was in love, because if Ross was good at one thing, it was self-delusion. At heart he was an optimist, as evidenced by his investment philosophy, and he hated letting people down, so that when he did—as he invariably did—he just disappointed them all the more. With the exception of Vera, of course, frozen forever in perfect youth; and Isabelle, who has her exaggerated Russian features, her canted eyes and full lips, and her unstable Slavic temperament.

And who, I remark to Jane, should be arriving any minute now. I am intimately familiar with my sister's itinerary, since I bought the tickets for her and the girls. Isabelle, like most free spirits, never has any money. Jane and Lucy and I meanwhile are moving the teak garden furniture Lucy ordered from an English catalog onto the patch of dirt that separates our house from the Costas' next door. Last year they got there first, colonizing our somewhat fancifully designated patio with a plastic lawn set that Lucy, whose finely honed aesthetic sensibilities cringe at the slightest hint of bad taste, declared the most vulgar thing she had ever seen in her life. The Costas have been a thorn in her side ever since they inherited the house two years ago from an uncle, the Costas being the kinds of French people who refuse to conform to her ideas of how the French ought to behave. I should explain that Lucy's notions of French culture are culled largely from Elizabeth

David, the great expert on French provincial cuisine, whom Lucy worships almost as much as she does William Morris. One thing is for sure, Elizabeth David couldn't have had Santerrans in mind when she wrote about Mediterranean *savoir-vivre*. The sight of Madame Costa returning from the Super-Géant in Canonica laden with cans of stew and ravioli would undoubtedly have pained her as much as it does Lucy—even more than their annexation of the patio, which, due to the incoherence of French inheritance laws, belongs neither to us nor the Costas but to Mr. Peretti up the road.

So, like most things around here, it's a big free-for-all, and under the nervous eye of Odette, who doesn't believe in alienating the neighbors, we dispose this very expensive-looking furniture in the shade of the fig tree.

"This must have cost a small fortune," I observe, running a hand over the fine-grained wood. Lucy isn't exactly cheap, but when she does spend money it tends to be on herself—plus, they had to have it all shipped from London at great expense, as Richard pointedly mentioned at lunch. He's off somewhere right now with Electra, who threw another fit when Lucy wouldn't let her have butter on her bread. How do you put a four-year-old on a diet? In any case, Richard seems to be the only person who can calm her down. My suspicion is that he feeds her candy bars when Lucy's not looking.

"Trust me, it's worth every penny," Lucy says grimly, dragging the final chaise through the dust. There's a canvas parasol, too, that Jim and Yves are assembling over in the corner.

Jim is fitting in much more smoothly than I'd expected. He climbed down the cliff for a swim this morning and declared the water amazing—on a day like today it takes on a spectacular shade of turquoise, and is so clear that you can make out every sea urchin underfoot—and then actually coaxed enough hot water out of our dribbling shower to wash *and* rinse his hair. The juxtaposition with puny Yves definitely works to his advantage. I never really got the point of European men.

Jim and Yves are just hoisting the parasol when a car door slams up the road and little Olga and Sophie come bounding down the path, followed in due course by Isabelle, who, hair flying and bracelets jingling, does not exactly cut a tragic figure. She is wearing one of her Esmeralda outfits, a full, vaguely Indian-looking skirt with red peonies splashed across a sea-green background and a cherry-colored bustier upon which the eyes of Yves and Jim become instantly fixed. My sister's breasts have been likened by their many devotees to peaches and apples and even melons, their implausible combination of weight and aloftness endlessly marveled upon. It kind of makes you wonder about the masculine mind, the fruit thing, but that's another story.

"*Ah, mes petits anges!*" cries Odette, rushing toward them, her heels clicking on the uneven flagstones and her small thin arms held out. She's so tiny that Isabelle practically enfolds her, making it look like it's Odette who's being comforted—and maybe it is. I, too, have run toward Isabelle, and one look at my sister confirms what I've known all along: that once again she has emerged unscathed from love's battlegrounds. Lucy, hanging back in the doorway, cannot entirely hide her disappointment.

chapter *five*

"God, that turnoff! We nearly went over the cliff!" Peals of laughter. Only Isabelle would find the idea of a car wreck with two small children screamingly funny. Olga and Sophie, after two hours of immobility in the little Renault, are bouncing around like Ping-Pong balls, babbling away in Czech and opening all the cupboards in the kitchen in search of last year's kittens.

"*Ravissantes . . . ,*" Odette trills, and they are indeed ravishing, with Isabelle's green eyes and their father's lighter coloring, so that their tangled curls are auburn instead of black. They're both wearing fairy outfits, with somewhat tattered wings and little tiaras, and I catch Lucy and Richard exchanging a glance—the one about how Isabelle imposes no discipline and lets her girls do anything they want, such as screech like banshees and bang cupboard doors and wear grubby fairy costumes on airplanes.

"Mommy! Mommy! There are no kittens!" Sophie shrieks. At six she's the oldest and definitely the most obnoxious. Isabelle had her girls barely a year apart—not that she planned it that way; she just, as she charmingly put it, kept getting knocked up. Another sensitive topic, this: Lucy and Richard tried for years to do the same, and in the end they had to get fertility treatments. The summer Lucy finally got pregnant, they showed up in Borgolano with a big box of fertility sticks, the kind you have to pee on every morning to see if you're ovulating. Of course it had to be Isabelle who found them in the bathroom cupboard behind a pile of towels and spent the rest of the vacation lewdly speculating about what Lucy and Richard were getting up to whenever they disappeared for more than fifteen minutes.

"But there *are* no kittens this year," Odette laughs. "That naughty Minette ran off with a big old tomcat and never came back."

"*Naughty, naughty* Minette," the girls intone, before collapsing into another fit of giggles. Another pregnant (pardon the pun) glance between Lucy and Richard. Ever since they were able to talk, Olga and Sophie have been shockingly wise to the carryings-on of the Minettes and tomcats of this world, as most egregiously evidenced last summer by Sophie's dinner-table remark that "Mommy once liked Daddy so much that she let him put his willie inside her." This delivered in the peculiarly accented English both girls have picked up in Prague, and which is definitely getting thicker.

"They're beginning to sound like Bela Lugosi," I remark to Isabelle.

"Yes, isn't it hilarious? I'm convinced they have a future in horror movies. God, I'm starving!" She leans across me and grabs a piece of bread on the table, a movement that simultaneously plunges her cleavage to dizzying depths and pushes her breasts upward, where they more or less remain as she slathers the bread with a half inch of butter before stuffing it in her mouth. Jane nudges me and winks in the direction of Yves: Caught in the grip of a strong emotion, he's forgotten all about his smoldering cigarette.

"Who made you the lovely costumes?" Jane asks. Sophie proudly informs us that it was Grandma Maria—Grandma Maria being Maria Orlik, the stage designer and legendary femme fatale of Prague's theater circles and mother of the philandering Jiri, who had to get it from somewhere. Most of the adults the girls know are famous in one way or another, in the Czech Republic at least, where it seems everyone including the president knows their father. Which is perhaps why Jiri and Isabelle have always treated them like miniature grown-ups. From the earliest age they've had the run of Prague's cafés and theaters, not to mention bars and nightclubs and even the Royal Castle, most notably when the Rolling Stones visited. Isabelle actually has a picture of them sitting on Mick Jagger's lap. Still, for all the lack of family values, they seem to have come out okay. For one thing, you can actually have a conversation with them—an impossibility, I find, with most kids.

"Where's Electra?" Jane suddenly asks. It seems I'm not the only one who's forgotten all about Electra, because Lucy looks panicked, until Jane says gently, "Ah, there you are, love. Aren't you going to say hello to your cousins?"

It turns out she's been hiding behind Richard's legs all along, from where she's observing Olga and Sophie with undisguised fascination. The girls stare back at her until Sophie breaks the silence by brandishing her fairy wand and yelling, "Electra! You are under my spell!"

At first Electra just stares back, and then her doughy face crumples up and I have a horrible feeling she's going to burst into tears. Instead she points back at Sophie.

"Zap!" Olga yells, running up with her own wand extended. Another look passes between Lucy and Richard, one of relief this time that strikes me as ineffably sad, much as I can't help but find a certain poetic justice in the situation. Even more, though, I'm relieved, as is obviously everyone else in the room, that Electra isn't going to throw another fit.

I shoo away Jim and Yves and help Isabelle up with her bags. In her room I open the shutters, flooding with light the marble-topped dresser with its clutter of antique perfume bottles from the Canonica flea market, and the faded Renoir poster on the wall. Odette must have cleaned up in anticipation of her arrival. The bed is covered with a nubby white coverlet, and the assorted cushions and stuffed toys without which my sister cannot find repose have been arranged in a neat row along the headboard. With a happy sigh she flops down and throws a pillow at me.

"I can't believe you took over Lucy's room, you sly dog. Did she have a cow?" Isabelle has always been big on animal metaphors. I think it has something to do with her European upbringing.

"You'd better start acting a little more dignified, you know," I retort, tossing the pillow back at her. "Odette was getting all the wailing women lined up and you breeze in looking like a lingerie ad."

"Oh no, am I being a pig?"

"No more than usual."

She stretches and rearranges herself amongst the bedclothes, then flashes me a wicked grin that reveals the gap between her front teeth that she always refused to get fixed. No fool, my sister. "To tell you the truth, it's a little difficult to play the grieving widow when you've been getting stuffed like an octopus for the past two weeks by *the* most devastatingly sexy playwright. . . . Hmm, you might even know him."

"I doubt it," I say. It's our little family joke that I only read the *Wall Street Journal,* while Isabelle, Lucy, and Jane have the monopoly on things cultural. Actually, I'm a big fan of the nineteenth-century novel, but I'd hate to give up my reputation as the in-house Philistine.

"Anyway, you're right. I'll go down and have a cup of tea with her as soon as I've unpacked. But enough about *me*. . . ." She makes an owl face. "Aren't you going to tell me about your *boyfriend?* What a dish: I love those green eyes!"

"What do you want to know about him?" I say guardedly. It's not that I don't want to gloat—I do—but confiding in Isabelle doesn't exactly come naturally to me.

She looks at me like I'm retarded. "What's he *like?* Where did you meet him? What's his favorite color? Does he have a big you-know-what?"

"He's nice. I met him at work. Blue. Not really."

"Thank you. Already I feel like I know him intimately. So, how long have you been going out?"

"It's called dating now."

"Really? That's not what *we* used to call it."

"Yeah, well, *you* didn't have to worry about AIDS."

"Ugh, thank God! We have it in the Czech Republic now, too, you know. Are you in love with him?"

"I don't know. Define *in love.*"

"Constance, you are hopeless."

"I don't get weak in the knees at the sight of him, if that's what you mean."

Isabelle clutches at her breast. "Would you sacrifice your life for him?"

"Oh, please, like *you* would sacrifice your life for anyone."

She considers this. "I would have for Jiri, once."

"Good thing you didn't," I remark.

"He wasn't always a shit. When I first met him he was sweet. He had this pair of black jeans that he wore all the time and I was washing them once and they had these patches on the inside of the knees. He'd sewn them in so they wouldn't wear out."

"You mean Maria sewed them in."

"Whatever."

"Wow," I say, "that's really moving. It completely changes my opinion of him."

Isabelle yanks the pillow out from under her and hits me on the head with it. "You're a heartless pig. I'm just saying he wasn't always such a big shot. Under communism he only had one pair of jeans, like everyone else."

"I'm weeping," I say. She whacks me again. We lie back on the white coverlet and stare up at the ceiling. A mildew stain has been spreading out from one corner over the years, its blistered edges assuming ever more fanciful shapes as it eats its way into the plaster.

"Definitely a camel," I say.

"No way, it's the Taj Mahal, the Temple of Love."

"Camel."

"Taj Mahal."

"You're both wrong," says Jane from the doorway. "It's the crack in the ceiling that had the habit of sometimes looking like a rabbit."

Isabelle sighs, "Don't you sometimes wish you were still little?"

Jane and I exchange glances. The crazy thing is that she means it: Isabelle would love nothing better than to be a child again.

CHAPTER *six*

In a Victorian novel I'd be the plain sister, but there's no such thing as a plain woman anymore, at least not in New York. It's too bad really; there must have been a certain comfort in not being beautiful, a sort of restful anonymity that gave you the space to develop your mind, like the Brontë sisters, or Jane Austen. Today if you don't look good it's your own fault, for not exercising or making more of yourself, all of which I do sedulously. I may not look like Isabelle but I am trim and athletic and even chic in a non-threatening American way. Why, then, did it take me so long to find a boyfriend? Based on the mating behavior I have observed around me, I've come to the conclusion that it's more an indict-ment of my character than of my looks.

For one thing, I'm too blunt. Isabelle, of course, is blunt, too, but in a charming way. I just put people off. What with that and my impatience with empty rituals, I was pretty much a disaster on the dating scene. I did manage to lose my virginity in college, with a frat boy called Rob whose face I don't remember—I'm not even sure he was called Rob, to tell you the truth—and I've had a string of one- or two-night stands ever since—I happen to like sex; it's not like there's something wrong with me—but Jim is my first de facto boyfriend.

I met him at work, of course. I picked him out early on, when he was a junior associate. Even though he'd gone to Harvard Business School, Jim was from Kansas and it still showed. The most exciting place he'd ever lived was Boston, and he was thrilled at actually having made it to Manhattan. That he was interested in my area, emerging markets, didn't hurt, either. He wanted to know more about the Czech mass privatization program, so one night I suggested a drink, which he could hardly refuse, since I was his senior.

Sometimes people will surprise you. It turned out that Jim, on top of being a genuinely nice guy, was also that other rarity, the man who doesn't freak out when you sleep with him on the first date. Personally, I've never seen the sense in waiting around, an attitude that I've noticed some guys find alarming, and apparently Jim was of the same mind as I was. Either that or, being a bit of a rube, he thought this was just the way people did things in the big city. In any case, we turned out, in bed at least, to be extremely compatible—he has the kind of thick, veined penis that I like—and soon enough we were as close to an official item as you can get in investment banking, working out together at the gym and spending the night at each other's apartment and, occasionally on a late night at the office, fucking in the thirty-seventh-floor utility closet. Then, by one of those coincidences peculiar to Wall Street, we both got headhunted by Solomon Pierson Webb, which allowed us to grab our bonuses and run, working in a four-week vacation in the interim. That was when I got the idea of luring him to Santerre.

Call it entrapment if you like. If I glossed over the business of Ross's memorial and somewhat misrepresented the island's charms, it was only in the service of seizing opportunity. I don't believe in fairy tales; that's Isabelle's department. Jiri actually proposed to her on his knees on the Charles Bridge with the castle in the background, shrouded in mist, and look where it got her. All the same, my sister remains a force to be reckoned with, and you wouldn't be entirely wrong in thinking that in some way, I hope to reel Jim in through her agency. I guess I think of her as a kind of good luck charm, even though I know that it could all blow up in my face.

CHAPTER *seven*

It's time for our first shopping trip to Flore, an undertaking necessitated by Lucy's announcement that she's cooking dinner tonight. As always, she has come equipped with sheaves of twenty-seven-ingredient recipes clipped from food magazines, much to the amusement of Odette who, being French, just throws things together with whatever she has on hand. Do you know how much frozen food the French eat? There's actually a supermarket chain in Paris that only sells the stuff. Lucy's gastronomic endeavors, on the other hand, inevitably require items not available at our local shop, such as dandelions or wild mushrooms or pumpkin seeds. Not that we'll find any of these in Flore, but Lucy retains a touching belief in the existence, and availability, of native organic products even though the selection at our village store strongly suggests that the locals live on frozen fish sticks and macaroni. This year she's brought new evidence: an article from *Gourmet* on the organic

Santerran olive oil industry, copiously illustrated with pictures of the author in the company of grizzled old men in berets.

"Remember the chestnut flour?" Jane whispers to me at breakfast as Lucy labors over the shopping list. Last summer we traveled seventy miles on some of the island's worst roads to a mountain village in search of this rare delicacy. The three-hundred-year-old mill was closed, of course, for the *vacances,* though we did in the end find a souvenir shop that sold bags of rock-hard traditional chestnut cookies at twenty francs apiece.

"I found the village charming, actually," says Lucy. "If we left things up to you lot, we'd never go anywhere." Lucy and Richard and even Jane share the English compulsion to go off on expeditions, preferably with a picnic. I can't count the hunks of Santerran salami I've gnawed on, perched on a rock, a glass of sour wine balanced precariously on my knee. I'm sure Jim will find it all very romantic. The assimilation process is going well: He and Richard went jogging this morning, a promising sign of male bonding.

"It's very expensive, Flore," Yves cautions us. "You should go to the Super-Géant in Canonica."

"I must say, I find it endlessly shocking, how cheap the French are," Lucy declares once we're in the car. "Frankly *he* should be buying the groceries, seeing he's getting a free holiday."

"Maybe he's paying his way through services rendered," Jane suggests.

"I don't care what you say, she had no right to invite him to our house."

"It's her house too," I point out.

"What's all the fuss about?" Isabelle asks.

"Lucy thinks Yves is Odette's fancy man," Jane says.

"No way: She wouldn't go for a little weenie like that."

"You're all hopelessly naïve."

"Well, why don't I just ask her?" Isabelle teases. "I'll tell her you were especially curious, Lucy."

"Don't be absurd."

Together again. . . . The children have stayed home with Odette, who has promised to take them blackberry picking, a prospect that left Electra indifferent, though Sophie and Olga went wild. So far they all seem to be getting along. Kids are so strange, you never know how they're going to react. I half expected the girls would blurt out something about Electra having gotten so fat, but they don't seem to notice—unlike Isabelle, who pulled me aside as soon as she got a look at her and wanted to know what was wrong, as if I would have any idea. I almost feel bad for Lucy. I know parents aren't supposed to make these kinds of comparisons, but it's hard to believe that she wouldn't look at Olga and Sophie, as bratty as they may be, and wonder where she went wrong.

The drive to Flore isn't as harrowing as the one to Canonica, where you have to take your life in your hands and cross over the *cap*. Around Ursulanu, the road stops hugging the coast and the landscape flattens out into a vineyard-filled valley, so that you can actually speed up on the way in to the town. Flore itself is your standard Mediterranean pleasure port, fringed with mountains and quite pretty in a picture postcard sort of way. It also has real shops, including several bakeries and a small supermarket, and a string of restaurants and cafés along the harbor that all serve the same *prix fixe* of Santerran charcuterie, followed by the purported catch of the day. Since we haven't had breakfast yet, we head to one of these for coffee and croissants.

"Un café au lait, s'il vous plaît," Lucy enunciates carefully to the waiter.

"Un grand crème," Isabelle orders with a dazzling smile. She speaks perfect French from her Paris days, much to the vexation of Lucy, who, for all her hours at l'Alliance française, still sounds like she's trying too hard. In what is partly a legacy of Vera, a fanatical Francophile like all Russians, the speaking of French in our family has assumed an importance ridiculously disproportionate to the language's actual utility. Not even I have been spared: As a part of my ongoing self-improvement program, I'm taking an evening class.

"Coffee," I nonetheless say curtly, eliciting a chuckle from Jane.

"That's right, little sister, wave the flag."

"Honestly, Isabelle," Lucy snaps, "you might as well walk around in your underwear. The poor man was practically drowning in your cleavage."

"Really? I didn't notice."

"Of course you didn't," says Jane.

"Isn't this bliss?" cries Isabelle, stretching out her arms. "Sometimes I think I could just drop everything and move here!"

"Right, and give up your fabulous lifestyle in the Disneyland of Eastern Europe."

Our coffees arrive and soon enough we're all companionably intent on the ongoing *pétanque* game in the square, until Lucy blurts out:

"Are you and Jiri really getting divorced?"

A little frown flits over Isabelle's brow. "That's what it looks like."

"But why? I mean, couldn't you have worked it out. It seems such a shame for the girls."

Lucy doesn't approve of divorce; she's a big fan of keeping up appearances and doing the right thing. Jane ascribes this to Protestantism.

"Well, it's beyond repair," Isabelle says sharply.

I often wonder if my sister really is as oblivious to life's slings and arrows as she makes out. I suspect that for all her bravado, she didn't take the breakup of her marriage quite as lightly as she would have people believe. For one, Ross, whom she worshipped, was a big fan of Jiri's. When they got married, he flew us all over and threw a huge party at Lvi Dvur in the Prague Castle, which was attended by all the local celebrities, including Havel. Ross saw a lot of himself in Jiri. Not only were they both alpha males, they were more or less of the same generation—Jiri is twenty-five years older than Isabelle—and, being one of the world's great bullshit artists himself, Ross always had a fine appreciation of this quality in others.

In the mini-mart, Lucy makes a beeline for a box of lemons with the leaves still attached. "Don't these look lovely and fresh!" she exclaims, picking one up. A sign over the box says that they're Santerran, which pleases her inordinately, though as far as I'm concerned they just look like lemons. "We'll have *pasta al limone* as a first course," she exults, piling them into her basket. What we are indulging here is Lucy's fantasy, fueled by Elizabeth David and *The River Cafe Cookbook,* of the harmonious communion with the seasons that dictated menu planning before the corruption of mankind by convenience foods and supermarkets. In this spirit we stock up on local tomatoes, too, and melons. Then Isabelle tries to slip some apples into the basket.

"Why don't we get some of these lovely peaches instead?" Lucy wheedles.

"Because I like apples," Isabelle says.

"I do think we ought to make an effort to support local agriculture," Lucy persists. "Those apples were probably grown in New Zealand and flown over unripe in a box."

Jane and I assume horrified expressions, but Isabelle is unmoved. "*What* local agriculture? When was the last time you actually saw a Santerran tilling the soil? I'll bet you those lemons came from Tunisia or somewhere," she says blithely, adding a bunch of grossly unseasonal bananas to the pile. I should mention that Isabelle is a complete barbarian when it comes to food, and can live for days on cookies and Diet Coke. Her eating habits moreover have only worsened in the Czech Republic, where the two main alimentary groups are pork and starch.

Which is why I know we're heading for trouble as soon as we pass the junk food isle. Sure enough, Isabelle heads straight for the potato chips.

"I wish you wouldn't," Lucy says tensely. "Electra isn't supposed to have them."

Jane and I glance at each other.

"Oh, come on, don't be such a spoilsport," Isabelle says.

I watch Lucy with interest. She looks like she's either going to hit Isabelle or burst into tears. Jane moves protectively toward her. It's something she does, I've noticed, without being aware of it. Not for the first time, I find myself wishing that Isabelle would grow up.

"Come on," I say, "it's not going to kill you to eat vegetables for a few days."

"How did Electra put on all that weight, anyway?" my supertactful sister chooses this moment to ask.

So it's out. Lucy's expression goes through a series of tectonic shifts; I'm beginning to worry that she's going to lose it, but she regains her composure and says, with icy dignity, "Don't you think if I knew, I would have done something about it?"

Isabelle puts back the potato chips and picks up a sack of Cheez Doodles instead.

CHAPTER *eight*

Lucy brings up the matter of the garden furniture at dinner aptly enough, since we're sitting on it. Since the Costas haven't shown up yet, we have the free run of the patio between our houses, which means being able to dine alfresco without having to listen to them scarfing down their pork chops and the Super-Géant's version of Tater Tots ten feet away to a soundtrack of pulsating Euro-disco. As for us, we are enjoying a healthful meal of *pasta al limone* and dandelion salad dressed with the balsamic vinegar Lucy brought from London and the extra virgin Santerran olive oil we finally found, and paid an arm and a leg for, in a display of traditional native products at the Esso station. Sophie and Olga are eating cereal in the kitchen, where Odette sent them for making barfing sounds over the dandelions. Electra, it turns out, will eat anything including weeds, probably because she's starving, Isabelle points out to me under her breath. Oddly enough, she doesn't seem to mind Odette's disciplining the girls—you might think out of some great respect for her authority, though I'm sure it's more out of laziness.

"I might as well bring this up while we're all together," Lucy announces after we've all dutifully lauded her cooking. "The cost of the outdoor furniture was fifteen hundred pounds. I think it's only fair that we split it five ways, which comes to three hundred apiece. Jane has already given me her share."

A silence descends, one that Isabelle and I simultaneously break by jumping in with hasty *Of courses*. The expression on Odette's face however can only be described as consternation. Yves' eyes have begun to wander, and Jim just looks puzzled. Richard stares at the wall. Lucy smiles.

"Of course we'll pay you back," I repeat. "There's no reason you should have to pick up the whole thing."

Odette clears her throat. "You might have consulted us before deciding to spend such a large amount of money," she says carefully. Odette's English gets very precise when she's flustered, though she never entirely manages to shake the Inspector Clouseau effect. "We could have found something perfectly adequate in Canonica. . . ."

Lucy's smirk at this indicates her opinion of the wares to be found in Canonica. "Well, actually, they were on sale, so I had to make an executive decision. But in fact you're quite right: It's high time we had a meeting to discuss common expenses. We can't just go on doing things in this haphazard way. The roof needs to be fixed and the stairs are falling down—"

Odette makes a *pfff* sound that I interpret as meaning that, as far as she's concerned, there's nothing wrong with the roof or the stairs. Actually, Lucy is right. The place has been falling apart since the day Ross bought it, having been used for years as a boarding-house for workers in the neighboring asbestos plant, one of the reasons he got it so cheap. She has once again, however, not antic-ipated the Gallic cunning of Odette, who chooses this moment to lift her glass and say, *"Mes enfants,* I think your father would be saddened to hear us squabbling like this. Let us remember why we have gathered here: to commemorate a man whose generosity and *joie de vivre* were legendary . . . and who never concerned himself with trivial details," she pointedly adds.

Well, that sure took care of the garden furniture. Isabelle, never one to pass up an opportunity for cheap sentiment, blurts out, "I totally agree! Look at us with our pathetic materialism! Dad would be so disgusted." Which is easy for her to say, since she knows I'll pay her share.

Odette is right on target about one thing: Ross left such a mess when he died that it took a whole team of accountants and lawyers to sort out the trivial details he was so unconcerned with. He didn't exactly leave her homeless and penniless—just nearly, so that she had to give up the New York apartment, which the bank had foreclosed on, and go back to Paris, where she'd kept a small flat. I do have to say that she handled the whole thing with sur-prising dignity, as opposed to Isabelle, who made a spectacle of herself, sobbing hysterically at the funeral and then getting plas-tered at the reception before slaking her lust on a waiter. As far as I'm concerned, Odette's gravity throughout the proceedings was a great argument for European formality. It confirmed my suspi-cions, moreover, that she did not, as Lucy has always insisted, regard Ross as a meal ticket but was actually in love with him. I don't see this as being incompatible with whatever financial expec-tations she may have had. I'm a banker; I don't get emotional about money. Odette isn't young anymore and she had every right to assume that Ross would take care of her. Marriage is a contract like any other, and frankly, Ross didn't live up to his end of the bargain.

What's the best way to let people down? Raise their expectations. My father was a master at this. He understood that, though there's no difference in value between a warehouseful of pork bellies and a thousand-year-old Persian *repoussé* cup, people want a little romance in their lives. Ross was never just interested in amassing wealth: If that had been his goal, he would have stayed in the foreign currency markets, where he'd done just fine in the sixties. What he craved was drama, and this he found in gold; and because gold made for such great spectacle, and because Ross could sell you anything, a lot of people got swept up in the grand folly of his vision. When I was little, my friends' fathers were stockbrokers and lawyers. Mine owned a gold mine in Borneo. He kept his pens in a chalice that had belonged to the Borgias, and his cigars in a Byzantine casket from Constantinople. His gifts were so lavish as to be almost unhinged: When I had to write a report about Patagonia, he flew me there. Lucy accepted the Rome Prize with Renaissance pearls dangling from her ears, and Isabelle graduated from college in an Etruscan necklace that had once graced the neck of a princess—or so Ross said, and we took him at his word, because everything he did always had a great story.

When the baubles big and small started disappearing one by one, sold off to pay his debts, I don't think any of us really believed that his luck had run out. He would bounce back, like he always did. He'd find another investor, a banker with more imagination, a fool with a buck, and he'd be off again. . . . When it all came crashing down, we were as surprised as he was. Even more bizarre, no one thought of blaming him: Not Odette, who had every reason to, nor I, who had to clean up the mess, nor Lucy, who adored him, and especially not Isabelle, for whom he could do no wrong.

CHAPTER *nine*

Jim and I run into the village cow this morning, breakfasting at the peach tree that overhangs the Paolis' garden wall. The Paolis have completely redone their house with the help of their local relatives and, in Lucy's opinion, with a shocking disrespect for native building customs. Most of the houses in Borgolano belong to émigrés who use them for the two-month summer vacation all French people seem to enjoy, and then for retirement. The reason for this is that there is no economy to speak of on the island except for tourism. This somehow manages to thrive despite the terrorists, whose puzzling desire for autonomy would result in the end of the French government subventions that support half the population. For all the malaise at dinner, I am feeling elated, by sex no doubt, which we've been having a lot of, and now by the sight of Linda, a legacy of some long defunct EC subsidy that had all Santerrans claiming for a while to be dairy farmers, and an inspiring symbol in my mind of the triumph of grit over destiny.

At first Jim thought it was a bit weird that I wanted to bring him along to my father's funeral, though I had explained that it was in fact a memorial, the funeral having already taken place. He's a pretty conservative guy—well, he's an investment banker—and he didn't really get the idea of having a party for a dead parent. After last night, though, I can see that he's beginning to appreciate where I'm coming from. I don't believe all this nonsense about dysfunctional families: If anything, our family is living proof that even the nuttiest people can function just fine. But that doesn't mean that they don't pose a social challenge. I can't say I didn't worry about Jim's reaction: Would he find them fascinating, or merely bizarre? What was his attitude toward lesbians? Would he like Isabelle better than me?

"So let me get this straight," he said in bed this morning. "First your dad married your mother, then Jane and Lucy's mother . . . ?"

"Daphne."

"Right, Daphne. And finally Odette, which would make her his third wife."

"Uh-huh." I was playing with his cock and was not all that interested in explaining the minutiae of our family tree at that very moment.

"She seems so young," said Jim, getting hard.

"It's called plastic surgery," I said, lowering my lips to his now purple glans and slowly running my tongue around it.

He moaned softly, like a girl.

At breakfast (the reason Jim and I were out so early was to get croissants and go for a run), Lucy has clearly not forgotten the matter of the garden furniture, so it's just as well that Odette hasn't come down yet. Or Yves.

"Shacked up together, I should think," she exclaims disgustedly. "God, what a miserable excuse for a croissant! Next time we're in Flore, we'll buy a sack at the bakery and freeze them."

"Freeze?" says Jane in mock horror.

"Actually," I say, "Odette's door was open this morning and she was definitely alone."

"How innocent you are, Constance: No doubt he crept back to his lair before dawn. I must say, one could live with the lack of morals of the French if they weren't so bloody avaricious as well: I doubt I'll ever get a penny from her—not that I care."

In our family, the Hundred Years War lives on, another thing Ross clearly didn't take into account when he was playing musical nationalities at the altar.

"What I can't bear is the hypocrisy: They all claim to be penniless and yet they dress head to toe in designer labels. That shockingly vulgar outfit Odette was wearing last night was a Dior, if you can believe it. I saw the label in the wash basket."

"I've always found him overrated, myself," says Jane, who is wearing her usual overalls and T-shirt. Lucy, a believer in timeless elegance, favors long floaty garments in colors like heather or sage.

"Actually," I say, "they don't have to pay for them. They get clothing coupons from the state; it's a way for the government to support the fashion industry."

"The laxative industry, you mean," Jane says. "How do you think they all fit into those teeny-weeny dresses?"

"What *are* you talking about?" A bleary-eyed Isabelle appears in her own idea of timeless elegance. Jane lets out a wolf whistle.

"Must you walk around naked?" snaps Lucy.

"I am *not* naked. I am clothed; my parts are covered. Do I smell coffee?"

Jane pours her a cup and slides it across the table. Isabelle sits down, causing her nightgown—more of a slip, really—to ride even higher up her thigh. Her big nipples press up against the thin silk.

"I'm putting the girls in that empty room upstairs," she announces. "Sophie snores like a truck driver and Olga woke me up at six this morning. Lucy, we can drag a cot up for Electra, too; it'll be like camp."

"I don't think Electra is old enough yet to be sleeping on her own."

"But she won't be on her own; they'll have a blast," my sister says.

"I just don't think it's a good idea," Lucy says tensely.

"Where *are* the girls?" Jane says. "I haven't heard them in a while."

"They are drawing seashells in the living room," announces Odette, who has just come down, perfectly coiffed and made up as always, her face dewy from moisturizer. She still pulls her hair back into what I think of as the Air France bun, a style that is very popular with French women, probably because it gives you an instant face-lift. This morning she's sporting her casual look: Capri pants and a sleeveless blouse, both creased and ironed, and little high-heeled mules that click on the tile floor. Her shoes are about a size three, an object of fascination to Isabelle and me, who both inherited Ross's big flat feet. Even more fascinating is her underwear, as we discovered when she first moved in with Ross by going through her drawers: layer upon frilly layer of tiny push-up bras (though she has no breasts) and thongs and peekaboo panties that only convinced us all the more that she got Ross through sex. Except for the black hair, which Lucy swears she dyes, she just wasn't his type, though for that matter neither was Daphne.

Olga and Sophie, however, worship her, and when they hear her voice, they come tumbling in to the room in a rattle of glass beads and pearls. The Czech Republic is the world capital of cheap costume jewelry, and the girls own boxes of the stuff.

"Ah, mes belles," Odette trills as they leap all over her. *"Mes princesses . . ."*

Electra, who has followed them, hangs back in the doorway, staring, and I find myself wishing that just once Odette would call her pretty, too, just to balance things out, which is exactly the thought that I read in Jane's averted eyes. Lucy just looks stonily ahead.

CHAPTER *ten*

The mayor is coming for *apéritif* tonight, a yearly ritual that sets our protocol-conscious Odette all aflutter. Ross and he were buddies. My father took a great interest in the local politics—he really thought that some day he would retire here—and, when we first came to Borgolano, he set out as a matter of course to seduce all the bigwigs in town, lavishly sponsoring the annual *pétanque* tournament and disco, and paying for the renovation of the *gendarmerie*. His efforts paid off: By the time of his death, Ross had become so popular that the proprietor of our café-bistro had named a cocktail after him: Le New Yorkais, a deadly mixture of cheap Scotch and the local wild-thistle–based liqueur.

The mayor is expected at six, along with his wife, Madame Benoît, and Yolande Van Langendonck, who owns several properties in town that she rents to fellow Belgians. Yolande is rumored to be the mayor's mistress. Lucy made a valiant attempt to take over the cooking but was rebuffed, Odette muttering darkly under her breath about seaweed and raw fish. This in reference to the one time Odette did let Lucy prepare the hors d'oeuvres, an event that would have gone down in the island's culinary history had Odette not whisked away the sushi (made from sea urchins hand-gathered by Lucy) in the nick of time and replaced it with bowls of chips and peanuts.

This year Lucy has been dispatched to Flore on a critical errand, dropping Richard, Jim, Isabelle, and the children at Orzo beach on the way. Jane and I stay behind to clean up. This is no easy task. In our eagerness to preserve authentic period detail (unlike the natives, who go wild with linoleum and Formica), we have condemned ourselves to living in a dustbowl. Practically every three-hundred-year-old terra-cotta tile in the house is loose so that the dirt underneath puffs up in little clouds with every step; add to that the drifts of plaster from the cracks in the walls and ceilings, and we're not about to appear in *House & Garden* anytime soon. All of which is a matter of great social humiliation to Odette, who, for all her cosmopolitan airs, is from a nice bourgeois family in Toulouse and would like nothing better than to give the place the same kind of makeover as the Paolis' up the street, with a shiny modern bathroom and kitchen appliances. It had been Ross's oft-stated intention to accede to this wish as soon as he retired, a promise that I imagine must make her doubly bitter. When I suggest that, in the absence of the Costas, we might as well avail ourselves of the patio *and* Lucy's fancy garden furniture, Odette looks downright grateful.

"*Quelle bonne idée,* Constance!"

"What happened to those old Chinese lanterns in the back closet?" Jane asks. "We could string them up on the fig tree."

"I don't know," Odette says doubtfully. "We don't want them to think we tried too hard. . . . And besides, it will be light," she adds, which is true: The sun doesn't set until nine in July and pre-scribed *apéritif* time is between six-thirty and eight. If you wanted people to stay later you'd have to invite them for dinner, which would constitute a major upset of the social order, dinner being second only to sex on the intimacy scale. As Odette keeps remind-ing us, this is not Paris. The not-trying-too-hard also extends to the menu, hence the banishment of Lucy. Odette has made a *pissaladière,* a sort of tarted-up pizza, with frozen dough from the Super-Géant now cooling in the pantry, and Jane and I have been delegated to scrub down the kitchen. This is fine with me. What with all the comings and goings, I haven't really had a chance to talk to Jane since she arrived. She's seemed a little subdued and I've been meaning to ask her if everything is okay.

"So," I say, pouring us both a glass of wine after we've scoured all the surfaces with Ajax—another Anglo-Saxon trait that Odette frowns upon: drinking at all hours—"how's Marge?"

Jane was sketching up on the roof earlier and still has a charcoal smudge on her nose. She pushes her hair distractedly out of her eyes. "Oh, busy defending the rights of minorities as always. . . . She's thinking of running for the local council."

"So I guess she won't be joining us again this year?"

She laughs. "Oh, God, no. . . . I'll be staying longer, though, trying to get some work done."

"Uh-huh?" There was a little pause at the end that makes me think there's more to this than she's letting on.

"Actually," Jane says, her eyes not meeting mine, "we've decided to spend some time apart."

"You mean you've broken up?"

"I don't think so." She looks wistful for a second, then brightens up. "It's more of a sabbatical. At least I hope so."

"Can I ask why? I mean, you've been together for years."

Jane sighs. "Oh, the same thing it's always been I suppose: I'm not politically engaged enough. She wants a lifetime partner who shares her ideals—not that I don't, but . . . well, I've never been much of an activist. . . ."

She looks so crestfallen that I decide not to open my big mouth. Although this would conceivably be a good time to do so, I am not going to confess that I've always found Marge insufferable with her incessant harping on the World Phallocracy and her insistence on bringing up genital mutilation at the dinner table, which is really what got her in trouble with Odette. I am not going to say that Marge has some nerve dumping Jane, who is way smarter and prettier and funnier, not to mention a distinguished artist of international stature. Who does Marge think she is, anyway?

"I'm really sorry," I say.

Jane pats me on the arm. "Thanks, honey. It's honestly not as bad as it seems. I'd be more concerned about Isabelle."

"Isn't it amazing how everyone is concerned about Isabelle except Isabelle?"

Jane smiles. "Well, no one will ever accuse her of practicing the examined life . . . but she seems almost too cheerful: It's a little disconcerting. To tell you the truth, I'm not sure she ever let herself properly grieve for Ross, and then to have the divorce on top of that . . ."

I shrug. "She says she's fine. She's got a new boyfriend already."

"How many men are going to take in a woman with two small children? Isabelle will never manage on her own."

"That's a very unfeminist sentiment you just expressed there."

"It wasn't meant to be a compliment," Jane says dryly.

"Alors," the mayor says, "have you heard? The Costas have sold their house."

"Ah, bon?" says Yolande, obviously as startled as we are by the mayor's announcement—which makes you wonder about the reliability of the local rumor mill—and miffed as hell, too, I'll bet, that a whole house changed hands right under her nose.

"Tiens," says Odette with studied neutrality, *"quelle surprise."* She's handing out pastis and the awful Santerran rosé that everyone dutifully drinks before dinner to support the local wine industry. Jim, obviously not aware that pastis tastes like liquid licorice, takes a big sip and tries not to make a face. I nudge him and pass him a glass of wine. Lucy, unlike Yolande and Odette, can't hide her astonishment.

"They've *sold* it? But it was never even put on the market!"

A pitying look passes between Odette and Madame Benoît. They're both wearing nice grown-up French lady clothes, unlike Yolande, who is decked out in some kind of Indian caftan with assorted beaded necklaces and amulets and whose purple eyeshadow has caked into the creases in her eyelids. Borgolano is not exactly famous for attracting normal people. On top of the usual tax evaders and Santerran nationalists, we have our share of jailbirds and sex offenders, though we don't normally see much of them outside the local bistro, La Marmite du Pêcheur, the one where Ross has a drink named after him and where it seems Yves has taken to hanging out. He must be there right now, since he's not here.

"Eh bien si, Madame!" The mayor winks jovially at Lucy. "Per-

haps they advertised at one of the Canonica agencies. . . . In any case, a Parisian has bought it, *un écrivain.*" Reverent pause here, to allow us to share in the mayor's delight that yet another interesting personality has chosen our little community. The mayor, I should explain, cherishes a vision of Borgolano as a kind of international artists' colony, a vision that Ross encouraged and that so far rests entirely on the shoulders of Jane *(artiste-peintre)* and of the Countess Fatulescu, the mysterious Romanian poetess who bought the estate above the old monastery last year. Like most Santerrans, the mayor is short and dapper and smells agreeably of cologne.

Further discussion of our new neighbor is aborted by the arrival of Isabelle, who, she charmingly apologizes, has been washing her hair, as evidenced by the damp ringlets that cling to her temples.

"Ah, Mademoiselle Wright, every year you look younger!" the mayor exclaims, tripping forward to kiss her on both cheeks and disregarding the fact that she is technically Madame Orlik. She flutters about now, butterflylike, dispensing kisses and trilling in her flawless French under the approving eye of Odette, who considers the rest of us to be socially retarded—especially Lucy, who can't resist competing and, as Isabelle relates to the mayor a droll anecdote from her journey, jumps doggedly in with both feet.

"Monsieur le Maire," she painstakingly enunciates, *"qu'est-ce qui se passe avec le hameau?"* A smart conversational move, you might think, since she is referring to one of the mayor's long-standing ambitions, the unloading on us of the abandoned shepherd's hamlet above Borgolano, but in fact a dumb one since the mayor would rather flirt with my sister right now than talk real estate. Plus, everyone wants to hear about this writer from Paris—includ-

ing, I should have thought, Lucy, who would like nothing better than to raise the social standards in the neighborhood.

"Madame Townsley, nothing has changed: The offer still stands. I welcome you at your convenience in my office to discuss the particulars."

I can see Lucy wants to forge on, but Odette takes the situation in hand: *"Alors,* what can you tell us about our new neighbor?"

The mayor smoothes his mustache. *"Eh bien,* Madame, he is called Philippe Kahn. You may have read his novel *La Cloche Fêlée.* I confess I only just started it myself; it is rather, shall we say, conceptual."

"Mais bien sûr!" exclaims Yolande. "A very good-looking man; I saw him on *Bouillon de Culture.* "

"Golly," says Jane, "won't he find our society a bit pedestrian?"

"I'll bet you he finds our society pretty stimulating," Isabelle says archly.

"I should imagine he'll be having friends down from Paris," Madame Benoît says eagerly.

"Surely he will have the house remodeled first," Odette demurs.

"I am not so sure, Madame. He was specifically looking for *une maison de charactère.* "

"Some famous French writer is moving in to the house next door," I explain to Jim, who is looking lost. Odette has noticed too.

"Jeem, would you be adorable and bring another bottle of rosé?"

Jim ambles off. Odette seems to have taken a liking to him and is always sending him on little errands, which is just as well, since he is the kind of guy who likes to feel useful.

"A charming idea, this *apéritif alfresco,*" declares the mayor. He clears his throat and grows solemn, our cue to pipe down. "I would like to take this opportunity to express the great loss we all felt at the news of Monsieur Wright's passing. I shall save my full remarks for the memorial. In the meantime, I wish to drink to the memory of a great man, a great friend to the Commune of Borgolano and to me personally."

"*Très bien,*" murmurs Madame Benoît.

"*Oui,*" Odette agrees.

"What did he say?" asks Jim, who has come back with the wine to find us all with grave countenances and raised glasses.

"*Cet enfant vous appartient?*"

We all turn to find Madame Paoli advancing onto the patio, a glum Electra in tow.

"Yes, of course she belongs to us," Lucy says irritably; then, as if suddenly realizing that something is out of order, "Where did you find her?"

"In my kitchen, Madame, eating our dinner."

"But I . . ."

Madame Paoli's expression conveys just what she thinks of these *anglais* who, while they themselves feast on hors d'oeuvres at ostentatious outdoor parties with public officials, leave their children to scavenge food from the kitchens of strangers—a sentiment evidently shared by Madame Mayor, whose eyebrows also descend a fraction.

"I am terribly sorry," Lucy says stiffly. "Thank you for bringing her back."

"*Pas du tout,* Madame. *Bon appétit.*"

"*Tiens,*" says the mayor, looking at his watch, "it is getting late. . . ."

CHAPTER *eleven*

Our guests quickly disperse, leaving Lucy free to fly off the handle.

"Where the hell were *you?*" she hisses at Richard.

Why does Richard put up with Lucy? you might wonder. Because he has to. They could never afford their lifestyle on his solicitor's salary. The reason they live in one of the most expensive parts of London, and buy teak garden furniture and take the whole summer off, is that Lucy is loaded. Jane too. When their father, Hugh Nicholson of Nicholson Breweries, died, he left them a trust fund, and it wasn't all tied up in African gold mines, either. Lucy has always had Richard under her thumb, but never more so than since Electra was born. If you ask me, she blames him. Not that there's anything overtly wrong with the guy: He's a perfectly average upper class Brit. He went to Cambridge and reads *The Guardian* and has so far only suffered minimal hair loss. But Lucy being Lucy, I'm sure she figures there's some sort of genetic flaw on his side of the family. She's always going on about how eccentric they are, which in England seems to be code for not-one-hundred-percent-there, and she loses no opportunity to intimate that there was nothing wrong with *her* results on the fertility tests.

"What do you mean, where was I? Where were *you?*"

"*I* was entertaining the mayor and *you* were meant to be watching the children. Oh, God . . ." Lucy bursts into tears. Richard observes her stonily.

"Calm down, Lucy," Jane says. "You're making a big deal out of nothing."

"I'm making a big deal out of nothing!" She's hysterical now. "The child breaks into a neighbor's house and—"

"She didn't break in, the door was open."

"You think this is *normal* behavior?" Lucy shrieks.

"We should have invited Madame Paoli," I remark. "Then she wouldn't have been such a bitch about it."

The conversation is getting too weird for Jim, who, seeing Yves coming down the path, hastens off in his direction.

"*You think* normal *children sneak into people's houses and steal food?*"

"I've had enough," says Richard through clenched teeth. He stalks off in the same direction as Yves and Jim. Lucy heaves another sob and shouts after him, "You were meant to watch her!" before running down the path toward the cliff, followed after a second by Jane.

"Why doesn't anyone have the guts to say it? There's something wrong with Electra."

We're in the kitchen cleaning up, Odette washing glasses

and Isabelle and me drying. "And I don't just mean the weight," Isabelle continues. "She hasn't spoken a word since we got here."

"You'd be fat and speechless, too, if you were Lucy's daughter," I say.

"Don't be so flippant, Constance. I'll tell you something: I have some friends in Prague whose daughter is autistic, and Electra behaves just like her."

Odette crosses herself. *"Ah mon Dieu!* Don't say such things. . . ."

"Why not? It's worse not to."

"For you, maybe," I point out.

"It's worse for Electra too. We're all going around pretending she's normal, beginning with Lucy. For all we know, she needs to be in an institution."

"Quelle tragédie . . ."

"You've been in Eastern Europe too long," I say. "We don't lock them up anymore."

"That's *not* what I meant. All I'm saying is that she probably needs treatment and she's not getting it."

"I agree with Isabelle," says Odette. "I have thought from the beginning that that poor child is *retardée.*"

"She said autistic, not retarded."

"Franchement, what is the difference?"

Jane comes in, putting an end to these deliberations.

"How is Lucy?" Odette asks.

Jane sits down and pours herself a glass of wine, causing Odette to frown. This idea of the French guzzling liters of Bordeaux daily is a myth, at least the women. Odette only drinks at meals and clearly thinks we're a bunch of lushes—especially Richard, who brought two bottles of vodka from London and has already polished one off.

"She's all right," Jane says wearily. "She's having a rest. Where are the children?"

"They are drawing nicely in the living room," Odette says sententiously. "All this fuss is not good for them."

"No, I daresay it isn't. . . ."

"I think we will just have salad for dinner, *non?* It is too late for a meal."

It's long past dinner when, through the open window, we hear voices and the rattle of loose gravel on the path.

"It seems the gentlemen have returned," Jane observes.

"Helloooo," Richard calls out, bumping his head on the lintel as he comes in to the kitchen. Jim has bashed his skull already on every door frame in the house, which was not built with strapping American farm boys in mind.

"Hi, girls," Jim says with a stupid grin. Yves just smirks.

"What did you do, crawl home?" I ask.

"Eddie gave us a ride. You know, the butcher. Great guy, Eddie. Here, we bought some meat for dinner: veal or something." Jim dumps on the table a bloodstained paper parcel containing what looks like ten pounds of pork chops. Odette wrinkles her nose.

"I suppose he gave you a discount too."

"Absolutely."

"Yes, I should hope so, considering that they are not of the first freshness. *Eh bien,* I suppose they won't kill us; we can have them for lunch tomorrow. Somebody will have to build me a fire for the grill."

"I'll be happy to," Jim says gallantly.

"It looks," says Jane after they've stumbled out, "like the local lads caught on to a good thing. I wonder how many rounds they got out of them."

Odette makes an indulgent clucking sound. "Like children . . ."

CHAPTER *twelve*

Surprise, surprise: Odette *is* sleeping with Yves. Lucy, our moral watchdog, caught them in the woodshed.

"Disgusting," she stammers, her eyes wide with indignation. "She actually had her skirt up around her waist and he—"

"Go on," Isabelle says eagerly.

"Well, you know." A furious blush has spread across Lucy's pale cheeks (she's allergic to the sun and doesn't leave the house without coating herself in SPF 45 cream). "It's perfectly disgraceful; one of the children could have walked in."

Isabelle giggles. "Poor old Odette. Why shouldn't she be getting some, even if it's only from dweeby Yves?"

"That's right, make a big joke out of it. Am I the only one who remembers that Daddy's been dead barely a year? Not only does she have the nerve to carry on with the little wretch in our house, I suppose she plans to bring him to the memorial service as well!"

I've never entirely gotten over the weirdness of Lucy calling Ross Daddy. Nobody else ever did, not even Isabelle. "Since when are we having a service?" I ask. "I thought we were just supposed to disperse his ashes?"

"Why are you being so horrible, Lucy?" Isabelle cuts in. "Odette has every right to go on with her life. She's not the Virgin Mary."

Lucy's on a roll now. "It's the lack of dignity that makes me sick: that they would carry on right there with Daddy's ashes on the shelf—"

"Is that where they are?" Jane says. "I was wondering where she put them."

"I thought you said they were in the woodshed," I interject. "Odette and lover-boy, that is."

"At least *someone* is getting laid around here, besides Constance," Isabelle says. "It's beginning to feel like *Bleak House.*"

"I don't think that's what *Bleak House* was about," Jane says.

"Well," Isabelle says, "I'm going to tell her that she has our blessing."

"I agree," I say. "We're all grownups."

"Well, you can count *me* out. For heaven's sake, this is the woman who threw Jane's girlfriend out of the house!"

"She did *not* throw her out," Isabelle says. "She just made tactless remarks that Marge was too humorless to brush off. It's what's known as a cultural misunderstanding."

Jane says nothing.

"If he moves into her bedroom, I'm leaving," Lucy declares before stomping out.

"What a grouch," Isabelle sighs, flopping onto the bed. Our little conclave has been taking place in my bedroom, formerly

Lucy's and possibly yet another of the little things that set her off. "I was wondering why Yves stayed out of sight when the mayor came. Poor Odette: She's probably afraid he'll think she's a hussy." She frowns. "It *is* kind of creepy, her keeping Dad's ashes in her bedroom. I mean, when you think about it."

"Where was she supposed to put them?" I say.

"I don't know. The living room?"

"She's French," Jane says dryly. "They're very pragmatic about that sort of thing."

This latest *affaire,* at least, has distracted Lucy from the matter of Electra's food raid. By dinnertime she's calmed down and even offers to cook, always a good sign with Lucy. Isabelle had a talk with Odette, who was mortified and protested that she wouldn't hear of Yves moving into the bedroom that she had shared with Ross. Go figure. Maybe they just like sneaking around. As for Yves, he pays meticulous attention to the food on his plate: a vegetable *ragoût* of Lucy's composition with, perplexingly, crushed peanuts sprinkled on top.

"*Délicieux,*" he murmurs, eyes cast firmly downward. Lucy tosses him a look of utter contempt. Richard remains glacial. He has obviously not forgiven her her little scene of yesterday. The only ones unaffected by the tense atmosphere are Isabelle and Electra, who has not behaved inappropriately since yesterday with the exception, as gleefully related by Sophie, of eating a big booger. Sophie and Olga are out of control as usual. They're dressed up as Gypsies, which, as Odette tersely points out after the salad, does not give them license to act like "*sauvages.*"

"Mommy! What's a *sauvage?*"

"An uncivilized person."

"Mommy! Are we uncivilized?"

"Yes," Isabelle laughs.

"When is Daddy coming to visit us?"

"I don't know."

"You said he was coming!"

"I did not."

"You *promised!*"

"Manipulative little beast," Jane whispers to me.

Everyone drinks too much, except Odette.

Later on, upstairs, Jim asks, "What was *that* all about?" I never got around to filling him in on the latest developments because he was gone most of the day hiking with Richard. It occurs to me that, except at night, we're not spending a whole lot of quality time together. I should have known that my family was going to be a distraction.

"Lucy caught Yves and Odette in a compromising position."

"Really? I kind of figured there was something going on there. So I guess you're upset because of her being your dad's wife and all?"

"No. Come here." I grab him by the belt and pull him down on top of me. "Take your pants off. I couldn't care less. Lucy flipped her lid, though."

"Oh."

"Hence the slight tension at dinner. That and the fact that she and Richard aren't speaking."

"Richard's a good guy."

"Yeah, whatever." I'm tugging at his boxer shorts. Unaccountably, I have a mental flash of Yves in the little bikini briefs I imagine he wears, with a big erection poking out. The bulge in his bathing suit suggests that he's rather well endowed.

Speaking of erections, Jim seems sadly distracted tonight, or maybe it's the wine. I let go of his penis and tickle his balls instead.

"Why are you all so dismissive of him? Do you think he doesn't notice?"

I give up altogether. It seems somehow inappropriate to discuss Richard while fondling Jim's scrotum.

"If Richard is looking for respect," I say, "he's going to have to learn how to stand up to his wife."

"Well, he kind of implied to me that he's going to."

"Nothing like male bonding for that testosterone rush, huh?"

"Are you ever *not* sarcastic?"

"Not about my family. It's a necessary defense mechanism: In case you haven't noticed, most of them aren't right in the head."

"I know it's none of my business," says Jim, "but you guys sure aren't very nice to each other."

"Oh, for Christ's sake," I snap. "Get over it. You're not in Kansas anymore."

It's our first fight. We sleep back-to-back.

CHAPTER *thirteen*

The next day, our new neighbor moves in. Isabelle, out hanging laundry, is the first to see him. She reports at breakfast that he is *most* attractive, very Paris Intellectual: longish black hair, Alain Mikli glasses, nice clothes.

"Uh-oh," Jane says, "now she'll start walking around completely naked."

"Not around *you* I won't, you old pervert. I wonder where we could find a copy of his book. . . ."

"We must ask Madame Peretti. Perhaps she has one stashed behind the tins of spaghetti sauce."

"Why don't we have him over for dinner?" Lucy suggests brightly.

"This is France," Jane says. "You can't just invite strangers over for dinner. He'll think we're mad, or desperate."

"We *are* desperate," Isabelle says.

"Speak for yourself," Lucy says.

Yesterday's crisis has dissipated. Jim forgave me this morning after I woke him up with a blow job, and then took off early for the beach with his new best friend, Richard, and all the kids. Odette has remarked on how good he is with children, so unusual in a man. I guess she's right, though frankly, the last few days have made me seriously wonder about the whole breeding issue. Who needs the aggravation? Yves and Odette are in Flore, doing *le shopping*. "About bloody time too," declares Lucy.

"Anyway," Isabelle says, "I told him he was welcome to use the patio."

"Big of you."

"The main question is, has he come alone? I saw no evidence of either a wife or a girlfriend."

"Mmmm, solitary brooding intellectual . . ." Jane says, winking at me.

"Alors, have you seen him?" Yolande Van Langendonck comes scooting in, in a long *djellabah* with a matching turquoise turban. Her eye job today suggests that she's been getting makeup tips from old *Star Trek* episodes. As our local eccentric, Yolande is exempted from the rules of decorum that forbid things like wandering into other people's houses, something Madame Benoît, with whom Odette is much chummier, would never presume to do.

"Only Isabelle," Jane says. "She contrived to be hanging up her wet underpants just as he arrived."

"Tssss, naughty girl. I saw him in the *parking*—*very* handsome. I understand that he is divorced. . . ."

"Do tell. What's your source?"

"Monsieur le Maire heard it from Countess Fatulescu. Have I

earned a cup of coffee?" Yolande, the only person in Borgolano to have actually gained an entrée to the reclusive Countess Fatulescu, has been trying ever since to make social capital out of this great good luck, imagining that we're all dying to meet her too. I have to admit, I wouldn't mind seeing her house, by far the grandest in the area and, in Lucy's opinion, one that *we* should rightfully inhabit.

"Oh, of course, I'm so sorry—here, Lucy made some chestnut-flour scones."

"*Tiens,* how *original.*"

"And how exactly," Jane asks, "is Countess Fatulescu privy to this information?"

"Well, she is a poetess. I expect they move in the same circles in Paris," Yolande says grandly.

The word on Yolande is that her husband died in the Congo under mysterious circumstances—he was some kind of explorer, apparently—and she never really got over it, hence her semi-exile in Santerre. Odette says more likely she's on the run from the Belgian IRS. She is, in any case, a local figure of some substance, especially given her friendship with the mayor. Personally, I think they may well be fooling around. Madame Mayor has a mustache and doesn't seem like the type who would wear frisky G-strings under her housedress. If I were Yolande, though, what with the Santerran predilection for vendettas, I'd be worried about her relatives.

"I must betray a secret," she now announces. "The countess is thinking of having *un petit cocktail,* to get to know the neighbors. She has asked me to make a guest list—you understand, she doesn't want to invite *n'importe qui*—and, naturally, I suggested your family."

"Too kind," Jane says with a straight face.

"I think now that I will also include Monsieur Kahn. Hmmmm, a Jewish name, *non?*"

"You can ask him yourself," I say, glancing out the window. "He's heading this way."

Philippe Kahn is indeed good-looking, if you go in for that sort of thing: I'll bet he wears a leather jacket in the winter. He also speaks good English, the result of having spent five years teaching at Columbia University in New York. He came over, he explains, to introduce himself and to ask if we knew the location of the gas and electric *compteurs,* both of which were shut off by the Costas. While clearly not a leering oik, he seems gratified to find that two of his neighbors are major babes, one of whom—Isabelle—is looking like lunch just walked in. Lucy has slipped into her ice queen act. She can't help it: She thinks it makes her look mysterious.

"Didn't they tell you?" Isabelle says with a smile that reveals her diastema to fetching effect. "They locked them up in the basement after they found out that the Paolis were siphoning off their current."

"A completely unfounded accusation, by the way," Jane points out.

"*Pas du tout,*" Yolande leaps in. "Some of these *retraités* will stop at nothing to reduce their utilities bills. I myself—"

"Madame Peretti up at the shop might have a key," Lucy coolly interposes, obviously aiming to rein the conversation back from the loopy regions where Yolande will take it if left unrestrained. "She was friendly with the Costas."

"Have you come alone?" Isabelle asks our new neighbor.

He smiles self-deprecatingly. "I'm afraid so. I have come to work. I suppose I could live without electricity, but I need it for my computer. . . ."

"I have just finished *La Cloche Fêlée,*" Yolande says breathlessly, returning to the charge.

Lucy cuts her off. "Then we must have your power restored. I'll call Madame Peretti." She gets up and glides majestically out into the hallway, her loose linen shirt floating behind her like a vestal virgin's train. Isabelle also rises, a motion that causes a gravitational shift inside her tank top and that is duly registered by our new neighbor, whose eyes flicker in acknowledgment.

"Will you have a cup of coffee while you're waiting?"

"Please. What a charming kitchen: I see you have kept it in the original state. I'm afraid mine has been ruined."

"Madame Costa was not known for her *bon goût,*" Yolande says primly. "You must come and see my house; I like to think I have found a happy compromise between tradition and modernity. Surely you will wish to make *travaux;* I have found a reasonable local *équipe,* though of course one has to watch them like hawks." She leans forward and lowers her voice. "The gentleman Madame Benoît hired last year to do her bathroom turned out to be a sexual degenerate."

Our neighbor represses a smile. "Did he? Good Lord! I'm afraid I won't be in any danger, though, as I really have come to write. I may rip up the linoleum in my spare time: There must be a stone floor somewhere underneath."

"You're in luck," says Lucy, returning. "Madame Peretti does have a key."

"Oh, good, I'll run right up. What delicious coffee." His eyes flicker again and I realize it's not Isabelle he keeps glancing at but Jane, sitting beside her.

"Mademoiselle Nicholson," he says, "I must confess that I am an admirer of your work. I own two of your paintings."

Jane blushes. For all her success—just last month there was a big feature on her in *Art Forum*—she's one of the most unassuming people I know.

"Though you must not think I am one of these stalkers. I promise you I only found out after I bought the house."

"I'm sure," Jane says, "that your intentions were entirely honorable."

"You must come to dinner sometime," Lucy says.

"I would be delighted."

"What's with the sexual degenerate?" I ask after he's gone.

"Oh, don't you know?" Yolande says eagerly. "It was one of the Simonetti boys. Madame Benoît caught him reading the label on her birth control pills. Can you imagine?"

"Weird," Isabelle says.

"These are not civilized people," Yolande says.

CHAPTER *fourteen*

That night we head out for dinner at the Marmite du Pêcheur, our local bistro. Even Lucy, with her undying faith in peasant cooking, has abandoned all hope of redemption for the Simonetti family's tourist-fleecing operation, where, under a canopy of moldy salamis and desiccated garlic bunches, diners are subjected to Madame Simonetti's lethal interpretations of Santerran cuisine. As summer residents, however, we have to pay our respects once, after which, like everyone else, we can stick to the café.

Of all the Marmite's pretenses, most cynical is its implied relationship with any kind of *pêcheur,* Monsieur Simonetti, now slumped at the bar in a drunken stupor, having long ago given up fishing for drinking. Whatever hapless sea creature ends up in Madame's pot has made a long journey from the Super-Géant in Canonica, as have the few vegetables on offer and the *charcuterie du pays.*

"Ah, our American friends!" the *patron* calls out as we file in the door, much to the disapproval of Odette, who, despite having married one, considers herself anything but. "*Alors,* what are you having?"

A bottle of the thistle-based local *apéritif* appears and is sloshed into glasses and handed around. The patron wisely sticks to whisky. Behind the bar, his son Fabrice grins toothily. It is rumored that he and Eddie the butcher are involved in nationalist activities, in light of which it's occurred to me that the attempted poisoning of tourists by Madame Simonetti may be part of a wider and more sinister plot. Eddie is also present, his hairy chest festooned with gold chains and a diamond stud winking in his ear, as well as Toto, the village halfwit and winner of last year's *pétanque* tournament.

Now that Ross is gone, Isabelle is the only one of us who has any meaningful contact with the natives. She's been known to hang out at the Marmite, tossing back *fines* and flirting up a storm, though so far her consumption has been limited to beverages. The hungry leer Toto the halfwit gives her when she pecks him on the cheek doesn't seem to disturb her, though, nor the rustle of Eddie's jewelry in his thickets of chest hair. But then, Isabelle doesn't find lust alarming.

"*Ça va?*"

"*Ça va?*"

Lucy, Jane, and I stick to shaking hands, cementing our reputation as frosty Anglo bitches, except with Albertine, the Simonettis' daughter-cum-slave-laborer, who hastens out of the kitchen to greet us. According to Isabelle, Albertine's ambitions to go to fashion school in Marseille were thwarted forever when her brother married the perfidious Marcelle, relegating Albertine to the bottom of the familial pecking order. Marcelle herself, a handsome woman in her thirties, now appears, every inch the hostess in her tight skirt and high-heel pumps. Her scheme, as I understand it, is to keep Albertine gravy-stained and aproned in the kitchen while she takes over the firm's management. It seems to be working.

"Terrible about Monsieur Wright," she murmurs. *"Une tragédie . . ."*

"Un grand homme," slurs the *patron.*

Under what I assume is Marcelle's influence, the menu has taken on a decidedly nouvelle cuisine intonation since last year. Gone are the chops and fish fries, the mucilaginous *soupe de poisson.* In their place, to Lucy's (premature, I'm convinced) delight, a saddle of baby lamb (local) with a crust of wild herbs from the *maquis,* a *méli-mélo* of garden vegetables, and even bouillabaisse.

"Hey, I've always wanted to try bouillabaisse," Jim says eagerly.

"I'd stick to the pork chops," I caution him.

Albertine stands dolefully by, waiting for us to make our selection. She used to be a snappy dresser, hoping perhaps that a man from the continent would walk in one night and sweep her off her feet. Tonight she looks resigned in a T-shirt and jeans. What must it be like, I wonder every time I see her, to be stuck in Borgolano all year with Eddie and Toto and the guy who sniffed Madame Benoît's birth control pills, waiting for the next tourist season, imploding with rage as your prospects inexorably diminish? At the next table, a group of vacationers from the mainland are tucking into one of Madame Simonetti's terrifying charcuterie platters, reviving my doubts about the new menu. The popularity of her fifty-franc *formule touristique* certainly puts to rest any notion of all French people being discerning gastronomes.

"I think I'll give the lamb a try," Lucy says. "Electra, *stop it!*" At the other end of the table, Electra is picking her nose with furious concentration, to hysterical giggles from Sophie and Olga. "Richard, can't you see what she's doing?"

Richard ignores her and goes on talking to Jim.

"*Richard!*"

"Sorry, darling?"

Electra belches, long and loud. Olga and Sophie scream with delight.

"Girls," Odette says severely, "if you do not stop, I will have to lock you in the car." Lucy, who disapproves of threats, opens her mouth to object, but just then Albertine appears with our first courses.

"I warned you," I tell Jim when his bouillabaisse arrives: two boiled fish in a viscous pool of Madame Simonetti's *soupe de poisson*. Lucy's rack of lamb turns out to be the familiar greasy chops dusted with bread crumbs.

"*Tinned* green beans!" she exclaims with disgust.

"Good thing you didn't order the lobster," Jane remarks.

After dinner, which we've washed down with several carafes of the gut-wrenching *réserve du patron,* Isabelle follows Albertine to the kitchen for a smoke. It's what Albertine's been waiting for all night: Isabelle seems to inspire people to confide in her—a mistake, since she has absolutely no discretion. I head off to the bathroom, which is to the left of the bar, and on my way out find our new neighbor ordering a Pernod. No sign of Eddie or Toto.

He smiles. "We meet again."

"Trust me, the novelty will wear off."

He seems to find this funny. He's got a navy blue sweater draped and knotted around his shoulders, a style that normally irritates me.

"Then I shall have to enjoy it while it lasts. . . . Cigarette?"

"No, thanks, I'm one of those American nonsmoker types."

"Of course. You don't mind?"

"Not at all. I like the smell."

He lights his cigarette and exhales in that unaccountably sexy way that has been exploited by every French movie ever made. "Borgolano seems a curious place for an American family to buy a summer home. I should think it would seem rather rustic."

"Oh, we like rustic. Besides, we're not really an American family: My sister lives in Prague and Jane and Lucy are from London."

"And how, if I may ask, did such an international group of people come together?"

"My father kept marrying women of different nationalities," I say.

"I see. I would argue with you that this in itself is very American."

"Yeah, I see what you mean. I guess he was more of a professional expatriate."

"You speak of him in the past tense."

"He's dead."

"I'm sorry."

"That's okay, it happened a year ago. We're here to disperse his ashes, actually; I think the mayor is going to make a speech. What were you doing at Columbia?"

"Teaching literary theory to alarming girls in black leather."

I laugh.

"You are familiar with the species?" he asks.

"I went to Columbia. For business school, though, not undergrad."

"Ah, yes, I shouldn't imagine there was much black leather in the business school."

"Only on people's feet."

Now *he* laughs. "Well, Miss Nicholson—"

"Wright. Jane and Lucy are Nicholsons, different fathers; I know, it's confusing. You can just call me Constance."

"Constance. How pretty. Well, Constance, I have held you up long enough. I think I shall go in and have some dinner—unless you would like to join me?"

"Thanks, we've eaten already. Don't order the bouillabaisse."

"Constance, there you are!" Lucy, also on her way to the bathroom. Her expression subtly shifts when she sees who I'm with. "Hello, Philippe. What a shame we didn't know you were coming: You could have joined us—though, to tell you the truth, you'd be best off going home and making yourself an omelette."

"Good evening, Miss Nicholson. Don't worry about me: My standards have been hopelessly adulterated by university cafeterias."

"I'm afraid you'll find Madame Simonetti's cooking several notches even below that. Constance, we're going back down, the children are getting wild. Perhaps you could drag Isabelle out of the kitchen."

"I'd be happy to walk back with you if you want to stay," Philippe says.

"That's all right. Isabelle might take you up, though."

"Ah, yes, your charming sister."

In the kitchen my charming sister is deep in conversation with Albertine, or rather, sucking intently on a cigarette while Albertine relates the latest string of indignities inflicted upon her by her sister-in-law. Isabelle is the kind of person who, at a catered party, will always end up in the kitchen with the staff. While I find this presumption of being more at ease with the commoners to be completely affected, she does seem to take a genuine interest in the pathetic details of Albertine's life.

"Hey, Constance, come and join us." Albertine doesn't seem to think this is such a great idea. My French isn't good enough for cozy chatting, and I don't have Isabelle's populist touch.

"Can't, we're going. You can go back down with our neighbor if you want to stay. He's in the bar."

"Oooh, really?" Isabelle drolly crosses her eyes. She has a slight strabismus, which intensifies when she's tired or drunk.

"Yup. I wouldn't make that face around him if I were you."

"My little sister," Isabelle says in French to Albertine, "is always picking on me."

Albertine shoots me a baleful look. I'm clearly ruining her evening.

"Have you seen him? He's *quite* the dark and mysterious stranger. . . ."

Albertine shrugs, no doubt figuring that if Isabelle's got her eye on him, he's out of her range. Besides, Marcelle has just come in and is wondering what all those dirty dishes are doing stacked on the table. Isabelle pats Albertine consolingly on the shoulder and, to me, whispers, "What a bitch"—none of which prevents her from abandoning Albertine and following me out, her big mouth stretched into her most seductive smile.

"Complete weirdo," Isabelle announces the next morning. "We talked about Czech theater and then he walked me home. D'you think he's gay?"

"Clearly," Jane says. "Otherwise how could he have resisted you?"

"Stop picking on me, you big old lezzie. Oh, well, I guess I'll have to resign myself to a month of celibacy. . . ."

"There's always Eddie the butcher," I suggest.

"*Please*, he's a child molester."

"I very much doubt that," Jane says. "It doesn't seem like the kind of thing the aborigines would put up with."

"Well, whatever—a teen molester, then. Remember the Danish girl?"

"I'd rather not."

"Anyway, I don't really think he's gay. I think his wife left him and he's still getting over it. He's got that shell-shocked look."

"Sounds to me like you have tons in common," I remark.

"Is Jiri keeping in touch with the girls?" Jane asks.

"They're supposed to be spending August with him in Krasna Hora," Isabelle says, meaning Jiri's spartan mountain dacha near the Polish border, which has neither hot water nor electricity and where I once spent a miserable week listening to them conceiving Olga in the attic.

"I sometimes think," she says dreamily, "that if Dad were still alive, none of this would have happened." By which I guess she means her divorce, though with Isabelle you never know. As she bends down to scratch a mosquito bite, exposing a patch of golden down on her lower back, I am thinking that our neighbor is indeed an odd bird, even as I am equally convinced that in the end he will succumb.

CHAPTER *fifteen*

Overnight, the air goes still. We wake up to a white haze that cloaks the sea in a metallic sheen. "God, it's hot," Jim groans. Our sheets, tossed off in the night, lie in a twisted heap on the floor, next to my discarded underpants and a spent condom that looks like a little shroud. It's a good thing Jim and I have been fucking so much, because our conversations haven't been anything to write home about. Not that they ever were: In New York we spend most of our free time at the gym, and how much meaningful intellectual exchange can you have on a StairMaster? Could it be that our relationship has been fueled entirely by sex and exercise? I don't even know anything about his family except that they have a farm, and I think he has a sister in Minneapolis. I've caught myself wondering of late if my lack of interest in the details of Jim's life is symptomatic of some fatal character flaw. Undoubtedly it is, but he shouldn't take it personally: The truth is, I find most people outside my family boring. What had not occurred to me until now is that this might present a problem.

"It's the sirocco," I explain, resolving to be a better person henceforth, or at least one who does not get irritated by nice midwestern American boys who can't tell one Mediterranean wind from another.

"The what?"

"A wind that comes from the Sahara. It'll be really oppressive for a couple days and then it'll start blowing—or not. Sometimes it changes its mind."

"Weird."

"Not really. Africa isn't that far away."

Jim yawns and gazes at the big crack in the ceiling. "Why did your father buy this house?"

"He liked to live on the edge. It's the only part of France with terrorists."

"Yeah, right," Jim says languidly. I'm noticing a change in him, a subtle but unmistakable erosion of his midwestern innocence—the beginnings of an edge? Maybe it's all the time he's spending with neurotic Richard.

"Actually, Odette found the house. She used to come here on vacation. My father was a big indulger of the whims of women."

"He must have been really in love with her," Jim says wonderingly.

"Oddly enough, I think he might have been."

Jim frowns. "What do you mean, 'oddly enough'?"

"Nothing," I say lightly. "It's just hard to imagine Odette inspiring a great passion."

"Well," says Jim, "I can see how a lot of men would find her glamorous and fascinating."

"Whatever," I say in a bored tone.

It's so stifling outside that we decide to walk down to the water after breakfast—even Lucy, who naturally suggests packing a picnic.

"This English tradition of eating outside is very curious, *non?*" Odette remarks to Isabelle.

"The idea is to make the consumption of food as uncomfortable as possible," Jane says. "It's a part of the Protestant experience."

"At least we eat our food and keep it down," Lucy retorts, with a meaningful glance at Odette: a bit rich, coming from a former bulimic, who even now, for all her obsession with fine gastronomy, fanatically watches what she and everyone else eats—unlike Isabelle, who has taken the mention of a picnic as a cue to start throwing potato chips and cookies into a bag.

"I thought perhaps some cheese and fruit," Lucy says testily, her eyes on Electra.

"I'm not eating Santerran cheese outside. The last time we tried, those dogs followed us home." Howls of laughter from Olga and Sophie, who start chanting, "Stinky cheese! Stinky cheese!" A pretty apt description, actually.

And so we're off, Richard in the minivan with the cooler, the kids, and Odette, who, not being a Protestant, doesn't see the point of walking if there's a perfectly good motorized conveyance available. The rest of us go on foot. Borgolano is perched atop an escarpment so that if you want to reach the water you have to go down, first past a series of disused terraces where, before EC subsidies, people supposedly grew vegetables, and then through the *maquis,* the scrub-wood that carpets the mountainside, on a path originally meant for goats. There is a road, too, which Richard has taken, but it's twice as long. Either way, getting to the water is a production, and once you're there, perils await in the form of jagged rocks and the irascible marine wildlife. Which is why we usually drive to Orzo where the beach is sandy—well, pebbly, anyway—and reasonably child-friendly, and the worse thing that can happen to you is drowning.

Not being a sun worshipper myself, I prefer our treacherous cove with its glinting pools full of crabs and minnows. The Borgolano *plage* was once an integral part of the village, as you can tell from the stone fishing cabins that cling stolidly to the final stretch of slope before the sea, and the cement dock where the daily catch was unloaded. Yolande owns three of these fishing cabins, currently all rented, to judge from the towels hanging out the windows, and the other four, entangled in inheritance disputes, are falling apart, which drives Lucy nuts. She's been trying for years to buy one, yammering on about stark purity of form and the sound of the waves at night, though we all know that what she really wants is to get away from the rest of us.

What luck: Eddie and Toto have also picked today for a swim. I catch sight of them as we round the bend, Eddie furry and oiled in tiny bikini briefs, and Toto, mercifully, in boxer shorts with *Malibou Beach* plastered all over them. The two of them are reputed to be inseparable—strange, you might think, considering Toto's mental handicap, but then, while he's not officially retarded, Eddie's IQ isn't jumping off any charts, either.

"Shouldn't they be at work?" says Lucy, frowning with disapproval as Isabelle waves in their direction. "Stop it, they'll want to join us."

"They're all right. . . ."

"I'm really not up to socializing with the local fauna."

"Why don't you just relax; it's not like you have to have sex with them."

"*That* is disgusting."

Too late: They're upon us. Isabelle pecks them both on the cheek, which means that the rest of us have to follow suit. The politics of kissing, as far as I can make out, are that you can get away with a handshake the first time, but on the second encounter it looks rude. Even Lucy submits, with barely concealed distaste. The guys all manfully shake hands, Yves netting a thump on the back, an indication of how much time he's been spending at the Marmite bar.

"*Attention les filles,*" Eddie says with a leer, "lots of jellyfish today. . . ."

"Both in and out of the water," Jane observes.

"Ssssshhh!"

We spread our towels on the flat area above the dock, Eddie and Toto sauntering around and looking helpful. They're both wearing blue plastic jelly sandals—a necessity, due to the sea urchins—which make them look childish in a way that is somehow more alarming than incongruous. Jim's fancy diving shoes from Paragon Sports in New York arouse much admiration:

"*Cool!*"

"James Bond," Toto says with an idiotic grin.

Once we've arranged our towels, we all stand around looking foolish, except for Eddie and Toto, who just look expectant. What do they want? Ah, of course: While we've all been waiting for them to leave to strip down to our bathing suits, Isabelle, never prey to bourgeois modesty, has tossed off her sundress and, in a flash, removed her bikini top. Toto's tongue doesn't exactly hang out but his eyes go glassy. Eddie's are hidden by his mirrored sunglasses.

His smile stretches wider. Poor Yves has gone all mottled and Jim has the bemused look of a tourist stumbling upon a natural wonder.

"*Must* you do that?" Lucy hisses.

"Whaaat?" my sister drawls.

"Don't you boys have anything to do besides block the sun?" Odette says briskly.

They shrug and amble off, Toto casting a longing look behind him.

"*Vraiment chérie,* you should not provoke them so. These are not civilized people."

"Odette," Jane says, pulling off her T-shirt to reveal her sensible blue bathing suit, "your political incorrectness is always refreshing."

Odette, undressing with her usual efficiency, looks at her blankly. She and Jane have never really gotten each other, and the incident with Marge didn't help.

"Anybody going in the water?" Jim asks.

"Would you take the girls, please?" Isabelle says lazily. "They're champing at the bit."

"Sure. Come on, last one in is a rotten egg!"

"Aren't you going to put swimsuits on them?" says Lucy.

"What for?"

Lucy glances meaningfully toward Eddie and Toto but says nothing.

Electra, squeezed into a pink bathing suit, waddles off after the naked and already toast-brown Olga and Sophie, followed by Richard, brandishing a bottle of SPF 30 sunscreen.

"Don't forget to do her shoulders," Lucy calls out. She herself is in the process of covering every inch of her skin with lotion, her face already protected by a huge straw hat. With a quick look around, she removes her bikini top, too, keeping it close at hand in case Eddie and Toto reappear. Lucy's breasts are small and elegant and tipped with dainty pink nipples. I always get the sense that it's torture for her, baring them, that she goes topless only because she's in France, the way some women feel obligated to wear a head scarf in Muslim countries. Meanwhile, Isabelle has changed her mind, jumping up and racing toward the water.

"Cor blimey!" Jane exclaims.

"She's had them done," Lucy says flatly.

"What?" I say.

"Her breasts. She's had them lifted."

"No way."

"They didn't look like that last year."

I try to summon a mental picture. It's not like I spend a lot of time staring at my sister's breasts, though I have to admit that there *was* something curiously gravity-defying about them as they bounced by. She *is,* after all, thirty-eight.

"Gosh," Jane says, "d'you really think so?"

"You can see the scar line when she's lying down."

"Bloody hell!"

Odette props herself up on her elbows and gives Lucy a pitying glance.

"Et alors? So what?"

"Well, I just find it rather ironic."

"What is ironic?"

"That our carefree Isabelle would try to cheat the clock."

Odette raises a perfectly plucked eyebrow. I don't suppose she's had her own breasts lifted, since they're of the neat and tiny French variety. But she's had her face and butt done, and no doubt some additional tightening here and there, judging by her drumlike stomach, which barely even creases above her bikini bottom when she sits up, as she does now.

"What an interesting expression, *cheat the clock.* A very English idea."

"Quite right," agrees Jane. "Laden with guilt, just the way we like it."

"Well, we French do not feel guilty about cheating the clock," Odette says serenely.

"That's pretty obvious," Lucy says.

"Yes, we want to look good, to embrace life's pleasures. This is a difference between us."

"Oh, please, spare us the clichés."

"But most clichés are true. This is why they become clichés, no?"

Yves saunters back, all dripping wet, and plops himself down next to Odette, who makes a playful show of pushing him away. Though he's still nominally residing in the attic, they both seem to have relaxed a bit on the public opinion front. Still, Yves continues to baffle me, as does Odette's interest in him. Beyond his generic Frenchness, he doesn't really seem to have a personality. Lighting his cigarette now with a cupped hand, even though there's no wind yet, and except that he's in a bathing suit, he could be any one of those men you see leaning up against the counter in Paris cafés on a weekday morning, their jeans a little too tight, one small loafer propped on the foot rail. It's almost as if he'd perversely decided to embody all of Lucy's stereotypes. Jim keeps saying he's a good guy, but Jim would probably think Mussolini was a good guy.

"Had a nice swim, Yves?" Lucy inquires, her voice dripping sarcasm.

"Yes, sank you."

"I'm delighted to hear it. Our father was an accomplished swimmer, as Odette has undoubtedly told you."

A scream pierces the air. Richard is running toward us, a howling Electra in his arms, followed by Jim and the girls, babbling in their strange Czech-English jargon. Lucy leaps to her feet. I guess she's forgotten that she's topless since Toto and Eddie, attracted by the commotion, also hurry over.

Electra, we are informed breathlessly by Sophie, has been stung by a jellyfish. An angry rash has begun to spread down her right cheek, which, with flailing arms pinned by Richard, she is frantically trying to scratch, all the while emitting panicked yelps.

"I thought you were keeping an eye on her!"

"Hey," Jim objects, "it wasn't Richard's fault: The thing just swam by!"

Lucy whips around. "Who asked *you?!*"

Jim backs off, a wounded look in his eyes. Richard tries to put Electra down, but as Lucy reaches for her, she burrows sobbing against him.

"Mean old jellyfish," Sophie declares solemnly.

"Bad," says Olga.

"Don't just stand there like a bloody fool!" Lucy cries. "We've got to get her to a doctor!"

"*Fais voir.*" Eddie the butcher puts his hand out to touch Electra's face.

"Get your hands off her!" Lucy screams. As if she'd just realized that she's half naked, her arms fly up across her breasts as her face turns as crimson as her daughter's.

CHAPTER *sixteen*

It's a good thing Odette is around to take control at moments like these. She produces a tube of anti-inflammatory cream from her beach tote and briskly sets about applying it. Once everyone has calmed down, even Lucy realizes the pointlessness of driving all the way to the emergency room in Canonica. She slathers Electra's face with more ointment and even allows Odette to give her a piece of candy.

I still can't believe that Isabelle would have plastic surgery. Not only does this fly in the face of everything my sister is supposed to be about, the source of the imputation is inherently suspect. Nonetheless, I find myself sneaking looks, as, I notice, does Jane. Finally I can't take it anymore. I corner her on the roof, where she's gone up to catch the sun's last rays. Isabelle has never minded the heat: You could say it's her element. She's lying on her back and I can clearly see now the two pale pencil lines.

"Have you had your breasts done?"

"Whaat?"

I gather from her disoriented look that she was asleep.

"Have you had your breasts lifted?"

She reaches for her sunglasses, puts them on, and slowly sits up, casting her shadow across me. "Yes," she says.

"You're joking." I stare at them. The nipples are perfectly symmetrical in a way that probably doesn't exist in nature. They are also, I now see, pointing at the sky.

She grins at me. "So, what do you think? Didn't they do a great job?"

"Have you lost your mind?"

"No. I'm not going to have any more children; I don't need all those milk ducts."

"Right, of course. That makes perfect sense. Make sure and remind me when the time comes so I can get mine done too."

She peers at me quizzically, or so I imagine, since she's wearing dark glasses.

"Why are you so upset?"

She has a point: Why *am* I so upset? It's her body. And yet, a thought flashes through my mind that she has diminished herself. I realize that I'm standing over her like the Grand Inquisitor. I pull over the beach chair that Odette keeps up here for sunbathing—she and Isabelle are both impervious to ultraviolet rays—and lower myself onto the cheap plastic webbing, not sure it will hold my weight.

"I'm just shocked, I guess. Why did you do it?"

Isabelle shrugs in a fatalistic way I associate with Czech women and lies back down, removing the glasses and laying them beside her on the dusty rooftop. "Why do you think? Because I want to stay young and beautiful."

How strange it's never occurred to me that my sister is vain, that she would remember to take off her glasses so she won't get raccoon circles around her eyes. That she would get her breasts sliced open and hoisted to look like an eighteen-year-old.

"Don't look so disapproving. It's no big deal in Prague: Everybody does it."

"Why? So you can keep on catching men? You do anyway; you didn't need to have surgery."

"I lost Jiri," she says.

"I thought you didn't care."

"Oh, Constance, you are so literal. Of course I care, but I also see the writing on the wall. He's always liked younger girls."

"Yeah, because he's a disgusting old goat."

"Honey, they all are. Even your nice Jim. One day he'll get old and he'll be a disgusting old goat, too, you'll see."

"Any other pearls of wisdom?"

"Use it while it lasts."

"Were you really in love with Jiri?" I ask her.

"Of course I was, dummy. Why else would I have followed him to a communist country?"

"Are you still in love with him?"

She appears to give this serious consideration. "I don't know," she finally says. "I can't figure out if I'm wounded because he ran off with that bimbo, or because I miss him. I feel bad for the girls. Since I told him to go to hell, he's been punishing me by not seeing them. I'm not even sure he'll really take them in August: I haven't heard from him since he mentioned it. I don't know what he was thinking—that we'd all go on playing happy family while he had it off with his little sex kitten? The Czechs are completely twisted: Maria thinks I should humor him; she says it's the kind of thing men do, especially famous men. Frankly, I used to think she was on my side, even though she's his mother, but now I'm not so sure." Oddly enough, she doesn't sound bitter. But then, Isabelle never was one to feel sorry for herself.

"Jane got dumped, too, you know."

"What, by boring old Marge?"

"Yeah, she's going into politics."

"Are they starting up a Ministry of Castration in England?"

"Yeah." We both start to giggle. "I wish you'd cover them up," I say. "Now that I know, I can't stop staring at them."

"That's *exactly* the idea. Do you think I should go parade them in front of Mr. French Writer?" She sits up again and jiggles them for my benefit. They are undeniably spectacular, if somewhat unreal-looking.

"Can I touch?"

"Go ahead."

I poke her right breast. It feels normal, but then, it's not like she got silicone implants. I guess all they did was tighten things up a bit.

"*What* are you two doing?" Lucy's head pops up through the trapdoor, followed by the rest of her in one of her long linen shifts.

"Want a feel?" Isabelle offers.

"You're disgusting."

"It's all right," I say. "She confessed."

"Where did you get the money?" our ever practical Lucy demands. "I thought plastic surgery was expensive."

"Oh, I had it done in Prague—by an old friend of Jiri's, actually. Lots of people come to him from the West now because it's so much cheaper: You can get yourself completely made over for under ten thousand dollars."

"Wow," I say. "That's one aspect of postcommunist economic development that I never thought of."

"You must tell Odette," Lucy says waspishly.

"Why are you always harping about Odette?" Isabelle says. "What has she done to you?"

"She belittles Daddy's memory."

Don't say it, I think, but of course, she does:

"He's not your father."

"Hey," I say.

Actually, Ross *is* Lucy and Jane's father legally, since he ended up adopting them, another one of his many baffling gestures in the waning days of his marriage to Daphne. They didn't even take his name, though I guess that, after inheriting that beer fortune from their biological father, it would have seemed a bit crass to completely disown the man.

Lucy's eyes have turned glittery with rage. "Why, you cheap little tramp!"

Isabelle closes hers and lies back. "Remember what *Daddy* used to say when we were little," she singsongs. "Sticks and stones may break my bones, but names will never harm me."

"Cut it out, both of you," I say.

"You can't hurt me, Lucy," Isabelle repeats serenely. "You can't hurt me because I don't care."

CHAPTER *seventeen*

I'm sitting on the patio, trying to read *Madame Bovary*, when our new neighbor appears. I took an evening course on the nineteenth-century French novel this spring, with the plan to improve my mind over the summer by rereading the syllabus in French. I have to say, it's been heavy going: I never really got Emma in translation, and so far she's just as vapid in the original. My idea of a great heroine runs more to Mathilde in *The Red and the Black*.

"Ah, Flaubert, those concupiscent descriptions of the bourgeois interior . . ."

I look up to find Philippe standing over me, grinning.

"It's wasted on me," I say. "In case you didn't notice, I'm reading it with a dictionary."

"Very commendable. I should think you might have opted for lighter fare, though, on such a hot day. *Bonjour Tristesse,* perhaps. . . ."

"I don't like Françoise Sagan."

"No?"

"No. I think she's shallow."

"Well, it was a simpler time."

"That's no excuse," I say. "You could say the same thing about Jane Austen."

This makes him laugh. "Well, I am not sure I would describe late-eighteenth-century England as a simpler time, but you are obviously a tough customer, Miss Wright. How are you finding the trials of poor Emma?"

"I don't feel sorry for her, though I do admire her determination."

"A very American point of view!"

"That's me," I say. "Actually, I was just thinking that there's not a single sympathetic character in the whole book, really. It's kind of amazing how he pulled it off."

"What about poor Charles, and the little girl?"

"Charles is weak."

"But he loves her."

"Blind love isn't a virtue."

"Such intransigence. . . ."

"I'm an investment banker," I say. "I look at the world in terms of the efficient allocation of resources."

"Now you are teasing me."

"Maybe," I allow, putting the book down and looking up at him. He's wearing a faded blue Lacoste shirt that clings damply to his chest. I can't be looking too fresh myself; the sirocco is still holding back, but the air is as thick as a blanket. He bends down to stroke the belly of the supine cat at my side—a daughter, we think, of the famously dissipated Minette, and one of three young females who spend their days sprawled on the patio wall, toasting in the sun while they wait for the next handout.

"Indolent beasts. I caught them yesterday hissing at that poor old fellow with the torn ear. He must've got too close to the food bowl."

"That's what I like about them," I say. "You know what to expect. How's your book coming along?"

He surprises me by sitting on the wall, sharing with me the shady patch cast by the fig tree. He stretches out his legs and crosses one long espadrille-clad foot over the other.

"Not so well today. If you want to know the truth, I saw you from my window and came down hoping for conversation. I am finding all this peace and quiet distracting."

"Really? I would've thought you'd be used to it, being a writer."

"Not at all. I am used to solitude, yes, but Paris solitude, with background noise. I haven't written a word since I've arrived."

"Writer's block?" I say sympathetically.

"Worse: boredom. Lately I am finding my book terrible."

"What's it about?"

"This will amuse you: It's about an American woman in Paris."

"What's she doing there?"

"She has come to study at the Sorbonne. She meets a Frenchman. A married Frenchman, naturally."

"Naturally. I got the impression you were more of a highbrow writer."

"Oh, but I assure you it is very highbrow indeed. Perhaps this is the problem."

"What are *you two* discussing so intently?" calls out my sister, who must have spied us from the house and is coming over to investigate. Philippe raises a hand in greeting.

"Literature."

"With Constance? You'd be better off asking her how to invest your money."

"Actually, I'm not a financial adviser," I point out, feeling all of a sudden irritated at Isabelle's ignorance.

"Well, whatever she does, it's terribly important," Isabelle says breezily. "Whenever she comes to Prague they put her up at the Savoy, which is *fiendishly* expensive."

"I have been to Prague," says Philippe. "It's a lovely city— almost too lovely, sometimes it doesn't feel quite real."

"That's just since they tarted it up for the tourists," my sister declares, plopping down next to him on the wall, much to the annoyance of the cat, who springs up and scampers away. "Normal people live in high-rises," she adds, with the blitheness of one who has never set foot in one. "Anyway, you should come again. I'll show you the *real* Prague."

"What a kind offer. I shall keep it in mind. Sadly, I must get back to the grindstone now." He rises. "It's been a pleasure."

"Why don't you come over for dinner some night?" Isabelle says in a challenging way.

"I would be delighted."

"Tomorrow?"

"I accept. As you can see, my social calendar is hardly overrun."

"Eight o'clock," Isabelle calls out as he ambles off. Then to me, "What a weirdo."

"I don't think he's weird at all; he's just quiet."

"Say what you will, *I* think he's hiding something."

"*I* think you have a one-track mind."

She yawns and extends her feet, their shell-pink nails freshly painted by Sophie, the rings on her toes catching the light. "I'll have him in the end," she muses, and I am suddenly stunned by her obliviousness to the possibility that someone, even a man, might find her irritating. But then, my sister has spent most of her life in a shimmery nimbus of male adoration. Why should she expect Philippe to behave any differently from the thousands of poor saps who've fallen at her feet? For that matter, why should I?

"I'll get Odette to make something really fabulous," she says dreamily.

CHAPTER *eighteen*

L ucy, naturally, has other ideas.

"I know, I'll make *vitello tonnato* for starters. Lovely and sim-
ple. . . . And then maybe that nice salmon with a fennel crust."

"Why don't you just let Odette cook?" Isabelle says.

"But I'd be perfectly happy to."

"Lucy can help me," Odette says magnanimously.

"Mommy!" Sophie shrieks. "Electra's face is all red again!"

Electra seems to have developed an allergic reaction to either
the jellyfish sting or the cream Odette put on it. The rash keeps
fading away and then flaring back up. It doesn't, however, seem to
bother her.

Lucy turns accusingly to Richard. "I thought you were going to
drive her to the doctor in Flore!" We are all, once again, sitting
around the breakfast table—except for the girls, who got up at six,
Lucy having finally relented and let Electra move into the extra

room with them, where they all seem to be having a fine old time getting up to whatever five-year-olds get up to without the benefit of adult supervision.

"We're going after breakfast. It's just a rash; she's not in pain."

"It's unsightly," Lucy says.

"Mind if I join you?" Jim asks.

"I think I will go too," Odette says. "I can shop for dinner."

"Oh, then maybe I'll go along," Lucy says.

"There's no more room in the car," Richard says pointedly. "I've already promised Jane a ride."

"I see," Lucy says.

What a treat: alone with Lucy and Yves. Since it's cooler today, I decide to go for a run. In New York, Jim and I jog every day, but it seems that all this Mediterranean languor is undermining our devotion to fitness, not to mention to each other. If you ask me, most people are together out of convenience; but, having now had a boyfriend for almost six months, I'm beginning to wonder if there's not something more to the equation. I have to say, however, that the couples around us offer few clues: I can't for the life of me fathom what Odette sees in Yves, and the less said about Richard and Lucy, the better. The only ones who ever made any sense were Isabelle and Jiri, in the way a combustible chemical reaction might make sense before you run for cover.

On the way up to the highway, I get a suspicious glance from Madame Peretti, out hosing down her patio in her housedress and slippers. Santerrans aren't big on physical fitness, not that you'd know that from looking at them: They're actually a fairly attractive people, lean and muscular in a way that you can't achieve working out twice a week. I guess risking your life in traffic just isn't their idea of a good time. The highway is, however, the only place where you can run, goat paths not being suitable for this purpose; and, if you hug the shoulder, it's reasonably safe. Much more lethal than the local kamikazes in their tiny Renaults are the tank-size recreational vehicles driven by Dutch and Germans, bristling with bikes and surfboards as they lurch like Cyclopes astride the one and a half lanes that snake around the peninsula. One of these rumbles by as I round the bend, missing me by less than a foot and causing me to wonder afresh why American tourists get such a bad rap when Northern Europe affords so many fine examples of obnoxious holiday-making behavior. Traffic aside, though, this stretch of the road is quite pleasant, canopied by trees that create a cool green nave. Rather less picturesque is the illegal garbage dump on the left beyond the village, a tangle of old car parts, defunct washing machines, and other inorganic refuse that is only partially obscured by foliage.

Ross was bedeviled by the Santerrans' indifference to the environment, not so much out of any deeply held ecological principles as out of incomprehension at self-defeating behavior. In this he found an ally in the mayor, who appreciated the dissuasive effect of rusted bedsprings on tourist dollars. They even devised a scheme together wherein people would get a tax break for the proper disposal of refuse, a brilliant idea that got nowhere since it had to be proposed via official channels to the central authorities in Canonica, where it has languished ever since. In the end, their only successful initiative was the green plastic recycling bin that sits halfway up the road to Borgolano, empty of all bottles and cans except those that Lucy dutifully lugs up every week.

I can feel the sweat trickling down my back as I pick up speed. After the next bend, the forest ends and the *pointe* comes into view up ahead, its black flank cascading into the sea. The magic of the moment is instantly dispelled by the appearance of Eddie's *camionette,* announced by a roar at my back and the screech of brakes. Toto is in the passenger seat.

"Salut, Constance," Eddie yells out before speeding up again. He drives like all Santerrans with his elbow sticking out the window; you'd think the island would be full of one-armed people. I wave back. Judging by the time of day, he is on his delivery route. Many of the smaller villages don't even have a store, so the groceries have to come to them—at a premium, of course—and both Eddie and the Perettis are happy to oblige. I reflect once again that there is something fundamentally disturbing about the thought of Eddie and Toto careening around the *cap* in a refrigerated van full of dismembered animal carcasses. A couple years ago there was some kind of unpleasantness involving a Danish tourist they picked up hitchhiking. The details are swathed in lurid speculations, but according to Yolande, Eddie spent six months in jail. Toto, it seems, was deemed not responsible for his actions—an even scarier concept, if you ask me.

The sun is starting to beat down in earnest, so I turn back, sticking again to the mountainside, though I'm not sure what makes me think that being crushed against a rock by a German Winnebago would be any better than being tossed over the cliff. This stretch being uphill, I'm panting for breath by the time I reach the woods before Borgolano. After the glare of the open road, the sudden plunge into shade is a little disorienting, which no doubt explains why I can't immediately make out the object hanging from a branch overhead. Squinting, I slow down and peer up. The object is a dog, or rather the corpse of a dog, hanging upside down by one hind leg. I stop, frozen by a visceral revulsion that quickly turns to outrage. I consider cutting the thing down until I realize I have neither the means/ of reaching it nor a knife. In the end I push on, deciding that I'll alert the police. Borgolano actually has a small *gendarmerie,* along with a post office. It's not until I've reached the village that I realize that the only car I saw coming from the direction of the woods besides the Germans' was Eddie's.

Back at the house, I find Lucy and Yves deep in conversation over coffee.

"Constance," Lucy says excitedly, "it turns out that Yves restores old furniture!"

"Imagine that." I pour myself a glass of water and gulp it down.

"Attention," Yves cautions, "you will catch a cold!"

"Right," I mumble, "in July."

"Amazing we never knew, and with all this work we need done—the dining room table, for instance."

"There's a dead dog hanging in the woods," I say.

"Really, Constance, how revolting!"

"Quoi?"

"And I strongly suspect that Eddie and Toto put it there, though I can't fathom why. I'm going up to tell the police."

"I don't think you should do that," Yves says.

"Why not?"

"It is not a good idea to interfere in the local customs. Besides, the gendarmes will do nothing."

"For Christ's sake, it's not like we're talking about some charming bit of local folklore!"

"Perhaps they are trying to warn someone," Yves says. "I would advise you to stay out of it."

"I think he's right, Constance," Lucy says with a worried look. "Yves knows rather more about these things than we do."

Well, well, when did this turnaround occur?

"I guess you're right," I concede. I'm not going to dispute the fact that Yves knows the locals better than we do, from all his hanging around at the Marmite. Besides, I am beginning to feel really creeped out. Suddenly I find myself wishing that Ross were here. This was just the kind of thing he knew how to handle.

By the time the others have returned from Flore, I've forgotten all about the incident. Odette is obviously as perplexed as I am by the sudden cordiality between Lucy and Yves, who are going over all the furniture in the living room with measuring tape and pencil.

"He restores antiques," I explain.

"*Ah bon?* I had no idea."

Some old friend, I think. At the sight of Richard, Lucy becomes even more gushy, making me wonder if this sudden interest in Yves is aimed at pissing her husband off. All the new attention, in any case, has rendered Yves positively expansive. I guess no one is at their best under a constant diet of withering scorn.

"Constance, please help me put the groceries away— Ah, thank you, Jeem, I think the wine is still in the car."

"No problem, I'll get it."

"Such a nice young man," Odette observes to me. "You are lucky, Constance."

"Why am *I* lucky?"

She ignores me. "How nice that Lucy has found a project. Perhaps it will keep her occupied. Now, Jeem has promised to build me a fire so we will have grilled lamb for dinner, and roasted potatoes—"

"Don't you think a gratin would be better?" Lucy pipes in from the doorway.

"Not in summer. I think *tomates farcies* as well, no?"

I wonder if our neighbor has any idea of all the hoopla he's causing. Isabelle, humming to herself, has already disappeared upstairs to wash her hair again and no doubt mull over whatever piece of undress she's going to appear in tonight. Odette, peeling an onion, is flushed and gay. Even Lucy seems caught up in the general good humor.

"Can someone chop the garlic?" Odette asks.

"I'll do it," hastens Lucy, who hasn't given up on sharing the culinary mantle. "Odette, if you want I could make the tomatoes . . ."

"*Ah là là,* go ahead . . . just don't put peanuts in them."

"Why on earth would I put peanuts in a Provençal dish?" Lucy says loftily.

"If I'm not needed, I'm going up on the roof," Jane announces.

"I'll go with you," I say.

I take a seat on the ledge and watch her set up her easel. In a typically schizophrenic display of Santerran weather patterns, the sky has turned periwinkle again and the air is lambent with late-afternoon sun.

"Are you going to do a pastel?"

"Yes, I think so. Watercolor wouldn't do it justice. Look at that yellow!" Swiftly, she traces the outline of the rooftops, the jagged mountains beyond, purple in the buttery light. Her big hands with their chewed nails are surprisingly graceful. "It's almost too pretty, isn't it?"

"What's wrong with pretty?"

"Ugly is more interesting. So, how's your romance coming along?"

"I don't know. He seems more interested in Richard."

"Poor Richard. He needs a friend," Jane says distractedly.

We sit in silence, Jane frowning as she rubs at the edge of the yellow wall with her thumb, smudging it with violet. When I was little I thought that art consisted of drawing the outline and then filling it in. In fact, if you look at Jane's work close-up, it's hard to tell where anything begins or ends. My eyes drift beyond her out to the water where one lone fishing boat bobs listlessly. I'm reminded that, for all its turquoise loveliness, the Mediterranean is an exhausted sea, overfished and depleted, old as the world. Our East Hampton house looked out over the rambunctious surf of the Atlantic—more Ross's element, you would think—and yet, he always preferred Santerre.

"Do you ever miss Dad?" I ask.

"Sometimes. We didn't have much in common."

"Neither did he and Lucy."

"Lucy has a weakness for big men." She frowns. "Shit, I've botched the Paolis' house. It's that bloody bougainvillea; I never get the color right."

"Right, that's why she married Richard."

"Not to marry. She always wanted a father more than a husband."

I watch the fishing boat some more. "Why did Daphne marry Ross?"

Jane looks at me like I'm stupid. "Why do you think? He was irresistible."

"Yeah, but she didn't have to marry him. I mean, you'd think she would've had more sense."

"She's just like anyone else," Jane says, turning back to her drawing. "She wanted what she couldn't have."

"Is that why Lucy hates Odette?"

"Lucy hates Odette because she can't bear that anyone so common could replace our mother," Jane says flatly.

"Well, you know, sometimes I think that's the secret of her success with Ross."

She looks at me. "You mean she lulled him with her banal feminine wiles?"

"Yeah," I say, smiling, though Jane isn't. "How *is* Daphne?"

"Oh, she's fine. She's got her garden and her dogs. I'm going out to stay with her in August; Lucy, too, I expect. Surrey's a nice change from Santerre."

Sometimes I think Jane is more interested in shapes than in people—that this is the secret to her equanimity.

"I guess I'd better go get ready for dinner," I say, but I don't think she hears me.

CHAPTER *nineteen*

"A barbecue!" Philippe says, accepting a whisky from Richard. "Takes me back to my days in the States. . . ."

"Better not tell Odette," I say. "She might infer that you're expecting a hamburger."

"But I adore hamburgers!"

Isabelle chooses this moment to make her appearance. In a silk slip the color of apples, she looks like a tropical Titania and smells like coconuts, from the hair conditioner that she can't get in Prague and that I bring over in big tubs from Duane Reade.

"*Salut*, Philippe. . . ."

"Ah, good evening, Miss Wright. You look charming."

"You're allowed to call me Isabelle, you know," she says playfully. "I'm glad to hear you're a meat lover; we don't think much of vegetarians in Prague. . . ."

"Then I am most relieved," Philippe says. "I would tremble at the thought of being held in low regard by you."

Isabelle plants herself in front of him. "That's why I had to leave America: If they think something is bad for you, they make it illegal. Who wants to live a life without vice?"

"We all know you don't," Lucy says, joining us. "How nice to see you, Philippe. I see you've been given a drink."

"*On n'est pas des sauvages,*" my sister says.

"Ah, the drama begins!" Philippe exclaims. We follow his gaze out to the horizon, which is gearing up for one of Santerre's spectacularly lurid sunsets. Personally, I've always found them a little over the top, like being stuck inside a postcard or a Douglas Sirk movie.

"Shockingly vulgar, isn't it?" Lucy says.

"Pure decadence. You must find it inspiring, Miss Nicholson"—Philippe turns to Jane, who has just joined us—"the thin line between the garish and the sublime."

"I'm not that subtle," Jane says.

"Oh, *please* let's not talk about aesthetics," Isabelle moans. "I get enough of that in Prague. . . ."

Lucy, evidently of another mind, opens her mouth but is instantly cut off—as is all further hope of bracing intellectual discussion—by the eruption of Yolande Van Langendonck on our little gathering.

"*Coucou, bonsoir!* Is the sunset not fabulous! Odette, get your camera, I will take a picture of the whole family!"

Odette demurs, claiming she has no film. Liar.

"*Ah, quel dommage* . . . it would have been nice for the girls."

"How nice of you to stop by," Lucy simpers with her fakest smile.

"Yes, so kind of Odette to invite me, taking pity on a lonely old woman . . ." Yolande winks, a motion that crinkles all the makeup around her eyes and makes her look arrestingly like a cockatoo.

"*Mais non . . .*"

Lucy glances furiously at Odette, though in fact Odette assures me later in the kitchen that Yolande invited herself, adding philosophically, "Besides, she harms no one."

"*Alors,* Monsieur Kahn, aren't you the lucky dog, with all these beautiful girls next door!"

"I count my blessing daily, Madame."

"And witty too!" She wags a playful finger in his face. "*Attention,* though: Odette watches over them like a hawk. . . ." Isabelle rolls her eyes toward me at this preposterous assertion, simultaneously indicating with a nod that I should follow her inside.

"Better get back out there," I advise her, having caught up with her in the kitchen. "Lucy's homing in on him."

Isabelle makes a dismissive gesture. "Look," she says urgently, "we've got to keep him away from Jane."

I eye her suspiciously. What kind of a threat can Jane possibly be? "I don't have anything to do with the seating arrangements," I say. "You'd better tell Odette."

"Oh, all right, just make sure and grab the other seat next to him. If he ends up by Jane, they'll talk about art all night and I won't be able to get a word in edgewise."

So that's what it's about. I don't suggest that maybe this wouldn't be such a bad thing.

With what I assume is the collusion of Odette, Philippe, in the place of honor at the table's end, ends up hemmed in by me and Isabelle, at a safe distance from Jane, who gets stuck between

Richard and Lucy and, I'm sure, would be most amused by all these machinations. Jim lands on the other side between Isabelle and Odette, leaving Yves at the other end with Yolande on his left.

"So," Philippe addresses me as Odette serves the salad, "still absorbed in Flaubert?"

"Not exactly. I haven't picked it up since you last saw me."

Isabelle leans forward. "What haven't you picked up?"

"My book. I keep getting distracted."

"Your sister is most commendably reading *Madame Bovary* in French."

"I never could finish it," Isabelle says airily. "Another novel about a bored housewife . . ."

"Well," Philippe says with a little smile, "Flaubert did say that she weeps in twenty French villages."

"I'm reading Gombrowicz's diaries. Do you know Gombrowicz?" Isabelle has been lugging Gombrowicz's diaries on vacation for three years now. Jiri considers them to be the highest flowering of Central European literature, along with *The Man without Qualities,* of which she also owns a virgin copy. Talk about boring.

"Intimately: I taught a course on him." Uh-oh, trouble . . . I'd be surprised if she's reached page ten. But my sister is not to be underestimated.

"Really? I thought people only read him in Eastern Europe."

"Oh, no, he's very popular in France. We're great appreciators of morbid Slavic humor."

"Believe me, if you lived there you wouldn't find them humorous. It's all a front for self-pity, really," my sister asserts.

"Oh, we French are quite comfortable with self-pity."

"What an interesting remark," calls out Lucy, who, though at the other end of the table, is still within earshot. "One doesn't think of the French as feeling sorry for themselves."

"But I assure you that we do. America has rather taken the wind out of our sails this past century," Philippe says with a mischievous smile.

"*Ah non,* no politics! Jeem, could you go check the meat, please?"

Jim hurries out. It seems they do a lot of barbecuing in Kansas, and he has, under Odette's tutelage, become something of an accomplished grill chef, taking to heart her admonitions on the inedibility of well-done meat. The lamb cutlets he reappears with are pink and succulent within, their fragrant juices oozing appetizingly onto the blue and white platter.

"*Bravo,* Jeem! And how lovely they smell." Jim grins happily. He's become Odette's little pet, which doesn't seem to bother him in the least. In fact, he laps it up.

The arrival of the food thankfully focuses everyone's energy on eating: Odette and Lucy in teeny, measured bites, Yolande with the gusto of one no longer concerned about her figure, and Isabelle like a slob. My sister has some of the worst table manners I've ever seen: You'd think she'd been raised in an orphanage. I read somewhere though that men equate all appetites, so no doubt Philippe will read the dribble of sauce on her chin as a sign of sexual voracity, as if she hadn't given him enough hints already. He turns to me again: "What does this impressive-sounding job of yours consist of, exactly?"

"I'm an equities analyst for an investment bank. I assess the worth of companies."

"It sounds terribly complicated and mathematical."

"It isn't, really. The computer does most of the work; I just plug in the numbers. It's all done by statistical models. . . ."

"That's not true," Isabelle says with her mouth full. "She travels all over the world and has a huge expense account."

"I wish," I say. "I'm in emerging markets, so I get to go to interesting places sometimes."

"Like Prague."

"That's the glamorous part. Then there's Warsaw in February."

"A capitalist who reads French novels and travels to exotic lands."

"I'm not sure Warsaw is exotic," I say.

Across the table, Isabelle widens her eyes at me. I make a little shrug as if to say, *I can't help it, he keeps talking to me.* Jim, on her other side, is absorbed in conversation with Odette, but Isabelle finds him boring anyway. Finally she leans right across the table. "Follow me to the kitchen," she hisses across a startled Philippe. I excuse myself and, picking up the empty bread basket for cover, head out after her.

"Can't you see that Odette is *flirting* with Jim?" she says indignantly as soon as I've joined her by the sink. Her cheeks are flushed, a sure sign that she's plastered.

"So what, she flirts with him all the time. It's the only way she knows how to talk to men."

"I'll tell you why you didn't notice: It's because you've been wrapped up all night in conversation with our mysterious neighbor—not that I *mind* you monopolizing the only available man in the house, even though you already have a boyfriend. . . ."

"You're drunk," I say.

"Of course I'm drunk: That's what people *do* at dinner parties—in Europe at least. I guess in New York you just sit around drinking mineral water and talking about the stock market."

I find myself observing her with almost scientific detachment. In the kitchen's sallow light, I notice for the first time the creeping signs of middle age: the fine webs at the corners of her eyes, the puffiness beneath, the softening chin. I wonder why this is so disconcerting until I realize that I must have believed she was ageless, like the goddesses she's so often been compared to.

I say, "Anyway, don't be silly, he's just talking to me because you intimidate him."

She hesitates. "Do you really think so?"

"Absolutely. Why would he be interested in *me?*"

Isabelle's face crumples with guilt. "Oh, Constance, I'm so sorry, I'm such a pig. Oink."

"Don't mention it," I say.

Back at the table, I stun Richard, who is on my other side and has been talking quietly to Jane all evening, by turning toward him and asking him about the Millennium Dome, the only topic that springs to my mind. Isabelle, I see from the corner of my eye, doesn't lose a second.

"It's good old British class warfare," Richard says. "The toffs hate it because working-class people enjoy it." Of course *Richard* is a toff, but like most Brits I know, he fancies himself a socialist.

"What *nonsense* are you spouting, darling?" At the sound of his wife's voice, an irritated spasm constricts Richard's brow. "The reason people can't bear it is because it is, quite simply, vulgar beyond belief."

"I see your point," I say to Richard.

"Actually," Philippe says, "the French felt the same way about the Eiffel Tower when it first went up. It seems that what we think of as good taste is just another product of acculturation." Isabelle, at this latest contretemps, glowers and sulkily slops more wine into her glass.

"I don't agree with you at all." Lucy's voice has grown animated. "Good taste has to do with an innate sense of aesthetic harmony!"

"What a snob you are, darling."

"I agree with Philippe," Jane says. "Good taste has become just another commodity. I think it's very healthy the way the Americans have debunked the myth of aristocratic graciousness with their Ralph Laurens and Martha Stewarts. It turns out it can all be bought."

"You can't *buy* good manners," Lucy exclaims, "or a sense of color, or perspective! How can you *say* these things as an artist?!"

"As an artist, I deal in illusion."

"And illusion is the same as reality?" Lucy says.

"The point *has* been debated," observes Philippe.

"God, listen to you," Isabelle says loudly. "Half the world is a total mess and you're worried about good taste."

"While you, on the other hand, are actively engaged in making the world a better place," Lucy says.

"More than you are."

"Yes, well, we haven't all had the great good luck of being married to an authentic Eastern European dissident," Lucy says sarcastically.

"You don't know what you're talking about. Jiri was more involved in the opposition than you'll ever know."

"When he wasn't off at the pub with the blokes."

"He was in *jail.*"

"No one is disputing the terrific glamour of Jiri; I was asking about your personal contribution to the greater good. . . ."

"Girls," Odette warns.

"Easy for you to criticize, sitting on your trust fund in Kensington."

"Delicious salad," Yolande says. "So clever to add orange segments."

"My wife has never found a recipe she couldn't improve upon," Richard remarks acidly.

I glance at our neighbor, who looks like he's finding this all very entertaining.

"At least she didn't add peanuts."

"Isabelle, *ça suffit!*"

"Golly, can't anyone take a joke anymore?"

"I think," Odette says firmly, "that it's time for dessert."

Jim and I have sex again that night. Maybe it's the only thing we have in common, the way others might share an interest in gardening or philately. In the middle of this detached coupling—all the more intense for its pure physicality, so that we both come violently—I close my eyes and picture Philippe thrusting inside me. When I open them, I find Electra staring at us from the doorway. We must have woken her up; the girls' room is right above ours. I know I should cover myself but instead I stare back, willing her to go away, though she makes no motion to do so. Her eyes meet mine and I detect something in her unblinking gaze, a fleeting expression that, accompanied as it is by a twitch of her pale lips, I could swear is amusement. Groggily, I lift my hand in a little wave—it seems to me then to shoo her away—but I wonder now if in fact I wasn't acknowledging a kind of complicity between us, as if, I in this animal state and she trapped in all that flesh, we had, for a moment, met in the same place.

CHAPTER *twenty*

The next day, the sirocco sets in, like a hot stale breath, so that I'm not sure whether to blame my headache on last night's wine or on the advancing low-pressure system. Jim is out of sorts himself. He's usually up earlier than me, but this morning he shifts restlessly in his sleep, muttering into the pillow. I tiptoe out, trying not to make noise as I creep down the stairs. Not that I have anything to worry about: Odette sleeps like the dead, and when I pass Isabelle's door, I hear her snoring.

A gust flaps the Perettis' canvas awning as I step out, startling the two cats who slink up when I unlatch the door. The dish the girls set out for them yesterday is empty but for a crusted bone that's already attracting flies. Monsieur Peretti's olive tree rustles irritably, its leaves silvery in the weird light. I head for the stone steps. On the way up I pass Madame, out hosing her patio again, her *bonjour* vitiated by the fish-eye that accompanies it. For all of

Ross's efforts, we're not from here and never will be. Even Yolande, with her obsession about the locals siphoning off her electricity, seems to understand this.

I emerge by the snack bar where Toto-the-halfwit's cousin Frédé peddles soft drinks and ice cream to passing motorists. According to Yolande, the mayor gave Frédé the concession after he came back from jail in Canonica, hoping it would keep him out of trouble. He's not allowed to serve alcohol, which suggests what at least part of the trouble may have been. At this early hour the stand is still shuttered, as are the four rather graceful turn-of-the-century houses on the main road that leads to the *place*. There was once a prosperous bourgeoisie in Borgolano, before trade with Genoa declined in the nineteenth century. The mayor is always going on about how today's youth have no interest in working, and if Frédé and Toto and Eddie are anything to go by, he seems to have a point. Above the still slumbering Marmite, I hear signs of matutinal stirrings: the creak of a shutter and a thwacking sound that, when I glance up, turns out to be old Madame Andreani beating a carpet on her balcony. Next door, Monsieur Paoli appears in a singlet at his window and thoughtfully scratches his armpit.

Since the Winnebagos aren't out yet, I head in the opposite direction of my jogging route, the more scenic choice, with dramatic sea vistas that are a favorite photo backdrop with the RV set. Just outside Borgolano, a weatherworn placard advertises the long defunct Auberge du Bon Pêcheur. Years ago the Marmite crew tried to branch out into waterfront dining, in one of the fishing cabins now owned by Yolande. A spray of rusted bullet holes pocks the sign's surface, a sad testimony both to the enterprise's downfall and to the mental acuity of Toto, who got carried away one night and forgot that he was supposed to shoot at French road signs, not placards advertising native-owned businesses.

I stop and peer down at the restless sloshing sea. I feel restless, too, distracted by my thoughts and the rustling underbrush, which is no doubt why I don't hear Eddie's van until it's right below me on the beach road. He must have swerved down from the highway while I was looking out at the water. Why, I wonder, is Eddie heading down to the beach on a day like this? At this hour of the morning he should be doing his rounds. I follow the little red van as it negotiates the first bend, disappearing for a few seconds and resurfacing on the last stretch before the fishing cabins where it comes to a halt. The air goes still again and I hear one car door slam, then another, then a third as Eddie and Toto pull a package out of the back and slam that door, too, before vanishing down the footpath. They must, I tell myself before turning back, be making a delivery. Maybe one of Yolande's tenants is having a barbecue.

I'm not all that surprised when I run into Philippe back on the square. What I hadn't expected is how flustered I feel, as if he could somehow read my mind.

"Hello, Constance," he says, that little smile playing on his lips. "You're up early."

"I couldn't sleep," I say. "It's too hot." He looks as if he's just woken up himself, his jaw shadowed with stubble and his hair unruly, and I repress the urge to reach out, as if touching him would somehow breathe life into our ephemeral intimacy. I notice that his eyes are not hazel but gray, and that he tans in the effortless way of Mediterranean people. His half-buttoned shirt reveals a fine tracery of dark curls. Jim's chest is as hairless as a newborn's.

"Miserable, isn't it? It's such an intemperate wind, the sirocco, very un-European."

"Well, it's from Africa, isn't it?" I say, looking into those strange gray eyes that, it strikes me, are the color of the pebbles on Orzo beach.

He meets my gaze and holds it. I'm sure women stare at him all the time. "Yes, our brush with the desert. . . . I was thinking this morning of those Bedouins whose skin turns blue from the dye in their robes."

"Are you writing about Bedouins now?"

"Oh, no, when I get bored with my story, my mind drifts off. I should pay attention, it's probably my subconscious speaking. . . . But I'm glad I've run into you: I wanted to thank you again for the superb dinner."

"Don't thank me, Odette did all the cooking."

"Well, then, it was terribly kind of all of you to take pity on a poor bachelor." His smile turns amusingly self-deprecating.

"*Are* you—a bachelor?" I ask.

"My wife and I have separated. I'm not sure what that makes me, technically."

"My sister is getting divorced," I say.

"Is she? How sad."

"Yes," I say, "I guess it is."

"Ah," he says, looking past me, "here is your fiancé."

"My what?" I follow his gaze across the *place* to where Jim has just appeared and is waving enthusiastically in our direction.

"Excuse me, is he not your fiancé? I thought your sister said . . ." His voice trails off uncertainly.

"Well, not exactly," I say, but Jim is already upon us, Odette's yellow string shopping bag dangling from his hand.

"Hey, guys! You headed toward the store?"

"As a matter of fact, yes," Philippe says. "And here is the bread truck—perfect timing!"

The blue *boulangerie* van has indeed just stopped outside Madame Peretti's shop, its back door flung open to reveal the stacks of plastic cases full of sticky pastries and floppy sheets of pizza that are dispersed daily around the *cap*.

"Dooz croysents ay weet bugettes seel voo play," Jim yaps eagerly. "Odette has been teaching me French," he explains. "How do I sound?"

"Very convincing," Philippe says.

"Hey, those peaches look good! How do you say peaches?"

"Why don't you just point?" I suggest.

"Pêches," Philippe says amiably.

"Hey, thanks, man: *ay oon keelow pehsh.*"

"Il est sympa, votre ami," remarks Madame Peretti, carefully picking out six bruised peaches and putting them in a bag.

"What did she say?"

"That you're a nice guy, and a sucker. She just unloaded all her beat-up up fruit on you."

Beaming, Madame Peretti offers him a bunch of bruised bananas.

"You're so cynical, Connie."

Philippe arches his eyebrows.

"Whew, it's hot!" Jim exclaims, but my mind is elsewhere. I just noticed the design on the strap of his Teva sandals: little rainbows, spanning his hairy toes.

CHAPTER *twenty-one*

For as far back as I can remember, the mayor had been trying to sell Ross the abandoned shepherds' hamlet above Borgolano, a bunch of ruins with spectacular views of the Mediterranean and, he kept assuring him, excellent water pressure. The fact that it was only accessible by beaten path was *un détail,* surely not the kind of thing to bother a visionary like Ross Wright. (Was Manhattan accessible when the Dutch first bought it from the Indians?) Ross never did take him up on the offer, but he enjoyed hiking up there and marching around the ruins, playing King of the Mountain and making plans, all with the enthusiastic participation of Lucy, who had visions of restored cottages and organic *potagers* and no Costas next door. Above and beyond that, she was tormented by the thought that someone else would snap it up if he didn't.

"Anyone up for a walk to the *hameau?*" she suggests that evening.

"Too hot," Isabelle moans, fanning herself with a copy of *Paris Match,* a topless Stephanie of Monaco on the cover.

"Nonsense, there's a breeze. Besides, it's much cooler up there."

"I'll go," Jim says.

"Okay," I say, "but just for a walk. No picnics."

"Then who will light the barbecue?" Odette coyly asks. I think she's joking at first but, the next thing I know, Jim has changed his mind and it's just me and Lucy.

We head up to the road and take the stairs behind the post office, which lead to the upper part of Borgolano and then onto a rocky path that wends its way up through several levels of ter-races and into the underbrush. "Ah, smell the air!" Lucy cries, throwing her head back and breathing deeply. The heat does seem to have concentrated the scent of myrtle and broom that gives the air on the *cap* its resinous sharpness; as we push deeper into the underbrush, I begin to feel light-headed. You think of nature as being quiet, but the Santerran *maquis* has got to be one of the loudest forests on earth, abuzz with bees and crickets, the ground underfoot rustling with skittish lizards and, all around, the sound of trickling water. It's also a great hiding place, as the Germans found out during World War II. It took them so many troops to police the island that they finally gave up.

At a brisk pace, the hike up to the hamlet takes a half hour, but Lucy keeps stopping to sniff the air or break off a rosemary branch or wax botanical: "We must come in the spring, when the gorse is in bloom. . . . You can't imagine how lovely it is, masses of bright yellow flowers, completely transforms the landscape!" or "Look at that, wild marjoram!" I'd forgotten how restful she can be in one of her expansive moods, if for no other reason than that she keeps the entire conversation going by herself. By the time we've reached the top, she's clutching various bits of shrubs and rambling on about how you could live for months in the *maquis* on roots and herbs and you wouldn't have to kill a single animal! Lucy is fiercely opposed to hunting—a generational issue in England, I gather, since her mother Daphne is an avid fox-murderer.

As we approach the hamlet, her brow furrows. There's a flat expanse before the entrance that's a favorite gathering place for Borgolano's teens, drawn by the beer-cooling properties of an old stone trough that abuts a collapsed stable. They must have had quite a party last night: The ground is black with the remains of a bonfire, the dirt littered with cigarette butts and beer cans and what looks suspiciously like a condom wrapper.

"Would you look at that! You'd think they'd have the decency to clean up after themselves!" With two fingers, Lucy lifts a can from the brimming trough—it's fed from an underground spring through an old pipe that sticks out of the wall—and, having glanced helplessly around, sets it upright on the stoop. I dip my hand in the icy water.

"I'll bet you it's the same bunch who broke into the house," I say.

"What?"

"Didn't Odette tell you? We got burgled."

Lucy frowns. "She didn't say a word to me."

"I guess she didn't think it was important," I say, wishing now that I hadn't mentioned it. "They didn't take anything."

"Why does she hate me so?" Lucy asks.

I look at her with surprise. "I thought it was the other way around."

The village proper begins through a little archway that leads up an alley with two half-crumbled buildings on either side and, farther up, a reasonably intact house built of the stacked schist slabs that Lucy finds so enchanting, and one of three that she inhabits in her fantasies, after she's reclaimed and remodeled the hamlet and turned it into Bloomsbury-sur-Mer. I wonder why she doesn't just go ahead and buy it; it's not like she doesn't have the money. I'm about to ask her this when she gasps. I follow her gaze up to a second-floor window, which I'm pretty sure was boarded up the last time we were here. Now it sports a red curtain, incongruously jaunty in these ghostly surroundings. As we gape up, a little dog comes scrambling out the door, yapping furiously. Lucy shrieks.

"Calm down," I say, "it's only a puppy." And a pretty sorry-looking one, too, already half-covered in mange and, judging by its uneven gait, lame. There used to be many more like him down in the village until the mayor decided that they put off the tourists. The dog skids to a halt before us, sticks out its jaw, and snarls.

"Pilou!"

The snarl subsides to a whine as it retreats back to the doorway, now obscured by a figure that I can only half discern in the shadow.

"Viens ici, connard!"

The figure steps out, blinking in the light. Being used to New York bums, I don't get upset by bad grooming or wine breath, but this guy is in a league of his own. I can see Lucy's nostrils dilating.

"How many times have I told you not to bark at pretty ladies?" He kicks the dog and, to my relief, misses. It scrambles off.

"Bonjour," I say, nudging Lucy to follow suit. The bum sticks out his hand. He looks like any number of vagrants I've seen hang-

ing around Paris metro stations, the ones with the plastic wine bottle and the cardboard sign informing you that they are homeless, jobless, HIV positive, or all of the above. I shake his hand, gingerly, and shove Lucy forward. The bum eyes her appreciatively. I guess it's not every day he gets visited by a Nordic goddess. Having grabbed her extended fingers, which I then catch her wiping on the back of her shorts, he turns back to the dog. "Well, Pilou, it looks like we have company. Come in, come in!"

I follow him, giving Lucy little choice but to do likewise. I know she's thinking Rapist and Murderer, but not only are there more of us, he's puny enough that I figure we can easily jump him if he turns out to have sinister intentions. This is definitely the house Lucy had staked out for herself. Our host leads us through the penumbra to a stone staircase (in excellent condition) and up to the second floor, where he has evidently settled in. There's a mattress on the floor by a litter of empty bottles, and a strange ripe smell, not unlike feet, that I trace to a row of sausages hanging from the ceiling beam. *"Charcuterie artisanale,"* I whisper to Lucy, whose eyes are fixed on a big hunting knife with bits of hair and blood still stuck to the blade. Through the shattered windows, the Mediterranean winks happily.

"May I offer you a drink?"

"Excuse me," I say, "but who are you?"

He swats himself on the forehead and beams, revealing crenellated yellow teeth. "What am I thinking! Jean-Paul Albertoni, but everyone calls me Jojo. Please wait here: The kitchen is a mess!" He darts through a grimy curtain and returns with a bottle and three glasses, motioning us to follow him. We go back down and out the rear door, onto a sort of terrace with a collapsed wall at the end, the very one with the fabulous view where Lucy had fancied herself sipping wine at sunset while discussing Proust. Jojo must enjoy cocktail hour out here, too, judging by the empty glasses on a makeshift table he's set up in a corner. What catches my eye, though, is a curious structure, like a big frame, upon which two animal skins are crucified, the raw side still glinting wetly in the sun. Yipping with excitement, the dog heads toward a plastic basin on the ground full of what looks like intestines and sticks his snout in. I decide to take in the view after all.

Our host uncorks the bottle and sloshes a brownish liquid into three glasses. *"Apéritif maison!"* I touch my lips to it; it doesn't taste any worse than the thistle liqueur at the Marmite.

"You must be the American girls," he says.

"Anglaise," Lucy demurs.

"When did you move in?" I say conversationally.

"Move in?" He laughs like this was a really good joke. "This is my family's house. Here, I'll show you." He leads us to back to the doorway and points up. On a mossy plaque encased in the wall, you can still make out the words *Famille Albertoni* and, below, an inscription: *Lungi da me i falsi amici.* Far from me, false friends.

"Our motto," Jean-Paul explains.

"Nice," I say.

He grins again.

"But"—Lucy hesitates—"this house has been empty for a long time. . . ."

The grin subsides, his expression now doleful. "Yes, I was away." From behind him I can hear the dog slurping away in the bucket.

"Ah," says Lucy.

"I killed a man."

Lucy's eyes widen. I smile pleasantly. Santerrans are always showing off about killing people; it's part of their mystique. The fact is, if they really ran around butchering each other right and left, people wouldn't come here on vacation.

"That's unfortunate," I say.

"Yes—yes, it is. But he was a bad man, and nobody can say I didn't serve my time." Jojo's gaze shifts pensively out to sea. "I have paid my debt to society." He fixes his eyes back on us. "Still, I live with the guilt."

Since there doesn't seem to be a whole lot to say in response, Lucy and I remain frozen in our best cocktail-party poses, glasses aloft, elbow cradled in palm. I'm beginning to wonder if maybe he's not kidding. There's something about his eyes, a sort of creepy blankness like a heroin addict's. If he's really a maniac, it occurs to me all of a sudden, he may not be so easy to overpower.

"But I intend to become a productive member of society again," he continues, brightening up. "I have a plan, to bring the *hameau* back to life, restore the houses, attract tourists. Look at this view!" He flings his arm out to encompass the vast turquoise swimming pool below, currently veiled in a milky heat haze, the green-black mountains, the *pointe* thrust up like a rocky fist. Then he stops, as if suddenly reminded of something. "Have you ever heard of agricultural tourism? I hear you can get a subsidy from the government."

"I think you have to have a working farm," Lucy says. "Goats and cows, things like that. . . . Maybe you should talk to the mayor."

"The mayor, eh? Good idea! I'm sorry, are you hungry? Would you like a peach?"

"Thank you," Lucy says, "but we mustn't trouble you any longer. We have to go home and make dinner, for our children."

"Ah, yes, the children. . . . It's all for them, isn't it, in the end?"

"Quite," says Lucy, who I notice has slipped into her Victorian nanny act. Meanwhile I'm the one who's getting nervous, warily eyeing the shotgun propped up against the wall and thinking that this guy is definitely nuts.

"But you haven't finished your drink," he protests.

"It's delicious," Lucy assures him, firmly setting our glasses on the table, "but we have to walk back down. We won't get very far if we're tipsy now, will we? . . ."

I'm thinking, *This is when he gets mad and shoots us.* Instead he says, "Come back and visit me, it gets lonely up here."

"Oh, we will," Lucy promises, extending her hand. "Thank you so very much for your hospitality; it was lovely to meet you."

"Let me walk you back—"

"No, no, you mustn't trouble yourself any further."

Amazingly, he doesn't insist. He just stands there, looking resigned.

"Bring the children," he calls after us. "I love children."

"Wow," I say, once we're safely back on the path. "How did you do that?"

Lucy laughs. "I don't know, I was trying to pretend I was Mum! Oh, my god, I thought for a moment that we were going to end up on those racks, guts to the wind. . . . D'you really think it's his house?"

"It has his name on it."

"Well, yes, but everyone has the same name around here. He might just be a squatter . . ."

"Or a poacher."

" . . . or an axe-murderer. . . ." We burst out laughing.

"How do you think he knew who we were?" I ask when we've calmed down.

"Heavens, I'm sure they all talk about us. . . . I mean, what else do they have to do all day?"

"Well, anyway, so much for the uninhabited hamlet. . . ."

"Yes, it's rather sly of the mayor, don't you think?" Lucy says. "I'm sure he knew all along."

CHAPTER *twenty-two*

Back at the house, Jim is blowing on the fire for the barbecue, trying to get the coals hot; Odette, like Lucy, is convinced that charcoal starter gives you cancer. He straightens up as we approach, his sweat-dampened chest visible though his open shirt. He's gotten really dark in the past few days—who would have thought someone from Kansas could turn that color?—and my breath catches momentarily as I remember fixing my eyes on those black nipples, the way you notice odd details when your mind is completely elsewhere, as I lowered myself onto him last night.

"Hey, guys!"

"Why do you call everyone *guys*, Jim?" Lucy asks coyly. "Do we look like men?"

"No way I'd ever mistake you for a man, Lucy," Jim says chivalrously. Odette comes out with a tray piled with lamb chops. "Ah, girls, did you have a nice walk?"

"Fabulous," says Lucy. "And we met *the* most interesting character, didn't we, Constance? Mmmmmmm, that marinade smells divine. Can I make the salad dressing?"

I can tell Odette is taken aback by all this good cheer. I've certainly never seen Lucy like this. You'd think she'd be devastated that her pet real estate fantasy has been usurped by a smelly and possibly homicidal vagrant. Instead she chatted and joked with me all the way down the mountain, and now she's actually flirting with Jim, whom she normally wouldn't look at twice. Maybe she just needs to get out in the fresh air more often.

In the kitchen, Isabelle is busy at the counter. "Oh, hi there, I thought I'd feed the girls early, they get so wild at the table. . . ." She drags on her cigarette and balances it on the edge of the table, ash poised to fall on the floor. When did she start smoking in the daytime? Before her is a box of crackers, a pot of Nutella, and a family-size jar of peanut butter—one of two she asked me to bring from the States.

"Oh, really? And what are you making?" Lucy asks.

"My specialty: peanut-butter–and–Nutella sandwiches. The girls adore them." She picks up the cigarette again; the ash falls.

"Electra is allergic to nuts," Lucy says.

Isabelle empties her wineglass and sets it down. "Oh, come on, Lucy, it's all in your mind. . . . It's such a neurotic Western thing; how come no one in Prague is allergic to nuts?"

"I don't know, Isabelle, I live in London. What I do know is that if you feed them to my daughter, she will become desperately ill. And you know it, too, because I've told you, many times."

Isabelle drolly rolls her eyes. "Well, sorry, it's hard to keep track with all the restrictions around here. . . ."

"I wasn't aware there were that many. Surely you can see that Electra's diet needs to be monitored."

Oh, God, I think, *please don't try to reason with her. . . .*

"You know," my sister says, like she's just had an epiphany, "I'll bet you there's nothing wrong with her. I'll bet you if you just let her live her life, eat what she wants, she'd be fine."

"Like you do with *your* girls," Lucy says.

"It's not like I'm the perfect parent or anything, but anyone can see that she's hungry all the time. . . ." Isabelle refills her glass and points the bottle at us. "Anybody want some wine?"

"I'm sorry," Lucy says. "I'm sorry if that's how she strikes you."

Richard pokes his head in. "Isabelle, the girls say you promised them a special treat."

"I just found out Electra's allergic to peanut butter."

"Oh dear, yes," Richard says, "terribly so. Can't you make something else?"

"I'll make her something," Lucy hastily interposes.

"Don't be such a spoilsport, darling. Can't we just pretend for one evening that she's normal?"

"I'm sorry, what did you say?"

Richard clenches his jaw; it's a tic he gets when he's being an asshole. "I said, can't you just lay off her for an evening?"

Lucy looks disoriented. "Have you been drinking, Richard?"

"No, darling, I'm as sober as a judge." He smirks. Sophie sidles past him and tugs at Isabelle's skirt. "Mommy," she whines, "we're hungry."

"Yes, honey, I know, but Electra can't eat peanut butter, so now I have to make you something else."

"Can we have scrambled eggs with ketchup and toast?"

"Oh, all right," Isabelle says with ill grace. "But you'll have to wait. She's not allergic to eggs, is she?" she adds.

"No," Lucy says quietly. "She isn't."

I go off in search of Jane and find her sketching behind the house, on the terrace Monsieur Peretti has annexed for his tomatoes. They look almost obscene in the molten evening light, red and swollen, straining at their vines. He doesn't like us coming here—I can see him up on his balcony, glaring in our direction—but the mayor, who is pissed off at his rampant colonizing, keeps encouraging us, saying that the land is for everyone to enjoy.

"Oh, hi," she says distractedly.

"I'm worried about Lucy," I say.

"Hmm. Why?" She squints at something in the distance and rubs at the paper. "Oh, bugger!" When I try to see what she's drawing, she snaps the pad shut. "Another one for the dustbin."

"I don't think she's very happy," I say.

Jane lets out a mirthless chuckle. "What else is new?"

"I was thinking maybe you should talk to her," I say. "Richard's being a real dick."

"Isn't that the nature of the beast?"

"What?"

"Sorry, bad joke. So, Lucy is unhappy."

Well, put that way . . . back when we all lived together, Daphne had a way of prefacing comments about her oldest daughter with a resigned "Poor Lucy . . ." I remember wondering what on earth she was talking about; as children do, I still equated happiness with good fortune.

"Poor Lucy, she does have a bottomless capacity for misery. . . ."

"I have a feeling she's trying to get pregnant again. There was one of those fertility sticks in the wastepaper basket in the bathroom," I venture. "It can't have been Isabelle's."

"You know, it's always amazed me about you straights, that you think having a baby is going to solve all your problems."

"Count me out. I have zero maternal instinct."

"Oh, you'll succumb like the rest."

"I will not. I'd be a horrible mother."

"Right, like that's ever stopped anyone."

"I think you'd make a great parent," I say.

"Well, thanks for the vote of confidence, but it doesn't seem too likely."

"Why not? Lesbians have kids all the time. I mean, you could adopt, or—"

"Get turkey-basted?"

"Yeah, whatever."

Jane smiles sarcastically. "That's very sweet of you, but to tell you the truth, I'm not all that fond of children. As Ogden Nash said, I consider that mankind achieved its zenith the day it achieved the adult."

Suddenly it hits me that she really is upset about the breakup with Marge: That's why she's been acting so strange. And I haven't exactly been supportive. "Why don't you come and stay with me in New York for a while?" I say on an impulse. "You haven't been in ages."

"And what would I do there?"

"Take a vacation. We could hang out, like we used to. Hit the clubs. . . ." Jane and I used to go dancing together all the time, to hokey dyke bars in the Village and the clubs downtown with the hot Puerto Rican babes. I even let myself get picked up a couple times, just to see what it was like. Jane thought I was a complete slut.

"Really, Constance, I'm a bit over the bar scene."

"Why not?" I press on. "Maybe it's just what you need, to get out, meet new people. There's any number of women who would die to go out with you. . . ."

"Marge not being one of them," Jane says bitterly.

This is too much. "I never liked Marge," I say.

"Really? That's too bad, she's quite fond of you."

"God, Jane, would you stop being so English!"

"But I *am* English, just like you're American and Odette is French. We're forced to get along by circumstance. Do you think any of us would be here if it weren't for this ridiculous memorial?"

"But," I protest, "that's not the way I feel about you at all!"

She pats my arm in a detached way that's not exactly comforting. "Don't mind me, I'm not myself today. I should go back to London. I have to sort out my life." She looks out at the water again. Why are people always looking out to sea? There's nothing there.

"Then why don't you?"

"I don't know. Cowardice, I suppose."

"I still don't think Marge deserves you," I say.

She turns to face me, her eyes cool. "How do you know?"

"She's just so grim and humorless. She's not like you at all."

"Really? And what am I like?"

I hesitate. "Well, you're great. I mean, you're thoughtful, and funny, and wise, and—"

"Rather daunting to be considered wise at thirty-two, don't you think?"

"I . . . I hadn't really thought about it that way. . . ." I'm beginning to feel as if I were being set up.

"What if that's not how I think about myself at all?" Jane says. "What if I considered myself to be wild and sexy? A bad girl?"

"God, Jane, you sound like one of those self-help books!"

"Why don't you just come out and say what you really think: that you find it impossible to think of me as a sexual being."

"For crying out loud, Jane, I'm your *sister!*"

"No you're not," she says flatly. "Oh, don't look at me like that! I am so *tired* of being considerate of the feelings of others." And without another word she turns back to her drawing, so that I have no choice but to walk away.

I feel so unsettled by this conversation that I skip dinner and head down to the water. Our little cove is empty, would-be bathers either put off by the sea's distemper or the jellyfish that wash up when the surf gets rough. I climb up on a rock ledge and watch the orange yolk of the sun, its shimmering reflection bisecting the water like a brushstroke. The mountains beyond Flore look dim and crepuscular in the distance.

"Mademoiselle Wright!"

I turn so sharply that I almost lose my balance. From the cement dock below, the mayor waves at me. I clamber down.

"*Alors,* Mademoiselle Wright, are you contemplating the forces of nature?"

He must have come down for an evening dip: He's clutching a rolled up towel and a pair of goggles.

"Isn't it a bit rough for swimming?"

"Not at all! I like a little movement in the water—makes it more lively!"

"Do you think there'll be a storm?" I ask to be polite. I don't have Isabelle's easy, bantering rapport with the mayor, but the weather always seems a safe subject.

"Ah, Mademoiselle Wright, you know as well as I how unpredictable our weather can be: We could wake up tomorrow to clear blue skies." He bends down and starts to take off his pants, hopping on one foot as he wriggles one leg out, then another. Having accomplished this, he stands there in his little French bikini briefs, beaming, and bends down again. I realize with dismay that he's about to take his underwear off in front of me.

"We were up at the *hameau* this afternoon," I blurt out, seizing on the first topic that leaps to mind. He straightens himself and peers at me through the thick glasses that weirdly amplify his eyes.

"Ah?"

"There's someone living there."

He eyes me speculatively. I'm convinced the mayor has always thought I'm a bit of a moron. "What? Ah, you mean Jojo!"

At least I got his mind off undressing. He smiles benignly, as if to say, *Well, and what of it?*

"We were kind of surprised to find him there," I say. "I thought the hamlet was supposed to be uninhabited."

"*Hein?* Of course it is uninhabited. Jojo is not a habitant, he is just residing there temporarily." I detect in the mayor's gaze a certain crafty blankness people get around here when they're trying to pull a fast one on you.

"He told us he killed someone," I say.

The mayor's eyebrows go up. "Now, why would he go telling you crazy stories like that?"

"It's not true?"

The crafty look again. "It happened a long time ago," he finally allows. "A regrettable misunderstanding! I assure you, he is as docile as a lamb. If you want to know, I have hired him as a sort of caretaker."

"Ah, there you are, *chéri!*" Madame Mayor comes trotting toward us over the rocks, a pair of plastic sandals in her hand. She must have been waiting in the car. "You forgot your jellies—you'll cut your feet up again. Why are you standing there in your underwear?"

"I was just telling Mademoiselle Wright about Jojo."

"He told us he murdered someone," I explain.

"It was completely justified."

"Really, *chérie* . . ."

"He was provoked," Madame says curtly. "Are you going to put on your bathing suit or not? Here, give me that towel." In the no-nonsense manner of a nurse, she shakes it open and holds it up before him like a curtain. Hastily the mayor finishes undressing. "Men are so impractical," she observes to me.

"This has no bearing at all on our little transaction," the mayor says. "If you buy the *hameau,* Jojo will naturally leave. Now, if you will excuse me . . ." He adjusts his goggles, hops up on a rock, and dives neatly into the water. Madame and I watch him paddling away. I glance up at Borgolano. In the gloaming, the village melts into the gray-green mountain, so that I have to squint to make out our house, which, for all the dramas roiling within, looks as stout and impassive as ever.

"What do you need with that bunch of ruins?" Madame Mayor says. "You have a perfectly good house already."

"It's not about need," I say.

CHAPTER *twenty-three*

The mayor was right: We wake up the next day to lucent skies. The fine weather so cheers me that I surprise Jim with a morning special and then, whistling to myself, head down to the kitchen where I find Odette and Isabelle. Judging by their hushed voices and the empty coffee cups on the table, they were just having a heart-to-heart.

"After the age of twenty-five, a woman cannot afford to be sentimental," Odette is saying.

Isabelle looks up at me with red eyes. "Oh, Constance, I thought you'd gone out."

"Any coffee left?"

"You girls drink too much coffee. It is terrible for the digestion."

"We're Americans," I say, sitting down. "Our digestive systems have been hopelessly adulterated by junk food."

"I'm going to leave Prague," Isabelle says.

"Ah, please do not start again! Constance, you must try to reason with her."

"Odette thinks I should use feminine wiles to get Jiri back."

"Sounds like a plan," I say.

"He is the girls' father," Odette says. "He will tire of this young actress, and if you act intelligently, he will come back to you."

"Isn't that amazing," Isabelle says bitterly. "It's exactly what Maria says."

"Maybe you ought to listen," I remark. "It sounds like they know what they're talking about."

"Oh, sure, that's why *their* marriages were such a success."

A hurt look flickers in Odette's dark eyes. "I have no regrets," she says.

"I'm sorry," Isabelle says with flagrant insincerity. "I didn't mean that. The fact is, I don't *want* him back. I'm going home."

"To New York?"

She looks at me like I'm dense. "No, to Paris."

"You haven't lived in Paris for fifteen years," I remind her. "You don't even know anyone there anymore."

"That's not true, I still have lots of friends. And Odette is there."

"You see, *ma chérie*," Odette says hastily, "Constance agrees with me." So she isn't all that eager to wake up and find Isabelle and her children on her doorstep.

"This is crazy," I say. "At least in Prague you have a support system. You have a great apartment, and friends, and Maria to help you with the girls. . . . What are you going to do in Paris? Where will you live? How will you pay the bills?"

My sister looks at me again like I'm stupid. "That's exactly why

I'm not going to New York. France is an enlightened country; the schools are free and—"

"Rent isn't free. What are you going to do, go on Welfare?"

"I'll get a job, of course," Isabelle says grandly.

"You've never worked a day in your life."

"Listen to your sister: You cannot start life again at your age!"

Isabelle's eyes widen. "What do you mean, 'at my age'?"

"Ah mon Dieu," Odette cries in exasperation. "You are not a young girl anymore! You are a mother of two children, alone. The world is a hard place!"

"But look at you!"

"I have no children. And I have a profession."

"Since when is stewardess a profession?"

"You do not mean what you say. When you think about it, you will see that it is better to act wisely than impulsively."

"She has a point," I remark.

"You're wrong, both of you! Anyone can start over! I'll be a waitress if I have to, I don't care!"

"Mommy! Look!"

We all turn toward the door where Sophie, who has inherited her Czech grandmother's sense of dramatic timing, pauses for a second before rushing up to the table, a beat-up metal box clutched in her hands.

"Electra found a treasure!"

Electra, following with Olga, doesn't seem all that excited. She chews forlornly on a cuticle while Sophie sets the box down before us and, with uncharacteristic delicacy, opens the lid. Inside are a folded index card and a little cloth Bécassine doll, which I recognize because Isabelle used to have one.

"Electra broke the floor," Olga says slyly.

"What do you mean, honey?"

Sophie explains: They found a loose floorboard in their room and Electra pried it up. The box was underneath.

"She's not going to get in trouble, is she?"

"May I see?" Odette says.

Reluctantly, Sophie slides the box toward her, no doubt figuring that, like most good things, it's going to be found unsanitary or unsuitable and taken away.

"Look at the paper," Isabelle says. "There's something written on it."

Odette hands me the index card. I would recognize Ross's handwriting anywhere; my father was a prolific dasher-off of notes, often embellishing them with apt quotations that he kept in a special notebook. It was the way he made up for his lack of formal education. *Banque Garnier,* I read, *Zurich, 1326905, Monsieur Samsa.*

"It sounds like some kind of bank account," Isabelle says.

"Mommy, may we have the sweet little doll?"

"Here," Isabelle says distractedly, handing it to Sophie.

"What now?" a voice drawls behind us. Richard, just back from a run by the look—and smell—of him, followed by Jim, who peers over my shoulder for a closer look.

"Looks like a bank account number," he says.

"God, don't you *get* it?" Isabelle cries. "The Bécassine doll—it's a sign! Dad put it there for us to find!"

Odette smiles indulgently. *"Chérie,* it's a lovely thought, but I think he would have said something, no?"

"Well, maybe he never said anything to *you.* . . ."

The wounded look again. "No, he did not, but I am quite sure he would have. There was nothing left when he died."

"But he didn't *know* he was going to die!"

"No, he did not."

"So maybe he never got a chance to tell us!"

"Look," I say, "I don't want to be a party pooper, but Dad had accounts all over the world. There was nothing in them."

"But not in Switzerland," Isabelle bleats, "and not with the number hidden under a floorboard!"

"I wouldn't get my hopes up," I say. "Anybody can open a numbered account. He was probably using it to hide money from his creditors. I'm sure it was liquidated ages ago. Trust me, he was broke when he died."

"Doesn't it come with an ATM card, so we can check the balance?" Richard asks sarcastically.

"You'd have to go in person, talk to this Mr. Samsa," Jim says.

"To Zurich?"

"Yeah, that's the way it works. It's not exactly a twenty-first-century kind of financial product."

"Tell that to Imelda Marcos," Richard says. "I must say, one has to hand it to Ross: cold in his grave and still pulling your strings—"

"What's that noise?" Isabelle interrupts.

I go out to investigate. In the hallway I come upon Lucy, trying to back her way through the front door with a giant aluminum pot clasped to her chest and grocery bags dangling from both elbows.

"Oh, hullo!" she calls out. "Give me a hand, would you?"

"What is *that?*" Richard snaps.

"A pot, darling, what does it look like?"

"What the hell for?"

"Bouillabaisse. I'm going to make a proper bouillabaisse, with masses of lovely *rouille* slathered on croutons . . ."

I grab the pot from her before she drops it.

"Whew, thanks! I'll just dump these things on the table."

Isabelle catches my eye and rotates her finger at her temple. "Such a gorgeous day! I got to Flore just as they were unloading the boats," Lucy babbles on happily. "Mind you, I did have to get up at five."

"Well, you can hang up your apron," Richard says. "Old Ross has left you millions after all; you just have to pop over to Switzerland and pick them up."

"What *are* you talking about, darling?"

"The old box-in-the-attic number . . . always a big hit with impressionable minds." He looks pointedly at Isabelle before walking out.

"You don't have to be such an asshole, Richard," Isabelle says to his back.

"Well," Lucy says briskly, "I'm afraid this fish can't wait, so you'll have to tell me about it later. There's masses of things to chop, if anyone wants to help."

Isabelle remains immobile. Odette makes her *The English are crazy* face and says, "I must go hang the laundry before it wrinkles."

"Oh, well, thanks a lot!"

"I help you," Yves says. I hadn't even noticed he was in the room; he must have just walked in.

"Why, thank you, Yves. Can you chop garlic?"

"I sink so."

"The fishmonger let me have all his fish heads. Wasn't that lovely of him?"

"Did you hear what Richard said?" I ask her.

"Yes, I did, but right now I am going to make bouillabaisse. If

I don't get the stock made, I'll never be finished by dinner. Here you go, Yves. . . ." She dumps a big pile of garlic out of a paper bag in front of him and hands him a butcher knife. Isabelle rolls her eyes again and walks out. Yves picks up the knife, whacks the garlic neatly with the side of the blade, and begins to karate-chop it the way chefs do on TV.

"Well, you certainly seem to know what you're doing," Lucy says, impressed.

"I worked in a kitchen, on a cargo ship, when I was a student."

"Oh, really?"

"Yes, I chopped much garlic," Yves says modestly.

"Elizabeth David says it's useless to attempt bouillabaisse anywhere but on the Mediterranean," Lucy says, ripping open a package and shaking out a cascade of fish heads onto a newspaper she's spread on the table. "It would be a sin not to have it at least once."

"Can I ask you what you're planning to do with those?" I say.

"For the stock—another trick from Elizabeth!"

"Very good," Yves says approvingly. "Gelatin in the bones."

"Exactly, I just need to get them in the pot. I can tell you, I had one hell of a time finding saffron. . . . Now, Yves, when you're done with the garlic, you can put it in this bowl. We'll need onions, too, and tomatoes. Constance, if you're just going to stand there, you might as well do something: Can you peel onions?"

"I guess so," I say doubtfully.

"Yves will show you."

While Lucy busies herself with the fish, Yves demonstrates how to peel an onion. Like most things about cooking, it seems more trouble than it's worth. "You know," I say, "in New York you can buy onions already chopped up."

Yves looked amazed. "Really?"

"Yeah. In fact most people don't even cook at all: They get takeout from restaurants."

"It must be very expensive," Yves says.

"Oh, well, you know Americans," Lucy says cheerfully. "They're all rich as Croesus."

Who is she kidding? I try to pry the skin off the onion the way Yves showed me, but the knife keeps slipping. Finally I just stab at it and tear a big hunk off. My eyes start to sting. I wipe at them with my arm, which only makes it worse. Pretty soon tears are streaming down my face.

"Heavens, Constance, you've wasted half of it. Do try to be more careful. . . . Here"—Lucy passes me a colander—"You can toss them in and hand them to Yves when you're done." She puts a big pan on the stove, lights the burner, and pours in a slug of olive oil. The smell of frying onions fills the room. "We'll have masses of stock," she exults. "We can freeze some!"

I glance doubtfully at our shoe-box–size freezer, which holds two miniature trays of ice cubes and Richard's vodka. Speak of the devil: Just then he comes back. He takes in the scene and, regarding us coldly, says, "Great, now you've got half the household enlisted in your mania."

"What's that, darling?"

"Cut it out, Richard," I say.

"That's right, encourage her. I'll be up at the bar, with the normal people." He stalks off again.

Lucy starts dumping fish heads into the pot, creating a great deal of hissing and sputtering. It's getting awfully hot in the close room with its one window. Not that she seems to notice: Her hair clinging in damp strands to her temples, she stirs energetically with a big wooden spoon, an ecstatic smile on her face.

"Do we have any leeks?" she calls out.

"I check," Yves says.

"I'm going to get some fresh air," I say. "It's too hot in here."

CHAPTER *twenty-four*

Richard is still gone by dinnertime, which is probably why it's such a pleasant meal, at least initially. If Lucy is worried that her husband is always running off to get drunk, she doesn't show it. She and Yves clearly bonded over that pile of fish heads, now rather more appetizingly transformed into a deep orange broth that she brings to the table in a porcelain tureen from the flea market. Yves follows behind her with a platter loaded with poached fish and potatoes and, extravagance of extravagances, two lobsters.

"*Langoustes,* actually," Lucy corrects Jim. "An infinitely subtler crustacean. . . ."

"Hey, whatever," Jim says gamely.

"Shockingly expensive, but you only live once, right? And besides, it sounds like we might have something to celebrate." She puts a couple pieces of fish into a bowl, covers them with a ladleful of soup, places a *rouille*-slathered crouton on top, and hands the composition to Odette, who graciously tells her how delicious it looks.

"What are we celebrating?" Jane asks. I realize suddenly that I haven't seen her all day; in fact, if I were the paranoid type, I would say she was avoiding me. From the paint on her nose, though, it seems she was just off somewhere working.

"The extremely unlikely event that Ross left us anything besides debts," I say. I explain about the girls finding the box. "Pretty crazy, huh?"

"Why is it crazy?" Jane surprises me by saying. "Why wouldn't Ross have had a stash hidden away somewhere? It would be just like him try to hoodwink everyone one last time."

"I'm not questioning that the account existed," I say patiently. "I'm questioning whether there's anything in it. I spent a month with a team of estate lawyers and accountants taking the empire apart, remember? I ended up paying for his funeral, in case you forgot."

"I still think it's worth looking into," Jane says. "Maybe you overlooked something."

I wish she would meet my eye; she's acting really strange. "Of course we'll look into it," I reply, trying to mollify her. "I'm just saying, don't get your hopes up."

"What if it were true, though?" Lucy says wistfully, a forkful of lobster halfway to her lips, which are dabbed, I now notice, with the palest of pink glosses. "Just think: We could buy the *hameau. . . .*"

"Right, with Jojo in it." I tell them about running into the mayor down at the beach. "You know, sometimes I think he must take us for complete morons. What authority does he have to sell a whole village, anyway?"

"I think there's a way he can declare it officially abandoned or something," Lucy says.

"Right, after collecting fifty thousand affidavits and submitting a dossier to the prefectural authorities in Canonica, which would bring us sometime into the next century. . . ."

"Hey, this is great stuff!" Jim says, slurping his soup.

"You must thank Yves," Lucy says. "He did all the work."

"Eet's not true," Yves says modestly, gazing at her with reverence. She certainly looks beautiful in the glow of the candles, her hair pulled back to reveal the perfect planes of her face. If I didn't know any better, I'd swear she was flirting with him.

"Look," my sister suddenly blurts out, as if she's been holding it in all evening, "I think we need to talk about who's going to go to Zurich."

"I'll probably be there on business at some point in the fall," I say. "I could check it out then."

Isabelle gapes at me incredulously. "What, you just want to sit around and *wait?*"

"I've been sent on enough wild goose chases by Dad."

"I don't believe you. Can't you see he's sending us a *sign?*"

"He's dead."

"Oh, stop it, you know exactly what I mean." Her eyes grow wide. "Don't you see, he knew we would all be here; it's perfect. . . ."

"How could he know?" Odette says reasonably. "He would have had to know that he was going to die."

"Oh, God, that's *not* what I mean!"

"Well, what *do* you mean, then?" I ask.

"I didn't mean for his *memorial!* I mean he knew we'd be here in the summer," Isabelle concludes, suddenly a tad hesitant. Perhaps she's becoming aware of the holes in her reasoning.

"It does sound like the kind of thing Daddy would do," Lucy observes.

"See?" Isabelle says triumphantly.

"On the other hand," Lucy continues, "I can't imagine him really thinking in terms of his own demise. I don't think he really believed that he was ever going to die. . . ."

"But he wrote a will!"

"Oh, everybody does that," Lucy says dismissively.

"*I* don't have a will," Isabelle says.

"You don't have anything to leave," Jane points out.

Jim raises his glass. "Ladies! I think a toast to the chef is in order. . . ."

"The chefs," Lucy corrects him.

"*Mais non.* . . ."

We all click glasses. Second helpings of soup are passed around. Sophie and Olga, having been told three times by Odette to stop chanting mournfully, "Beautiful SOUP! Who cares for FISH!" are sent to bed.

"I'll go to Zurich if you want," Jane says.

I'm not exactly surprised when Isabelle follows me into the bathroom. My sister has never considered peeing to be a private activity. She slams the door now, however, and leans against it, as if to ward off intruders.

"Can you *believe* that!"

I congratulate myself on having put on a skirt rather than jeans: At least I've spared myself the indignity of having to wriggle back into them in front of her "What?" I say, pointedly flushing the toilet. In fact, I was as amazed as she was by Jane's offer.

"The nerve!"

I observe her with bemusement.

"Oh, don't be so *naïve,* Constance! Can't you see what she's up to?"

"You mean Jane?"

"Yes, *Jane!*"

"Oh, *her,*" I say, turning on the tap to wash my hands.

"Stop being so superior. You always act like she's your real sister, not me!" I half expect her to stamp her foot for good measure, but she obviously thinks better of it and, instead, rearranges her features into a beguiling pout.

"Will you lend me the money to go to Zurich?"

"Why? Jane just said she'd go."

She pauses for a beat, then changes tack. "Okay, so we're just going to leave it at that?"

"Why not? I think it's a dumb idea, too, but better her than me. I don't even like Switzerland."

She eyes me craftily. It's a good thing Isabelle was dissuaded by Jiri from going into acting, though *she* thinks it's because her Czech accent wasn't good enough. "And if she finds something, she's going to come back and tell us."

"That's the general idea. Can we go back to the table, please? I hear Lucy made chocolate mousse for dessert; I'd hate to miss it."

But there's no distracting her, she's like a dog with a bone. "Why do you think she would even be interested? She's got her trust fund, not to mention all that money she makes from her paintings. Why would she even care if Dad had left us anything?"

"Well," I say, "I guess because part of it would be hers. People are strange that way." I keep forgetting that you just can't joke around with people who have no common sense.

"Exactly!" Isabelle slaps her hand down on the counter, upsetting Odette's neatly lined-up vials of homeopathic medicine and the sordid jumble of her own cosmetics case, gaping open to reveal a hair-matted brush and several greasy pots of the Romanian face creams that keep her eternally young. "And now ask yourself: Why would Dad leave Jane and Lucy anything? He *knew* they were loaded!"

Ah, so that's what she's getting at. "Let me see if I follow you: You want to make sure that Jane doesn't take off with the loot that is rightfully ours?"

"Well, I wouldn't put it that way exactly. I'm just looking out for our interests."

"Well," I say, drying my hands, "I'm perfectly comfortable with Jane looking after mine."

I can practically see the gears turning while she digests this. "They're not even his daughters, really," she says.

"Except for the minor detail that he adopted them."

"Yeah, well, that was because he felt sorry for them, with that pasty-faced mother of theirs. . . ."

"Whom he married."

"Yeah, whatever. . . ." Her eyes alight on Lucy's zippered sponge bag. She snatches it up and opens it. "Ha, I knew it: fertility sticks! You'd think she'd just give up. . . ."

"You are completely out of line," I say.

She narrows her eyes confidentially. "You know, Richard made a pass at me the other night."

All of a sudden I feel queasy. "I don't want to hear about it."

"He was drunk out of his mind, but he pawed me, right on the stairs. I think Lucy stopped putting out years ago; poor guy must be desperate. In a way," she muses, "it would be kind of funny . . . but charity sex really isn't my thing." She smiles at me like an angel. "Let me have the money."

"Okay," I say.

She gives me a little hug. "You'll see, you'll be glad."

CHAPTER *twenty-five*

When Isabelle announces that she's prepared to go to Zurich, invoking the flimsy pretext of an old friend of Jiri's who runs an émigré press there, Jane just looks amused and says, "Be my guest," meeting my questioning glance with a bland smile. Isabelle, meanwhile, armed with my credit card number, has already booked her ticket over the phone. I offer to drive her to the airport—not out of any charitable impulse but because I wouldn't mind getting away for a day.

"I really have a good feeling about this," Isabelle says as we get in the car the next morning. It rained during the night and the air is rinsed and sparkling.

"Seat belt."

She pouts. "Oh, come on. . . ."

"Seat belt," I repeat.

And so we're off, all the windows down and the radio blaring

French pop songs to which Isabelle knows all the words from her teenage years. She can actually tell the difference between those twin icons of seventies easy-listening rock, Julien Cler and Michel Sardou; and, it goes without saying, she worships Serge Gainsbourg. As we pass the black beach at Orzo, Johnny Halliday's immortal hit *"Que je t'aime"* comes on. "God, I love this song!" she cries, closing her eyes ecstatically and humming along. At the refrain she joins lustily in: " *'Que je t'aiiiiiiiiiiiiime, que je t'aiiiiiiiiiiiiiime, que je t'aiiiiiiiiiiiiiiime!'* " she belts out. " *'Que je t'aiiiiiiiiiiime, que je t'aiiiiiiiiiiiiiiime, que je t'aiiiiiiiiiiiime!'* "

"He sure had a gift for lyrics," I observe.

"Oh, come on, it's *brilliant!*"

"Did I hear correctly? *'When your body on my body, heavy like a dead horse . . .'?*"

"Don't be such a prude; it sounds different in French."

"Huh."

"Oh, you are such an American, Constance. Do you know the main difference between us?"

"Ten thousand dollars' worth of orthodontia?"

"No, silly. You're such a product of New York—and I don't mean that in a bad way—whereas I will always think of myself as a European."

It's funny she should say that, because I've always thought of Isabelle as having a hokey American side that I completely lack but that Ross also possessed. I've noticed that expatriates are often more American than anyone in America, as if they'd picked up their sense of national identity from *Happy Days* reruns. But I'm not going to burst her bubble.

"But then, of course," she concludes, "I grew up in France."

"What was Vera like?" I ask.

She looks confused. "What do you mean?"

"I mean, what was she *really* like?"

Isabelle hesitates, as if describing our mother were somehow sacrilegious. "She was . . . well, she was lovely—graceful and elegant, and so beautiful. . . . Men used to stop and stare at her on the streets."

"But what was she like as a *person?*" I persist, because in fact, I have no idea. When I was little, I made her into a fairy-tale character: the beautiful ballerina mother I never knew. As I got older, though, her glamour took on a touch of the sinister. I suppose I was jealous that Isabelle had real memories. I hated the way she and Ross turned Vera into a goddess—it seemed such a cheap trick—and so I distorted her, giving her ugly, calloused feet and a bad temper. Suddenly it occurs to me that maybe those *are* my memories.

Isabelle takes the deep and fatalistic breath that, I'm sure she's convinced, is the indispensable prelude to weighty revelations. "Well, you know, she was Russian. She had a real sense of style. I used to watch her dress in the evening—she and Dad went out practically every night—and it was like a performance. Everything she did was really dramatic somehow, even the way she smelled. She used to spray herself with clouds of Shalimar," she adds wistfully, as if this were a definitive personality trait.

"I don't remember any of that," I say flatly and focus on driving. After the vineyards of Ursulanu, the road starts to wiggle its way up in a series of hairpin bends as it traverses the mountainous spine that runs up the *cap*.

"Well, she didn't really spend that much time with us. You were so little you still had a nanny, Dominique. She was from Côte d'Ivoire."

I do remember Dominique, though more as a vaguely recollected sensory presence than an actual person.

"And she spent all day in her dance studio. It took up the whole downstairs of our building. The lobby was always full of little girls in pink tutus; they were so cute. It was one of the top ballet schools in Paris, you know?"

It strikes me suddenly that what I resent is not so much Isabelle's enchanting European childhood as her immutable sense of place. I sometimes I feel as if, like Athena, I just sprang one day fully grown out of Ross's head.

"So, did you go there too?" I ask.

"Me? No, I had no talent."

"How do you know?"

"She told me. I mean, I had to audition like everybody else. She didn't take just anybody."

"Well, well," I think.

Safely over the peak, we begin the looping descent into Canonica. At points the drop down is so sheer that it feels more like you're in an airplane than a car. I can already see the city below, shimmering in its delicate haze of smog. "Ugh," Isabelle exclaims, "that smell!" We quickly roll up our windows as the municipal dump comes into view. The huge open pit cascades right down the mountainside into the swamplands, the sky above it woolly with seagulls.

Isabelle says, "It always catches you by surprise, doesn't it?"

Skirting the center, we swing on to the N74, where Santerre's affinity with central Long Island is revealed in the garish string of gas stations, discount furniture warehouses, car dealerships, and hypermarkets that extends all the way out to Calmetta Airport. Odette gave me a list of things to pick up at the Super-Géant on the way back: toilet paper, mineral water, UHT milk, coffee, and the teeny cartons of wildly expensive Tropicana juice that Jim tosses back by the dozen, an extravagance that both dismays and fascinates Yves and that Odette seems to find endearing. Maybe I'll go into town after I drop Isabelle off, check out the flea market, have lunch in the old port.

"Maybe I'll meet someone on the plane," Isabelle says jokingly as I pull up to the Departures area, "A dark, mysterious stranger. . . ."

"You're going to Switzerland."

"Okay, a dark, mysterious banker. Have you ever heard of the Mile High Club?"

"Look," I say, "if you need money, I'll always give it to you. You know that, don't you?"

"Oh, I know, honey. You're such a good sister. . . ."

"I just don't think you should get your hopes up."

But she's already out the door, which she slams, too hard as always, before leaning down and sticking her face in the window. She's wearing makeup—not a lot, just blusher and mascara—and she looks fresh and young and eager for adventure. "I'll call you when I get to Zurich," she promises.

As she strides into the terminal on her long brown legs, I see the hungry eyes of the parking attendant following her.

CHAPTER *twenty-six*

I don't believe in accidents; I think people know what they want and plan accordingly, just as I have been doing since I realized, when I ran into him on the *place,* that Philippe was mine for the taking. The thrum of anticipation has been building in me ever since, a pleasantly languid sensation that I'm sure there's a word for in French and that I've been basking in like a cat in a sunbeam. All obstacles removed, I pick up the groceries and race back to Borgolano, where, finding the house empty, I stack them hastily in the pantry. Then I walk across to Philippe's. I was never inside when the Costas lived there, but now I see it's essentially a smaller version of our house, with a kitchen and a main room downstairs and, upstairs, a big bedroom in the back with windows on the sea, flung open, and two smaller ones on the other side, one of which he's turned into a study. He's sitting at a scrubbed plank desk by the window, the top empty but for a pile of books and a laptop, and an old bentwood chair, the kind you can pick up for a couple hundred francs at the Canonica flea market, where I would be right now if I had any morals. Hearing me, he turns and rises. I stay in the doorway. He looks perplexed for a second, one hand still on the chair, then he smiles. I think, *Why should I trust him?* But he extends his palm and there's something about this gesture, about its hesitant welcome, that makes me advance. I walk right to him and we kiss, hesitantly, then hungrily, until I pull back and stare at him hard and say, "Why don't you want my sister?"

"Because I want you."

I just had to make sure.

I follow him into the bedroom. It's as bare as the study with just a mattress on a boxspring. We kiss again, our tongues dancing. His saliva tastes like tobacco and wine.

"Sit, right here," he says.

I lower myself onto the edge of the mattress. He kneels down and pushes me gently back so that my eyes fill with the blankness of the ceiling. As he unfastens my skirt and spreads it open like a kite, I realize in a disconnected way that everyone is sleeping; that's why I can hear the sound of his breath. We're in that still part of the middle of the day where time stretches into infinities, and this liquid sensation seems to have extended to my skin, which registers the touch of his trailing fingers as if it were detached from my body.

"You're trembling," he whispers, bowing his face like a suppliant. "Don't move." I close my eyes and he remains suspended, hovering over me, his breath caressing me, until, swollen to bursting, I shudder and sink.

Later, I prop myself on my elbow and tug at him, trying to pull him toward me, but he shakes his head. "No, there's plenty of time for that. I wanted to give you a gift." He removes the rest of my clothes, placing them neatly on the chair as he finishes, and the thought half forms in my mind that he might be fussy.

"Aren't you going to undress?" I say.

"No. Not yet."

This time he strokes me with his hands, laying me down again and spreading me open with nimble fingers, his eyes fixed on my cunt as if it were a marvelous flower.

"You are so beautiful," he marvels. "You are fine and supple like a tree; I could touch you for hours, I could bury myself in the scent of you— No, don't say anything. . . ." He slips into French, he talks and talks, his voice low and sinuous, fucking me with words. Some, like *encore,* I can make out, but mostly they blur into a cajoling susurration that flows though me in waves so that, when he finally undresses, revealing the long, concave chest I had imagined, its filigree of black curls dipping down below his navel to swell again at the base of his penis, the rest feels like an afterthought.

CHAPTER *twenty-seven*

"Well, look what the cat dragged in," Jane says pleasantly when I slip home the next morning. As the kitchen fills with the smell of toast, she takes the tray from on top of the fridge and, humming to herself, loads it with jam and butter and our ubiquitous sticky jar of Santerran honey, along with two cups and saucers and cutlery. On the stove, the kettle starts to rattle.

"Coffee?" I ask.

"In a sec, this one's for tea."

Tea? Jane never drinks tea. The only person I can think of who drinks tea is—

"Oh, hi, honey, breakfast coming right up," Jane sings out. I turn around. Marge, her hair all spiky from sleep, is standing in the doorway, a typical disapproving Marge look on her broad, pink face. "Hullo," she growls.

"Hi, Marge," I say. "What a surprise."

"Yes, isn't it?" Jane twitters, encircling Marge's waist and giving her a big smooch on the mouth. "She just showed up out of the blue!"

"And in the nick of time, by the looks of it," Marge says. The thought strikes me, as it does every time I see her girlfriend, that Jane might as well be going out with a man. Not only is Marge utterly devoid of feminine charm, she possesses, in abundance, that uncanny ability guys have to take a woman's admiration for granted. Not that Jane is any help: From the way she eyes her as she pours water into the teapot, you'd think Uma Thurman had just walked into the room.

"I brought some herbal tea," Marge says, eyeing the box of Lipton with displeasure.

"Oh." Jane looks crestfallen. "I'll just boil up another kettle, won't be a sec!"

"That's all right, I'll have a cup of that while I wait," Marge says magnanimously. She lowers herself onto a chair and crosses one big hairy leg over another so that her Birkenstock sandal dangles in the air.

"Biscuit?" Jane chirps.

I'm going to throw up.

Marge slurps at her tea—table manners, like depilation, are a tool of class oppression—and looks around. "This place is every bit as much a tip as I remember," she observes, her eyes wandering from the big crack in the wall to the makeshift shelves stacked with the chipped crockery that Lucy buys with abandon at the flea market in Canonica.

"If we'd known you were coming, we would have redecorated," I say. Jane shoots me a warning look.

"Shame really, letting it fall apart," Marge goes on. "Probably be worth a fortune if you tarted it up a bit. Sell it to some yuppie toffs. . . ."

"Lucy's looking into getting some work done," Jane says.

"Huh, I can just imagine."

"She has a couple rather good ideas," Jane says defensively. "She and Yves have drawn up some plans and they look quite sensible."

"Ah, yes, Odette's new bumboy." Marge helps herself to a cookie and shifts her gaze to me as she chews. "So, still swindling the poor?"

"If you mean am I still working for an investment bank, yes," I say affably. Not even Marge can dampen my mood this morning. "I'm in emerging markets now," I add.

Marge brightens up instantly. "Ah, yes—quite a windfall for you people, I should think, all the commies going bust at once."

"Not all, we're still waiting on Cuba and China."

"Huh." She takes another cookie. If I were her, I'd go easy on the carbs and sugars. "So, just how *are* you raping the third world these days?"

"Oh, you know," I say, "buying up tractor factories and coal mines, firing all the workers, that sort of thing."

"Really, Constance," Jane says with a frown. "When did you get so cynical?"

"I was just at a conference on women's health in the former Soviet Union," Marge announces. "Really shocking stuff. D'you realize that infant mortality has actually *risen* under capitalism?" she asks in the rhetorical tone she always adopts when embarking on an ideological rant. Rhetorical because Marge couldn't care less about the plight of post-Soviet babies, or Eritrean lesbians, or any of the other causes she has espoused in her unending quest to break the world record in conference attendance. What Marge cares about first and foremost is getting her opinion heard.

Still, I can't entirely resist the bait. "I'm not sure what they're doing in Russia really qualifies as capitalism," I remark.

Marge snorts with derision but is prevented from skewering me to the wall by the appearance of Jim, who, if he's surprised I didn't come home last night, isn't letting on. As he grins disarmingly at Marge, I feel a completely unanticipated stirring of remorse. Marge scowls. "Who's this?"

"Constance's boyfriend," Jane says, grateful for the distraction. "He works at the bank with her."

"Aren't there rules about you people fraternizing outside the office?"

"This is Marge," I say to Jim. "She thinks we're raping the third world."

Jim looks perplexed.

"Water's boiling!" Jane cries desperately. "Shall we sit in the dining room? It'll be more festive."

"I thought we were having breakfast in bed," Marge says with a leer, just in case anyone had missed that, on top of being an expert on everything, she's also a demon lover. I'm about to follow them—into the next room, not into bed—when Jim holds me back. "Constance, we need to talk," he says urgently.

"Look," I say, "I'm sorry, I—" But I don't get a chance to finish because just then there's a bang on the door, followed by a booming voice I would know anywhere—"Hallo! Anybody home?"— which sets off a cavalcade on the stairs as Olga and Sophie, shrieking with joy, come tumbling down to jump into their father's arms.

"What now?" Jim says.

"Vere is my vife?!" Jiri shouts, striding into the kitchen with his daughters hanging off him like grapes. Jane and Marge look dumbfounded.

"Hi, Jiri," I say. "She's in Zurich." He shakes off Sophie and hugs me, mashing my face into his T-shirt. He smells like a bear but it's another one of those things Jiri gets away with in the service of pure masculinity.

"What the fuck is she doing in Zurich?" he roars.

Marge, still soldered to her chair, shoots Jane a *What the hell is he doing here?* look, but Jane in turn is now being helplessly pressed to Jiri's chest.

"Marge, you old dyke!" he bellows over Jane's head.

"Daddy, Daddy!" Sophie yells. "Mommy went to get a treasure!"

He grabs Sophie again, releasing Jane—"*You're* my treasure! Come here and give me kiss"—and Sophie, swooning with ecstasy, hoists herself up like a monkey and plants her lips on his stubbly chin.

"I need a shower!" Jiri roars. "Would you believe I drove all the way from Prague in one stretch?"

"How very manly of you," Marge says.

"Just had a short nap on the ferry, then on to these fucking crazy Santerran roads! I almost ran over a cow: Stupid thing was sleeping in the middle of the road!"

"Oh, no, Daddy!" the girls scream with glee.

"That's all right, I slowed down just in time. Who's this?" Jiri says, indicating Jim, who is gazing at him with the naked admiration my brother-in-law always inspires in not-quite-so-manly Westerners. I introduce them.

"Ah, got your hands on Constance, eh?" he exclaims, thumping Jim on the back. "What's your secret? She wouldn't have me!" Once again I am reminded that it's awfully hard not to like the guy, a feeling that has always been shared by Odette, who, attracted by the ruckus, now appears and comes skittering over. Jiri makes a big show of kissing her hand.

"Odette! Every year more beautiful!"

"Ah, stop it, teasing an old woman. . . ."

"Old woman?! I've thrown younger women out of bed!"

Marge rolls her eyes. The last time she and Jiri were together, they spent the whole vacation taunting each other like two guys in a bar, much to the distress of Jane, who I don't think was aware of the frat-boy element of Marge's personality. As for Marge, she's never quite been able to wrap her mind around the concept of a reactionary revolutionary.

"I didn't know your cave was furnished," she says. Jiri, who has dropped into the other chair, leans over and slaps her on the thigh.

"My good lesbian friend Marge, how goes the struggle against male oppression?"

"Coming soon to that backwater you call home: Guess where our next empowerment conference is taking place?"

"Ha! Very good! I'll have to hook you up with the old trouts from the Central Committee for Ladies' Affairs."

"I'm in touch with a number of Czech *women's* groups already, thanks," Marge says.

"I wouldn't bring up the muff-diving, though: You don't want to get slapped in the head with a handbag."

Marge settles herself more comfortably in her chair, under the desperate eye of Jane.

"I see you're still operating under the delusion that the Czech

Republic is the only country on earth with a gay population of zero?" she says.

"Absolutely not! Homosexuality has doubled under capitalism—it's just that none of the girls seem to be interested."

"Who can blame them, with strapping lads like you around?"

"That's exactly what *I* think," Jiri says with a grin, turning back to the girls, who are buzzing around him like mosquitoes. "Now, why did that silly mother of yours run off to Switzerland? Shall I go get her?"

"No!" Sophie and Olga wail in unison. "Stay here, Daddy!"

Jiri hoists his daughters onto his lap, which is when Electra makes her timid entrance, hesitating in the doorway. Jiri observes her with interest.

"And who is this young lady?"

"Oh, it's Lucy's daughter," Odette says hastily, almost apologetically. "Don't you remember her?"

"But of course! And what is your name?"

And just like that, out of the blue, and with neither of her parents in the room to record the occasion, Electra, loudly and clearly, says:

"Agnes."

CHAPTER *twenty-eight*

"She doesn't like her name," Sophie says.

"How do you know?" Odette asks.

"Because she told us."

"But—she can't talk," Odette says, reasonably enough.

"She talks to us all the time, don't you, Agnes?"

Electra doesn't answer.

"Jesus," Jim says.

"Could somebody," Jiri says, "please explain to me what is going on?"

I turn back to him. "We weren't exactly expecting you, you know."

Jiri looks shocked. "You thought I was going to miss my good friend Ross's memorial? What kind of a man do you take me for?"

"Daddy!" Sophie yells. "Wait right here! We have something to show you!" She races out of the room with Olga and Electra in tow.

"Well," I say, once they're out of earshot, "we were kind of under the impression that you and Isabelle had split up."

"Why would I split up with the mother of my children?" Jiri asks with a look of genuine amazement.

"You see," Odette says with satisfaction.

"I don't know," I say. "I think you and Isabelle might be having some communication issues you need to sort out."

"Female nonsense," Jiri says genially, grabbing a handful of cookies off Marge's plate. "What the fuck is she doing in Switzerland, anyway?"

"Jiri, *vraiment!*"

Jiri smiles disarmingly, revealing the gap from the tooth that was knocked out in an antigovernment demonstration in '68. "I am truly sorry, Odette, I forgot myself."

We explain, once more, about the bank account. I have to say that, with every retelling, the story sounds more preposterous.

"Ha! This is good! So my wife has run off to Zurich to see what is in this account, yes?"

"Daddy, Daddy!" The girls burst back in, Sophie clutching the box to her chest with an air of extreme and unbearable trepidation.

"And what do we have here?"

"Treasure!"

"Indeed," Jiri says, peering with great seriousness at the doll inside. "Come here, you little ape!"

"It's ours!" Sophie squeals. "Mommy gave it to us!"

Which is when we hear the explosion.

We all fly outside, where we find Lucy, Richard, and Philippe peering down over the edge of the terrace toward the fishing cabins, where the sound seems to have come from. Up on the square, the church bell is ringing in alarm. The only other times you hear it is on Sundays and for weddings, upon which occasion shots are also fired in the air.

"*Ah mon Dieu!*" cries Odette. "Terrorists!" Jim drapes his arm reassuringly around her shoulder. I glance over at Philippe. He makes a little sign at me and then looks back down, though you can't see anything through the dense cover of the *maquis*. The girls are beside themselves with excitement, except for Electra, who you would never know had just reached a developmental milestone.

"Daddy, Daddy! Is it a *bomb?* Let's go *see!*"

"Jesus," says Jim. "Aren't there people living down there?"

The skirl of a siren interrupts him: Borgolano's one police car, which also doubles as an ambulance. We can see it careering down the road from where we're standing.

"We'd better go down and see if we can help," Jim says.

"God, of course," Richard exclaims. "Philippe, got your car keys on you?"

"*Attention!*" Odette calls after them.

"Come on, we'll follow them down," says Jane, who has suddenly appeared at my side with Marge. "I'll get the keys and meet you at the car."

Marge, Lucy, and I pile into the little Renault, and within seconds we're tearing down the road to the water. When we reach the bottom, Philippe's car, doors gaping, is the only one in the parking area.

"A good sign," Jane says. "They must've all been off somewhere. Can you remember how many of the cabins were rented out?"

"Only two," I say. "I'm pretty sure the Germans left last week."

We make our way down the path, a strange acrid smell intensifying as we come closer. Up ahead I can hear Jim's voice.

"Jesus, what a mess! There doesn't seem to be anyone around, though."

Through a haze of dust, the first of Yolande's rental properties comes into view—or half of it, anyway, the top floor having been reduced to rubble. "Fuck!" Jane shouts. I look over to where she's standing, by the tree that shades the hut's entrance. From one of its singed branches, the corpse of a dog sways dismally in the ashy air. Philippe, Jim, and Richard come running toward us.

"What the— Oh, Jesus!" Jim stands rooted to the spot where he stopped. "What is *wrong* with these people?"

I want to go over to Philippe but I don't move. Jean-Michel and Pascal, Borgolano's two gendarmes, come racing down the hill.

"*Allez, dégagez!* Everyone clear out!"

"It's all right," Jim says. "There was no one home, and there doesn't seem to be a fire."

"Dynamite," Jiri says, sniffing the air.

"*Allez, dégagez!*" But except for ordering us to clear out, Jean-Michel and Pascal seem unsure what to do next, until they spot the dog. A look passes between them. I consider mentioning the one I saw when I was jogging but think better of it. Everyone knows the gendarmes are useless in a crisis. I'll just end up in the station— one room in the *mairie,* actually—for an hour, filling out statements in triplicate. My instinct is confirmed by the arrival of Yolande and the mayor, Yolande hysterical and the mayor looking troubled, especially when he sees the dog.

"Who is responsible for this? *Charles, what is going on? Ah mon Dieu,* my beautiful house . . ."

"You might ask if anyone was home," Jane says dryly.

"I *know* no one was home," Yolande snaps. "They all left yesterday. The new tenants are arriving tomorrow, and what am I to tell them? Charles, I *demand* that you find the culprits! *Ah mon Dieu,* I don't even have insurance!"

"Calm yourself, Yolande," says the mayor. I catch the gendarmes smirking at each other.

"*Allez,*" the mayor snaps, "you might as well call off the fire truck."

Lucy is staring at the dog. "It's a warning," she says.

"*Allons,* Madame Townsley, these are schoolgirl imaginings."

"*Charles,*" Yolande cries, "it is not as if we did not know who is responsible!"

"Madame," the mayor says coldly, "I think you should let me handle this through the proper channels. This would be best for everybody."

Yolande glares at him. "It seems to me that things have gotten rather beyond your control, *mon cher.*"

"I have everything under control," the mayor says through gritted teeth.

Lucy bursts into tears. "God, I hate this place!"

Yolande goes over to her and pats her on the back. "*Ah là là,* it is bad luck, *hein?*"

"What are *you* so upset about?" Richard snaps.

"I was going to buy it!" Lucy blurts out, dissolving into sobs again.

"It's true," Yolande says. "She gave me a down payment." All of a sudden, I notice, she's looking rather less devastated.

"What nonsense is this?"

"Oh God, it was meant to be a surprise, for your birthday!" Lucy wails.

"I hardly see—" Richard says.

"It wasn't just for us! It was meant to be for everyone!"

Richard stares at her in disbelief. "You bloody idiot."

"It's true," Yolande says. "She thought it would be a nice extension to the main house, a little *pied à terre* on the water—a charming idea, really, very practical."

Lucy sobs again. "Yes, another lovely idea in ruins!"

"Ah, well, who knows . . . perhaps you can rebuild," Yolande says cheerfully. Now she's got Richard's attention.

"What do you mean, rebuild? It doesn't belong to us."

"Ah, but you see, it does, does it not, Charles?" Then, turning to Richard, she says, "Your wife made a payment."

"I—ah—I shall have to look this up in the statutes," the mayor mumbles.

"There is nothing to look up," Yolande says primly. "She signed a contract."

"Lucy, is this true?"

"Oh God. Yes! Yes, it's true! How was I to know they would *blow it up?*"

Jane breaks the ensuing silence. "I really don't see that it matters either way. Lucy is entitled to buy a house if she wants to."

"Stay out of this please, Jane," Richard says.

"It *was* meant to be a present for you," I point out.

"For Christ's sake!" Lucy screams. *"Would you all shut up!"*

Since there doesn't seem to be anything we can do, we disperse. I start heading toward Philippe, but Jim pulls me aside and tells me again that we need to talk, urgently, and in private. I tell him to meet me at the Marmite.

CHAPTER *twenty-nine*

I find Jim at a back table, a cold beer before him. I'd like one myself but there's no sign of either Fabrice or Albertine. From the kitchen come the sounds of running water and the clatter of dishes. They must be cleaning up after the lunch rush. The place smells, as always, like bleach and fried potatoes.

"What a day, huh?" I say, pulling out a chair.

Jim nods. He looks preoccupied. "I have to admit, I didn't taken you seriously, about the nationalists. . . ."

I shrug. "They're not nationalists, they're just thugs: The whole movement degenerated a long time ago into organized crime. At this point it's mostly about protecting smuggling routes."

"You mean drugs?"

"Yeah, and diamonds, too; Africa's just a couple hundred miles away. There's a lot of money involved and it's not a nice business. I guess it's a natural for the mob."

"But what does any of this have to do with Yolande?"

"I don't know. She owns a lot of property, and she's pretty tight with the mayor, who isn't popular with everyone. Maybe they're trying to get at him through her: He's been trying to clean up local politics, so he's got a lot of people pissed off. Or maybe she wasn't paying enough for protection, who knows? One thing I'm pretty sure of is that they didn't know Lucy had bought it. Poor Lucy."

"Yeah, that really sucks, huh?"

"I'll say."

He swallows some beer. "Anyway, that's not what I wanted to talk to you about."

"Yeah, I figured."

He gazes at me intently. "Obviously, we aren't working out as a couple."

"Look," I say hastily, "it's all right, I—"

"Let me finish," Jim says, raising his hand, an anguished look in his eyes. "I'm really grateful you brought me here. This is kind of a new development because at first I was wondering what you were after—I mean, you seem a lot more interested in your family than in me, and frankly, they're a little intense. I know it's none of my business but, based on the past few days, I think you and your sisters have some issues to work out. Anyway, it's been an education." He grins at me in that disarming way of his.

"But the fact is," he continues, "I'm not in love with you, Constance. I'm in love with Odette—please don't say anything. She's changed my life. I've never known anyone like her. I'd feel terrible for Yves—he's a good guy, by the way, you should give him a break—except it turns out they had more of an arrangement, for companionship. I have to tell you that this kind of thing probably would have shocked me before, but I feel like I've learned more about human nature over the past ten days than in my whole life. I know I have you to thank for that, by the way."

My first reaction, I confess, is indignation: How could he fall in love with Odette over *me?* This is undoubtedly what people mean when they talk about a double standard. Then I start to laugh: My god, how could I have been so stupid!

"Why are you laughing at me? If it's the age difference, I have to tell you that—"

"No," I gasp, "It's not that at all! I'm thrilled for you, I—"

Albertine comes out of the kitchen and I wave and point at Jim's beer. She looks disappointed. No doubt she was hoping to find Isabelle.

"Terrible about the bomb, *hein?"* she nonetheless can't resist saying as she puts the bottle and glass down before me.

News sure gets around fast. *"Tragique,"* I agree.

Fabrice appears with a fresh ashtray, even though no one is smoking. Probably making sure Albertine isn't running off at the mouth around the foreigners. I haven't forgotten that I saw his buddies Eddie and Toto creeping around down by the fishing cabins the other day.

"Not good for tourism," I remark.

Fabrice shrugs. He does the stone-faced thing quite well; I'll bet he watches lots of gangster movies.

"It's those *petits cons* from Orzo. They won't get away with it."

Albertine slides him a molten glance but remains silent.

When we've finished our beers, we walk out and cross the square to the parapet that buttresses the far end. Up here, the view is even better than from the house: more mountains, more sea, more endless sky. "Sure beats the Hamptons, huh?" Jim says, but he's not really here. His eyes are alive with a secret excitement, and I think of Léon, after he's finally seduced Emma Bovary, that line about him savoring the inexpressible delicacies of female elegance. What dizzying worlds has Odette opened to him? But of course I know: Since last night, I've felt as if my skin were humming. I look down at Philippe's house, pretending I have magical powers and can see through walls. I picture him sitting at his desk, head bent, little black hairs curling on the nape of his neck, his own eyes looking out over the water, searching for words, missing the din of the city. I told him I would come back tonight.

"And anyway," Jim says slyly, "you have a crush on that writer." I actually blush.

"I'm not *that* dim, you know," he adds, and I realize that I do know he's not dim, he's just never set me on fire.

"I'm going with Odette to Paris after the memorial."

"That's great," I say. "I'm really happy for you."

"Thank you. That means a lot to me."

"I can actually kind of see you two together, if you want to know the truth. I mean, I think you make a nice couple."

"Yeah, well, it feels right. It feels really good."

"What about work?"

"I'm not going to start that new job after all," Jim says.

"What?"

He fixes me with those earnest eyes again. "I've discovered all sorts of things about myself in the past two weeks, and one of them is that I'm not cut out for investment banking."

"Could've fooled me," I say.

"Oh, don't get me wrong, I liked the work all right, and it was fun getting to know you, but I don't love it—like I don't love you. Oh, I'm sorry, I didn't mean it to come out that way."

"That's okay," I say magnanimously. "I don't love you, either, though I think you're a really nice guy."

"I think you're a good person, too, Constance."

"Okay, but we have to stop this, because I'm going to start squirming."

"What about you? Your vacation's just about up too."

"I haven't decided yet. To tell you the truth, I'm not so sure I'm cut out for investment banking, either, but I've gotten so used to being Constance the Banker, I don't know what else I could do. What are *you* going to do?"

"I'm thinking of going to culinary school."

"Wow," I say, and then, ever practical, "How are you going to pay the bills? Don't you have loans from business school?"

"Well," Jim says bashfully, "to tell you the truth, I'm independently wealthy."

"What? I thought you grew up on a farm."

"It's kind of a big farm," Jim says, blushing a bit. "More like an agribusiness—hogs, if you really want to know. My dad sent me to Harvard with an eye to my running the company someday, but I don't think I ever will."

I laugh out loud. "Oh, this is so great! Good old Odette . . ."

"Pardon me?"

"Nothing; it just amazes me sometimes how things work out. Look, we'd better get back: I have to deal with Jiri before Marge plunges an ax in his back."

"He's a real character, huh?" Jim says.

"Yeah, he sure is."

We turn off the *place* and walk down the street, past the newsstand and the *boucher,* both shuttered for lunch. The butcher shop's driveway is empty, but just as we round the bend, Eddie's van comes tearing around the corner. As if on cue, the mayor, old Mr. Peretti, and one of the Costa uncles emerge from the pink house opposite. When Eddie gets out of his van, they're waiting for him.

"Looks like they mean business," I remark.

"What was that all about?"

"Santerran law enforcement. We'd better get out of here: They might not want any witnesses."

Jim shakes his head. "Constance, you have one weird sense of humor."

CHAPTER *thirty*

"How positively Stendhalian!" Philippe says when I tell him the story that night. "She must be at least fifteen years older than him!"

"Actually, nobody has any idea how old Odette is. She was younger than my father, but that's not saying much."

"Yes, she has that ageless French quality, does she not? In another century she would have been a courtesan."

We're lying on his bed, a warm breeze wafting over us, cooling our sweaty skins. Through the wide-open window, a nightingale trills in the fig tree. Philippe traces his finger along my stomach. "I love how muscular you are. . . . Do you know, when I first saw you, you reminded me of a statue of Artemis."

"Anyway," I say, "it's nice not to have to feel guilty—not that I did exactly, but I did come here with Jim."

"Ah yes, the noble American. . . ."

"He's actually a really decent person," I say.

"Of course he is; they always are. You know, I love watching your family: Do you realize that they are all perfectly formed characters?"

I narrow my eyes. "What are you going to do, put them in a novel?"

"My prickly Constance. . . . Don't worry, I deal exclusively in tired old Europeans."

I stretch and gaze at him. I've never enjoyed looking at a man so much—the jut of his Adam's apple or the black mole on his hip, where the skin turns bluish from stretching over his pelvic bone. I run my finger over it.

"You drive me mad!"

"Don't say that."

"But you do. I feel like a teenage boy, a mass of seething, uncontrollable hormones."

He grabs at me, though in fact we're both too sated and sleepy to do anything but play around.

"Listen," I say, suddenly serious, "I saw Eddie's van down by Yolande's place the other day. And this afternoon he was paid a visit by the mayor and a couple of the village elders, and it didn't look like they were ordering a veal roast."

"Aha, so you think our *sympathique* butcher is the culprit?"

"Well, I think it's more likely someone would have put him up to it. Eddie isn't exactly the sharpest pencil in the box."

"A delightful expression, I must write it down—but you see, this is the charm of Santerre: If they didn't blow something up every now and then, it would be like any other Mediterranean island. I am sure the matter will be handled in the time-honored fashion, with no summer residents incommoded further. . . . Still,

I grant you, it *is* rather decadent of us to be wallowing in concupiscence while poor Yolande lies roofless in the night."

"It was a rental."

"Indeed. And one suspects that Madame Van Langendonck, who is not descended from generations of Flemish merchants for nothing, will recover. To tell you the truth, I would much rather hear about your new guests: that extraordinary surly lesbian, and your sister's magnificent husband. I can't imagine what she could possibly have seen in me; if I were a woman, I'd be mad about him."

"That's part of the problem."

"Ah, an Eastern Bloc Don Juan. . . . Actually, I seem to recall that he has a bit of a reputation."

"You know him?"

"My dear, I've heard of him. He *is* a fellow *homme de lettres*—not exactly on Kundera's level, but his early poetry isn't half bad if you go in for that particular brand of testosterone-driven Slavic sentimentalism."

"Well, whatever. He's a lousy husband and an irresponsible parent, not to mention a gambler and a slob."

"You disapprove of him?"

"No, I like Jiri. I just think you'd have to be nuts to marry him."

"Yes, I suppose these types work best as lovers. . . . Still, the combination of art and raw masculinity is awfully alluring, no?"

"Not to me. I guess they deserve each other, though; I mean, Isabelle isn't exactly easy to live with."

"Ageing beauties seldom are."

"That was a little harsh," I say.

"Was it?"

"There's more to Isabelle than her looks."

"I stand corrected—she is ravishing in all respects—but you'll have to forgive me for preferring your subtler charms. Now, tell me about the lesbian!"

"Marge? Oh, she's a pill. Nobody can figure out what Jane sees in her. By the way, do you really own one of Jane's paintings?"

"Oh yes, a very pretty one of a naked lady with a geranium. She intrigues me, your Jane: Those Raphael Madonna looks and what I suspect is quite a nasty mind underneath. If you ask me, what binds those two together is good old sex."

"You've got to be kidding: Jane could have anyone she wants."

"Undoubtedly, but that's beside the point. Maybe you are a little in love with her?" he says slyly.

"With Jane? Of course I'm not, what a dumb idea! We practically grew up together."

"Well, you know, stranger things have happened," Philippe says, beginning to stroke my stomach again. I have a feeling that the thought excites him.

"I don't do lesbian fantasies, in case you're getting ideas."

He laughs. "Please, Constance, you must try to be more oblique."

"I wouldn't get my hopes up," I say. "Why don't we talk about you now?"

He feigns dismay. "Me? What do you want to know?"

"Why did you split up with your wife?"

"Oh, the usual reasons. Actually, she left me."

"Really?"

"You sound shocked. Is it so unfathomable?"

"I don't know, I don't know you that well. Were you cheating on her?"

"Young lady, marriages do occasionally break up for other reasons."

"Such as?"

"Heavens, where to begin: listlessness, dissatisfaction, deceit, petty grievances, financial worries, professional rivalry, excessive ambition, insufficient love, diminishing sympathy, and, of course, the ineluctable monotony of the quotidian. My wife, however, fell in love with my best friend."

"That sounds like it came out of one of your books."

"Not one I ever published: Autobiography disguised as fiction is very boring, you know."

"I sometimes worry," I say, "that I'm not a nice enough person to get married."

Philippe laughs. "My dear, I am living proof that that has *nothing* to do with it."

CHAPTER *thirty-one*

"Constance, *there* you are!" Lucy, looking agitated, grabs my arm in the hallway. I try to adopt an expression of dignified aloofness but she isn't fooled. "Oh, stop it, I know perfectly well where you've been—that's not what I want to talk to you about. How *could* you not tell me about Electra?" she cries, her wide blue eyes boring reproachfully into mine. It hits me all of a sudden that, now that we're friends, certain things are expected of me.

"I'm sorry, Lucy, there was a lot of stuff going on."

"You can say *that* again," she says bitterly. "*Agnes!* Of all names. . . ."

"Aren't you happy that she started talking?" I say, though in fact that's a bit of an exaggeration. It's not exactly like the floodgates have been unleashed.

"Oh God, of *course* I am; it's just, well, one almost gets the impression that she's known how all along but was just being obstinate. Oh dear, do you think I'm mad?"

"Maybe she's trying to tell you something," I suggest diplomatically. "I mean, Electra *is* kind of a heavy name for a kid."

"But it's a lovely name! I would have *loved* to have been called Electra!"

"Lucy," I say, "most people don't name their daughters after members of the House of Atreus."

"It's because she can't bear me, isn't it?" Lucy says quietly. "Mind you, it's hard to blame her; I don't seem to be any good as a mother. Look at Isabelle: Her daughters adore her and she barely knows they exist. But *she's* fun and silly, and *I,* well, I depress people."

"No you don't," I say loyally.

"Yes I do. I depress my own husband—he told me so. He says I'm responsible for Electra's problems, that I've bullied her into silence, and that I'm trying to starve her. And now he's so angry about my having bought Yolande's fishing cabin, even though it was with my own money, that he's stopped speaking to me entirely."

I open my mouth to suggest that she tell Richard where to put it, but she stops me: "No, please listen, Constance; for some reason I feel you're the only one I can talk to. Tell me the truth: Do you think he's right?"

I consider the question. "No," I say. "I don't think anyone has that much power over another person, even a child. Kids survive all sorts of abuse. . . . Most people probably shouldn't be allowed to have them, but you're not such a bad mother; you just get a little overwrought."

"Thank you, Constance," Lucy says gravely. "I know you're being kind, but thank you."

From where we're standing by the kitchen door, we can hear Jiri and Jim talking in the living room. Suddenly Jiri raises his voice, which he tends to do when he's getting enthusiastic.

"No, no, my friend, communism wasn't *all* bad; in some ways it was like being a student forever: We got to live in shabby flats and drink too much and fornicate with delightfully loose girls— contrary to popular opinion, the socialist state did not breed virtue; quite the opposite, in fact—and occasionally, *pour le moral,* stage a little demonstration. Every now and then, one of you nice Westerners would drop in and drink vodka with us all night and then go home besotted with the depths of the Slavic soul. Believe me, now that we've become just another nation of shopkeepers, you won't find us so romantic."

"Uh, but what about political repression?"

"Jim, my friend! Let me tell you a secret: I was never so popular with women as when I was being persecuted by the authorities."

"I don't know, it seems like a hell of a way to get a date."

"Ah, but you see, it's all in the context—excuse me," Jiri says, reaching for the phone, which has just started to ring. "YES?" he bellows into the receiver. His expression changes to a delighted smile. "Isabelle! When are you coming home?!"

"You know what I find most amazing about Jiri?" I remark to Lucy. "The total freedom from self doubt. Do you think it's part of the artistic persona?"

"Hardly," Lucy says. "Look at Jane."

"Listen, *koteczko,*" I hear Jiri say, "you come back and I do anything you want, okay?" Catching sight of us in the doorway, Jiri motions me over and, clamping his hand over the receiver, announces cheerfully, "She is still angry," before handing me the phone.

"*What* is he doing there?" Isabelle hisses.

"Why don't you ask him?"

"This is really too much! After everything he's put me through . . ."

"What's going on?" I ask.

She takes a deep breath and pauses a second. "There are two million dollars in the account."

I stare out the window at a boat on the horizon—the car ferry to Livorno, probably. Jim and I were supposed to be taking it back, spending a couple days in Florence before we went home. I guess that's not in the cards anymore. "What?" I say.

"You heard me. Mr. Samsa was very surprised to see me, by the way: He didn't even know Dad had died. You'd think someone might have told them."

"Maybe it wasn't in his best interest to find out."

"Anyway," she says impatiently, "it doesn't matter. I can't do anything without your signature, so you need to come to Zurich: There are fees and things that I need you to help me sort out."

"I'm not going anywhere. You come back here and we'll decide what to do. This doesn't just involve you and me."

"I thought we'd already discussed this!" Isabelle says angrily.

"Yes, and I haven't changed my position."

"Well, I won't budge," she declares, though I can hear in her voice that she knows she's stuck.

"Okay, then I'll send Jane."

"You wouldn't!"

"Watch me."

Another pause as she reviews her nonexistent options. "Oh, all right, all right! I want you to promise me one thing, though."

"What?" I say, knowing what she's going to ask.

"Don't tell anyone."

"I'll see you tomorrow," I say, before putting down the phone.

CHAPTER *thirty-two*

As soon as I've hung up the phone, I convene a meeting in the kitchen.

"About two million dollars," I repeat.

"Are you sure?" Lucy says.

"Well, she's bringing the documents with her. Even Isabelle can read a bank statement." I glance over at Odette, who is wiping down the cutting board with an inscrutable expression. She's closed the shutters against the sun, but it seeps in between the uneven slats, throwing long stripes across the walls.

"How extraordinary," Lucy says. "I was convinced she'd come back empty-handed."

"Before we get all excited," I say, "can I just point out that it's not really that much money?"

Marge snorts. "I can assure you, Constance, that in most people's eyes, two million dollars is quite a lot of money indeed."

"Constance has a point," Lucy says. "Divided by five, it doesn't amount to much."

"I must say, this is awfully amusing, the nonchalance with which you toss about sums that would sustain an entire third-world village for decades," Marge says.

"I believe this *is* a family matter," Lucy says.

"Lucy!"

Lucy turns to Jane. "I'm sorry, but it's really none of her business."

"Thank you very much," Marge says huffily. "I know when *I'm* not wanted." She stumps out. I've never seen Jane so angry. She plants herself in front of Lucy, her chin shaking.

"How could you say that?"

Lucy is unrepentant. "She hasn't been here for years! What makes her think she can just walk in and tell us what to do?"

"Oh, really?" Jane cries. "Shall I tell you why Marge hasn't been here for years? Because you've never made her welcome—none of you!"

"*Oh là . . .*"

Jane swings around. "Don't you *Oh là* me, Odette—I know perfectly well what you think of us!"

Odette makes that little French shrug. "Do not flatter yourself, my dear."

"I'm not your bloody dear! You have made it clear from the moment Marge, my *lover,* stepped into this house that you consider us an embarrassing blemish on the family, something to be hushed up before the neighbors—"

"We are all civilized people. It is your business what you do in your bedroom."

"I can't believe this!" hoots Marge, who must have been hanging around in the hallway listening. "What is this, the fucking Proust-appreciation society?"

"Please do not use such language around me."

"Oh, that's rich. What's the matter, Odette, you find the word *fuck* shocking? I'm surprised that you of all people would have such delicate sensibilities," Marge says sarcastically.

"It is not such a bad thing to maintain appearances; perhaps you will learn this someday," Odette says.

"Ha, appearances!" Marge barks. "Women like you simply amaze me, Odette: You spend your entire life on your back and you worry about appearances!"

"This is enough, I think."

I decide it's time to intervene. "Look, Marge," I say. "No one invited you—"

"*I* invited her!" Jane cries furiously, and I notice with dismay that she has tears in her eyes. "And she has as much of a right to be here as that boy toy of yours, Constance, the one you seem to be sharing with half the household, or that self-satisfied prick Richard, or that buffoon Jiri—"

"Hallo," Jiri says, coming into the kitchen with a shopping bag full of wine bottles. "Did someone call me?"

"You all make me sick!" Jane shouts before being led out by Marge. Jiri takes in the scene with a raised eyebrow. "Have I interrupted a family gathering?"

"I thought you were at the beach," I say.

"The sun was too hot, and the girls all had mustaches. I went to the café, where I had a most informative talk with the *patron* about his theories regarding the explosion: He blames foreigners, in particular this Fatulescu woman who has taken up residence in that castle up the hill. He thinks she's an Arab."

"Oh!" Lucy exclaims, slapping herself on the forehead. "The cocktail party—it's tomorrow!"

"Cocktail party?"

"I completely forgot: Yolande stopped by to tell us; it's tomorrow at six."

"Isn't she going to send out engraved invitations?" I ask.

"It does seem rather odd, doesn't it?" Lucy says.

"The Romanian nobility is known for its oddities," Jiri says. "Think of Count Dracula."

"Well," Lucy says, "I for one am ready for a bit of diversion. I hope she's terribly grand and eccentric."

"Oh, I wouldn't worry about that," Jiri says. "Does anyone want an *apéritif?*"

CHAPTER *thirty-three*

The following day, Isabelle calls and tells me not to bother picking her up from the airport, she'll take a taxi. She doesn't mention Jiri. Jane and Marge have vanished, as has Richard, though he's probably just up at the bar, drowning his bile. Lucy decides to drive to the flea market in Canonica, and Yves offers to go along. She asks me before they leave if I've decided what I'm going to wear to the countess's party, then she glances at our neighbor's house and gives me a knowing look. "You're being awfully naughty, aren't you?"

"I'm hardly the only one who's being naughty around here," I retort, which for some reason causes her to turn pink, but she quickly grows serious again.

"I've decided to call Electra Agnes if she wants," she says. "What do you think?"

"You might as well try it," I say. For all the fuss, Electra hasn't exactly been running off at the mouth lately. Maybe she's just being obstinate.

"Though why she had to pick such a dreadful name . . . Perhaps she'll change her mind if we indulge her," Lucy says hopefully.

"It could have been a lot worse," I say. "She could have picked Barbie or Maude."

"What's wrong with Maude?"

"Forget it," I say.

Odette has been avoiding me. When I told Philippe about it, he laughed. "It's not shame, you know. You must try to view her through the prism of her ego: More than anything, she is terrified of appearing ridiculous."

"Well," I say, "I don't see any reason for her to feel guilty."

"My dear, you are intoxicating in your obtuseness."

"Oh, stop it," I say, though no one has ever called me intoxicating.

"You realize, of course, that she knows all about us."

"I really don't care who knows."

"Even your sister?"

"Well—"

But when Isabelle finally shows up, she has other fish to fry. She sweeps past me and marches straight up to Jiri, who has come out with the girls to greet her.

"What are you doing here? Did your bimbo throw you out?"

"Isabelle! *Les enfants* . . ."

"No, Odette, it's about time they learned the truth about their father!"

"Why, Mommy?" Sophie bleats. "What did Daddy do?"

"Nothing, sweetheart." Isabelle rustles through her bag and

pulls out a gift-wrapped box and a giant bar of Toblerone. "Here, Mommy has brought you a present. Why don't you go inside and open it?"

"We want to stay here with Daddy."

"I said, *go inside.*"

"No," Sophie says stubbornly. I'm afraid for a second that Isabelle's going to hit her, but she can't with all of us watching. "See what you've done," she hisses at Jiri instead, picking up her bag and stalking into the house. Jiri makes a helpless little shrug at me. I guess he really thought he was going to get away with it again. Strangely enough, I find myself feeling sorry for him; after all, it's not as if Isabelle had never cheated on *him.* It all seems so pointless all of a sudden.

I follow her upstairs and reach her room just in time for her to find Jiri's bag on the floor. "There was nowhere else to put him," I say.

"What about out on the street?"

"Look, I really don't want to get involved, but maybe you should give him another chance. He drove all the way from Prague—"

"Oh, please," Isabelle says disdainfully. "I can't believe you've been taken in by his act."

"I kind of got the impression before you left that you wouldn't mind getting back together."

"Well, things have changed," Isabelle says, fluffing out her hair in front of the mirror and making a show of inspecting her nails, which are freshly manicured and bloodred. She didn't used to go in for that kind of thing.

"You mean you no longer have two kids and no professional skills?"

"Excuse me," she says, affecting an air of puzzled incomprehension, "are you saying that I should go back to Jiri because I can't support myself?"

"Something like that."

"Right, because I'd have to be mad to give up the life of *decadent luxury* that he's accustomed me to."

"Jiri hasn't done so badly for a poet," I say. "It's not like you've ever had to work."

"Oh yes, that's always the bottom line for you, isn't it? Just because you have a dull boring job, everyone else has to suffer too."

"My job's not so bad," I say.

Isabelle whirls around, her eyes shining like a pirate's. "Yes, that's exactly it, it's *not bad*—but you can't stand the thought that someone like *me* would have a fabulous, wonderful, *interesting* life that doesn't involve going to a stupid office every day, can you? You know, Dad told me once that you have no imagination—" As soon as it's out, her face crumples. "Oh, Constance, I'm *sorry*, I didn't mean it!" She opens her arms the way she does to Sophie and Olga when she's forgotten to make dinner, or showed up an hour late for the school play.

"I have all the imagination I want," I say.

But already her eyes have grown huge and drowned and her hands have flown to her chest—where, unfortunately, her breasts get in the way. "Oh God, I can't believe I said that. Dad thought the *world* of you!"

"Well," I say, suddenly exasperated, "he thought the world of Jiri, too, so maybe, in his honor, you should give the guy a break or at least be civil to him until the memorial."

"Why can't we just have this memorial and get it over with!" Isabelle cries. "It's so morbid, all this sitting around waiting!"

"I thought the whole idea was to get together for a family vacation and then cap it off by celebrating the reason we're all here. Why would Ross deprive himself of one last chance to manipulate us?"

Her eyes narrow again. "You can't stand that I was his favorite, can you?"

"No," I say, "what I can't stand is having to pretend all the time that you're *my* favorite too."

CHAPTER *thirty-four*

By six o'clock everybody's ready for a diversion except for Lucy, who bought a chest at the flea market and is still on an antiquing high. Isabelle seems to have decided to grin and bear it. Alternating between sulking and sliding me molten glances laden with self-pity, she gets the girls all dressed up and, in an access of generosity, even curls Electra/Agnes's hair. We still haven't talked about the money.

To my surprise, Jane and Marge decide to come. Having been gone all day, they showed up flushed and disheveled with twigs in their hair, claiming to have been on a nature hike in the *maquis*, though anybody could tell they'd just emerged from a gigantic roll in the hay. Maybe Philippe is right and Jane just needs to get laid like the rest of us. Whatever their differences were, they seem to have worked them out. Jane is positively starry-eyed. She's wearing a flower-print hippie dress that really does make her look like a

Madonna, and Marge, in a major concession to the occasion, has slicked back her hair and put on a clean shirt. When Jiri asked her if she wanted to borrow a tie, she called him a prick, but it sounded almost affectionate. I've always suspected that in her heart of hearts she admires him.

At first I think Isabelle is going to behave herself and go with Jiri and the girls in the Škoda, but when she spots Philippe coming out of his house, she runs over to ask him for a ride, in a voice so nakedly suggestive that he winks at me before opening the door for her with a little bow. Jiri is not so amused. "Who's that?" he growls as I get into the passenger seat. I'd sort of hoped to travel with Philippe, but it doesn't seem worth the bother now. Jane and Marge squeeze in the back.

"Philippe Kahn," I say. "You met him at the explosion. He bought the Costas' house."

"He looks like a hairdresser," Jiri says.

"Actually, he's a writer."

"Never heard of him."

"Borgolano's turning into a regular intellectual colony," Marge says from the backseat. "Isn't this countess some kind of poet as well?"

"What was her name again, Fatalescu?" Jiri says.

"Fatulescu."

"I never heard of any poetess called Fatulescu," Jiri says grouch-ily.

"She must be pretty bloody rich, whatever she is," Marge observes as the manor comes into view atop its bluff, shrouded by a fringe of palm trees.

"I wonder," Jane says, "how she managed to get her hands on it. I thought it wasn't for sale."

The manor's gates have always been padlocked when I've driven by, but this evening they're flung open onto an oleander-lined driveway that winds through a lot of tropical-looking shrubbery before arriving at a bunkerlike structure topped with cement pineapples. We get out and look around curiously. Up close, the place has the vaguely decrepit look of all old houses in hot countries, the stucco dry and brittle and the green paint on the shutters blistered by the sun. Albertine, who must be on loan for the evening from the Marmite, stands guard at the door in a maid's uniform with a lace cap. Without a word, she leads us through a marble foyer with a burbling fountain and out through a bank of French windows onto the terrace where a table has been set up with drinks and the Marmite's special-occasion spread of toothpick-speared cheese and salami cubes, the lot presided over by a grinning Fabrice in a maroon bartender's jacket. Admiring the view from the balustrade are the mayor, the retired German couple who bought the old Paoli house last year, and Yolande in a kente-cloth–inspired outfit that makes her look like she's about to perform a ritual circumcision. She comes rushing over the minute she sees us.

"*Ah, enfin,* there you are! I was beginning to worry that you would not come. Where are the others?" She frowns as her eyes fall first upon Jiri, who hasn't shaved in three days, then upon Jane and Marge, the nature of whose relationship Yolande has never entirely been able to fathom, though what little she does understand she finds alarming in the extreme.

"Madame Yolande," Jiri booms, "our Flemish rose!"

Yolande smiles uncertainly, not sure whether this is meant as a compliment but in the end deciding to take it as one. "Monsieur Orlik, you are a naughty boy. . . ."

"Yes, Madame Yolande, I am a *very* naughty boy," Jiri roguishly agrees. I'm beginning to wonder if he didn't knock back a few before leaving the house. I'm about to steer him away to safer harbors when Philippe appears with Isabelle on his arm. I find myself staring at his hair. It's swept back in glossy dark waves that just might, I have to admit, have been sculpted with a touch of gel.

He kisses my cheek as he whispers to me, "You look enchanting," which is complete nonsense, even though I am wearing a rather nice silk shift that I spent an arm and a leg on, but pleases me anyway. And who's to say I'm not enchanting? Even Jim told me before we left that I looked great, though he hastily added to Odette that *she* looked ravishing in a green dress that I personally find a bit fussy. I'm relieved that she hasn't tried to say anything to me. It seems we're just going to let things slide in the French way, as opposed to going on *Oprah,* which suits me fine. I did feel a little bad for poor Yves—talk about the fifth wheel—but I heard Odette telling him not to be silly, of course he should stay and enjoy his vacation. I guess he was offering to leave, now that he's been relieved of his stud duties. He and Lucy have embarked on another home-improvement project. He's going to strip down that old chest she bought and grease the lock. Maybe he'll grease *her* lock while he's at it.

With Isabelle having gone off to say hello to the mayor, Jiri marches up to Philippe. "I don't think we've been properly introduced," he says loudly. "I am Jiri Orlik. My wife was just hanging all over you."

"Pleased to meet you," Philippe says imperturbably, shaking his hand.

Jiri grins, showing his broken tooth. "The pleasure's all mine. I always enjoy meeting a fellow *auteur.*"

"Thank you, I—"

"Especially one who is such a big hit with the ladies." Jiri winks. "Ah, but you must excuse me, my wife seems to have slipped away again." He lets go of Philippe's hand and darts over to where Isabelle is standing with the mayor and the German lady.

"This is really rather embarrassing," Philippe hisses once he's out of earshot.

"Maybe you shouldn't encourage her," I say lightly.

He looks surprised. "My dear Constance, your sister requires little encouragement."

"Anyway," I say, "I don't think Jiri is going to make a scene in a public place, if that's what you're worried about."

"I wouldn't be so sure of that," Philippe says.

"I guess you're not finding him so magnificent all of a sudden, huh?"

"Don't be silly," he says crossly.

The raised voice of the German lady suddenly reaches us. "—and in broad daylight! I ask you, how can you expect to attract tourists when you cannot even guarantee their safety!"

"*Quand même,* Madame," the mayor smoothly objects, "no one was hurt. . . ."

Yolande fluffs up like a hen: "And the tens of thousands of francs in damages?"

The mayor pops an olive in his mouth and assumes a remote expression. He must have thought it was pitted because I see him looking around before discreetly spitting into his napkin. "Well, Madame, not to put too fine a point on it, but I understood the damages are no longer your problem."

"And my honor, Monsieur? Am I to sell Madame Townsley a

ruin in good conscience?" Catching sight of Madame Townsley now stepping out onto the terrace with Yves and Electra, however, Yolande evidently decides it's time to change the subject, which the German lady is only too happy to do for her. "I must tell you," she says, turning to the mayor, "that our friends the Kistenmakers were thinking of buying Madame Albertoni's house but were discouraged in the end by a number of irregularities in the deed, were they not, Heinrich?"

"When did the Albertoni house go on the market?" Yolande asks sharply.

"Allons, Mesdames . . . ," the mayor says.

"I'm sorry, Charles, but this is a perfect example of the lack of transparency that plagues—and I do not think this is too strong a word—the real estate market. Borgolano will never become a proper summer community if people are continually discouraged from buying houses by legal irregularities."

"Especially if the houses they do buy are subsequently blown up," Jiri observes, eliciting a furious look from Isabelle.

"In Hamburg these hooligans would be arrested, is this not so, Heinrich?" the German lady says. Her husband, who looks like he might have had a stroke recently, nods vigorously. "And I regret to say, Monsieur le Maire," she continues, "that if this is the most egregious example of the lawlessness that is allowed to prevail in Borgolano, it is not the first. I remain convinced that Monsieur Ystres next door is siphoning our electricity. How else do you explain a bill of six hundred thirty-three francs and fifty-seven centimes for the month of February, when we were in Hamburg?"

"Is this some kind of local obsession, with the electricity?" Philippe asks me.

Isabelle chooses this moment to return, Jiri hot on her heels.

"There you are, Philippe. I see you've met my *ex*-husband," she says loudly.

"Not in the eyes of the law," Jiri remarks, placing himself between them and smiling broadly.

Philippe looks irritated as hell but is obviously not going to take the bait. "I wonder," he says coldly, "where our hostess is." For, though all the guests seem to have arrived, there is still no sign of Countess Fatulescu.

"Perhaps," Jiri says, "she plans to descend in a balloon like the Count of Monte Cristo."

Everybody except Jiri looks relieved when Lucy and Yves join us. "We were just having a look at the garden," Lucy announces. "*Very* interesting use of local flora: There's definitely been an attempt to integrate the *maquis* into the landscaping."

"I think this is probably accidental," Yves says with a smile.

"Well, perhaps, but it does give one an idea of the possibilities. . . . I was rather hoping we'd get a tour of the house," Lucy adds in a disappointed tone. "Oh dear, there's that dreadful old German woman; I wonder why *she* was invited."

"I'm sure you could have a look around if you wanted," I say.

"Well," Lucy says, lowering her voice, "I did get a peek at the parlor off the entrance: It's all done up in red and gold like a bordello!"

"Did you see the fountain?"

"Yes, fabulous, isn't it? I must say, I'm dying to meet this lady; I didn't know they had countesses in Romania. . . ." Lucy says, picking up a cheese cube from a tray sullenly proffered by Albertine and then hastily putting it back.

"I think I have seen this cheese before," Yves says.

Yolande's voice drifts over again. "Take the *hameau*, for

instance. How many such spots are left in the Mediterranean? And yet, it sits undeveloped for years, when all you have to do is declare it abandoned. I know, Charles, you will say these administrative procedures take time, but one has to start somewhere, and now that creature is squatting up there, that criminal—"

"*Criminal?*" The German lady gasps.

"A murderer, actually," the mayor says.

"Yes, *exactly*, and then you wonder why people hesitate to buy property. . . ."

"Hm," the mayor says, locking his hands behind his back and rocking on his heels. "Yes, I see your point."

Lucy pulls me aside. "Did you hear that? The old fright has her eye on our *hameau!*"

"Yes," I say, "but *we* have an in with Jojo."

She lowers her voice. "Listen, you know the money in the account: Maybe we could . . . ?"

"Haven't you given up yet on Santerran real estate?" I ask.

She brushes this off. "Don't be silly; the fishing cabin wasn't that expensive, to tell you the truth, and I was going to remodel anyway. . . . The *hameau* would be a much better investment, and if we all pooled our money together . . ." she continues excitedly.

"Count me out."

"No, listen, Yves is absolutely brilliant with his hands—"

"Are you being *serious?*"

"Of course I'm serious," Lucy says indignantly. Just then Albertine reappears with the cheese and salami cubes. "Really, Albertine, can't you see no one is eating them? You'd think they'd be ashamed," Lucy adds, turning back to me, "trying to fob off their leftovers like that!"

Albertine shrugs and moves on, making way for Jim and

Odette, who sniffs dubiously at her glass and says, "I think this champagne must be from Romania as well."

"Do you know that Odette can tell a wine's vintage just by its smell?" Jim says, as if this were simply the most amazing thing in the world.

"Not exactly," Odette demurs, "though one does learn a thing or two about wine in first class."

Lucy and Odette start to argue about who serves better champagne, British Airways or Air France, and Jim volunteers that, when he flew on the Concorde, they served Dom Pérignon, garnering a perplexed look from Lucy, who I guess doesn't know about the agribusiness empire. It dawns on me that a lot of people would look upon Jim differently, given this information, beginning with my sister Isabelle—who, having tried unsuccessfully to lure Jiri away, perhaps over the cliff, is heading toward us with him still in pursuit. Albertine darts her a lovelorn glance as she goes by, but Isabelle ignores her.

"Anyone want a drink?" Philippe says, making a beeline for the bar.

"Can't you see you're not wanted here?" Isabelle snaps at Jiri as they bear down on us.

Jiri bows. "You must forgive my wife: It seems my arrival has foiled her plans to seduce that French hairdresser—I mean writer, sorry—that writer with the pretty hair. Now, where did he go running off to?"

"He's completely drunk," Isabelle announces.

Jiri looks offended. "Yes, I am drunk—but, in the words of Winston Churchill, tomorrow I will be sober; you, however, will still be a slut."

"You're not making a very good impression, you know."

"I don't need to make a good impression, I am a hero of the opposition!"

"God," Isabelle cries, "can't you see nobody here cares about your stupid opposition?"

"I find it highly irregular," the German lady says loudly, "that our hostess has still not appeared."

"Perhaps she has been delayed," her husband says.

"Has anybody seen the children?" Lucy asks.

"Who does these childrrrrren belong to!" an angry voice demands from behind us in a thick Balkan accent. We all turn toward the French doors, where a lady in a yellow dress and black beehive hairdo has just emerged on the highest pair of heels I have ever seen, one red-taloned claw fastened around the arm of a furious Sophie, who, at the sight of Jiri, yells, "Daddy! Help!"

"Ah, dear Countess!" Yolande cries rapturously. Jiri rushes forward, practically knocking the woman over, and yanks Sophie back. Suddenly he bursts out laughing.

"That's no countess, you idiots," he exclaims. "That's Lupa Romesco!"

CHAPTER *thirty-five*

"**S**o you're saying this lady is some kind of gangster?" Jim says, gazing with naked admiration at Jiri across the kitchen table, where we have gathered for breakfast.

"Well, not exactly a gangster; more like a—how do you call it—ah yes: a con man."

"Con *woman,*" Marge corrects him.

"Well, this is one of the few things we can be sure of: that Madame Romesco is a woman. An international woman of mystery, you might say. Some believe she ran off with half the hard currency reserves of Romania, after they did away with that nice couple, the Ceauşescus, whom she was friendly with. I think they even made her minister of culture for a while."

"It sounds like we should be calling the police, or Interpol, or something . . . ," Jim says.

"Ah, but you see, the problem is that nothing was ever proved.

It is all most unclear, beginning with her real identity; maybe she is not even Romanian," says Jiri, who is obviously relishing being back in his role of chief raconteur, even if he did get us all thrown out of the party, the countess haughtily insisting that he was out of his mind and demanding payment for the Sèvres vase the girls broke while playing hide-and-seek in the bordello room, much to the indignation of Lucy, who declared that if that glorified chamber pot was a Sèvres, then *she* was a bloody countess. "The only thing that is certain," Jiri continues, "is that wherever Madame Romesco appears, money disappears, followed in due course by the lady herself."

"What an extraordinary story," Jane says. "But why have none of us ever heard of her?"

"This is because you live in the civilized West. We had all sorts of crazy characters running around Prague after '81," Jiri says, "didn't we, darling?"

Isabelle shrugs. I guess she hasn't entirely come to terms with Jiri's newfound popularity—especially with Philippe, who, after we'd been shown the door, slapped him on the back and congratulated him on his brilliant performance before pulling him aside and explaining that it was all very much a misunderstanding about his wife, seeing that it's *me* he's dallying with. Or so I gather from the appraising glances Jiri keeps sliding in my direction, as if, now that I'd joined the ranks of the officially desirable, I might be worth a closer look. As for Isabelle, she's been sending me dagger looks all morning.

"It was quite a scene," Jiri continues. "Russian gangsters, Israeli pimps, Sicilian businessmen, and all sorts of fantastical Balkan aristocrats who hadn't been heard of since the twelfth century. . ."

"You're making it sound a lot more interesting than it was,"

Isabelle snaps. "I just remember a bunch of tacky people in track-suits."

"Yes, but that is what makes horse races, as my good friend Ross used to say."

"What *I* don't understand," Lucy exclaims, "is how that awful woman contrived to buy the manor. Daddy tried for years and was repeatedly told that it was mired in inheritance disputes."

"Maybe," Jiri says, "she made a more attractive offer."

"*That* I very much doubt. There's something fishy going on here, if you ask me."

"Lucy, just because the lady got the house you wanted doesn't mean there was skullduggery involved," Jane says with a smile. She and Marge are snuggled up on the sofa by the window, which was wide open again when we got home, prompting Odette to reflect once again that one of these days we are going to have to replace the latch.

"Didn't you hear what Jiri said? She's an international criminal!" Lucy insists.

"Borgolano is really turning into a classy place," Marge observes. "Might be worth investing in some seafront property after all. . . ." She gives Jane's thigh a possessive squeeze that is duly registered by Odette, who looks pointedly away. With a wicked smile, Marge nibbles Jane's ear prior to kissing it.

"Would you two stop it—there are children in the room!" Lucy says. Sure enough, Electra has just appeared in the doorway, where she pauses, staring at us with a calculating expression.

"Why shouldn't they witness a bit of wholesome adult sexuality for a change?" Marge says tauntingly, glancing at Odette, who I would swear has just inched away from Jim on the settee.

"I don't see why they should have to witness *any* sexuality,"

Lucy says primly, pronouncing it *seksuality*. "What is it, darling?"

Silence.

"Oh, all right: What is it, Agnes?"

"Can I have a cookie?" Electra says slowly and precisely, as if she were worried she might not get it right.

"Biscuit, darling. Yes, you may, but just one, please—you don't want to spoil your appetite before supper." Electra darts off to the kitchen, where the girls must have been waiting because all of a sudden we hear loud giggles.

"She's becoming a regular chatterbox," Jane remarks.

"It's maddening," Lucy whispers, leaning forward. "She'll only talk to me if I call her Agnes."

"I think Agnes rather suits her," Jane says.

"It is a very nice name in French," Yves says.

"What we should ask ourselves," Jiri says, "is, what is Lupa Romesco doing in Borgolano?"

"Same thing we are, I should think," Jane says.

When I head downstairs much later to slip over to Philippe's, Isabelle is lying in wait in the hallway. Everyone else has gone to bed.

"And where are *you* going?"

"Oh, cut it out," I say. "You know perfectly well where I'm going."

"I have to hand it to you," she says with a nasty little smile. "You had me completely fooled."

"It's not about you," I say, but she's already followed me out. On this windless night the darkness is almost velvety, the only sound that of Muddy Waters drifting out of Philippe's open window. Like all cool Parisians, my lover feels a special and mysterious connection to the Mississippi Delta.

"Not that I care," Isabelle says, "but doesn't Jim-boy wonder where you're sneaking off to in the middle of the night?"

"I doubt it, seeing that he's sleeping in Odette's room."

"Ha, I'm supposed to believe that?"

"They're in love with each other. They're moving to Paris together after the memorial."

Isabelle makes a barking sound. "That is *so* grotesque."

"I don't think so."

"Well, I do. I think it's disgusting—she's twice his age."

"Jiri is twice *your* age."

"It's not the same thing!"

"Whatever . . . I have to go." I start to move away but she tugs at my arm.

"Don't do this to me," she pleads.

I stop. I can afford this small kindness. "I think you should go back in to your husband," I say. "He came all this way to get you."

From the way her breath catches, I can tell that she's crying. Sometimes I wish I were a nicer person, but I've seen all of this before. Like Odette says, there's a reason for clichés.

"He didn't come for *me;* he's just evening the score!"

"Look, what does it matter? Just pretend to believe him."

"I *can't!*" She looks so beautiful, even in the dark. Philippe must be crazy.

"I have to go now," I say.

"Wait!" she cries, but I'm already across the patio. "We haven't talked about the money!"

CHAPTER *thirty-six*

"*Laissons les belles femmes aux hommes sans imagination.*"

"Thanks a lot."

Philippe nudges me in the stomach. "You must stop taking everything so personally. . . . Your sister seems determined to test the adage that women are made to be loved, not understood."

"Who said that?"

"Oscar Wilde."

"Wasn't he gay?"

"Always so literal. . . . What I meant is that I am perpetually amazed by how different you and your sister are; you don't even look alike."

"I look like Ross. Isabelle looks like our mother."

"Ah yes, the Russian ballerina with the studio on the Rue Vavin. I must have walked by it many times; perhaps you were even inside, in your little pink tutu. . . ."

"Not likely, I was still in diapers. It's funny you should mention it, though, because Isabelle said something the other day about Vera, that she wouldn't let her in her class because she wasn't talented enough."

"Perhaps she was trying to uphold standards."

"I think it sounds bitchy and mean. Why couldn't she have just let her give it a try, even if she was a complete klutz?"

"I don't believe it's part of the Russian mentality to encourage the ungifted," Philippe says.

"And there's something else: I've checked out all the Russian ballet sites on the Web, and I've never found any mention of a Vera Shubin. You'd think, if she was this big Kirov star, she'd rate a mention."

"Maybe she was erased from the records. Didn't your father smuggle her out of the Soviet Union? Terribly romantic story, by the way."

"Exactly, it's a great story—so great that you start to wonder how much of it is true."

"Interesting: So you think your father and your sister made her up?"

"Not exactly—she had to exist, we had to come from somewhere—but frankly, the way Isabelle carries on about Vera, she doesn't sound real, and she certainly doesn't sound like the kind of woman who would have put up with my father."

"And so, over the years, they created a lovely fantasy. . . ."

"Something like that. I mean, I'm sure she was a dancer, but not necessarily a famous one. And I'm sure she was beautiful, but—"

"Paris is full of beautiful women," Philippe finishes my sentence.

"Yeah, not to mention Russian ballerinas. And Ross was such a mythomaniac. Plus, when you think about it, it's awfully convenient having this perfect wife who died young. It keeps all the next ones in line."

"How Machiavellian!"

"Well, maybe that's not how he put it to himself, but it did absolve him of ever having to make an effort again in a relationship."

"He must have been quite a character, your father. I regret not having had the chance to meet him."

"I'm not sure the two of you would have gotten along," I say.

"Oh really?" Philippe looks amused. "And why is that?"

"Well, you know, he was a big American guy."

"And I am a small Frenchman?"

"You're too intellectual. He probably would have found you pretentious."

"As you would say, thank you very much." To my surprise, Philippe sounds wounded. To make up for it I grab his cock. It pulses in my hand like a warm animal.

"Anyway," I say, "he's dead."

"Ah yes, but he keeps coming back. This money, for instance, causing all sorts of unpleasantness . . ."

"Not for me. I've decided to give my share to Isabelle."

He shifts, slipping out of my grasp. "My dear Constance, you are either being very noble or very foolish."

"She wants it more than I do, and it won't make much of a difference to me. It's not really that hard to make half a million dollars. When you work with money, all those zeros get kind of abstract after a while."

He smiles. "Something tells me that your sister may not find all those zeros, as you so charmingly put it, quite so abstract."

"You really don't like her, do you?" I say, surprising myself by how much this bothers me.

"My dear, the world is full of women like Isabelle. Come here."

I want to tell him that he's wrong, that my sister is unique, a goddess among women, but I don't. I reach for him, despising myself slightly.

CHAPTER *thirty-seven*

Philippe starts writing at six, a habit that he claims he picked up in New York. According to him, the French don't believe that there's any virtue in getting up early, or eating low-fat food, or exercising. Still, although he claims to delight in all things American—including, presumably, me—he can't altogether suppress the little edge of old-world superiority that I'm sure would have driven Ross crazy. I decide to go for a run. As I'm heading back to our house to change, I notice Jane sitting on the stone bench in Mr. Peretti's garden. She turns around when she hears me approach.

"Oh, it's you," she says, not looking exactly thrilled to see me.

"Hi," I say plopping myself down next to her. "Where's Marge?"

"Sleeping. I thought I'd come down and do some watercolors—I wanted to capture that ghostly pink the water turns at dawn."

"Can I see?" I say, reaching for her pad.

She hands it to me. "I mucked it up."

I think it looks fine, especially the way she's done the lemon tree that overhangs the ruined wall, its fruit tirelessly coveted by Lucy, but there's no point arguing with Jane about the insanely high standards she sets for herself. We sit in silence for a while, looking at the heat haze beginning to form over the water. Over in Mr. Peretti's vegetable patch, the tomatoes hang fat and heavy, tied to their stakes with yellow rags that match the color of the lemons. It's going to be a beautiful day.

"Constance," Jane says suddenly. "Are you sure you know what you're doing?"

"What do you mean?"

"You know what I mean: with Philippe."

"I'm in love with him," I say, though I hadn't meant to, but it's the easiest way to describe the relentless craving I feel for him.

"Oh, Constance . . ."

"Why do you sound so worried?" I say lightly.

She gives me a penetrating look. "Because I wonder if you know your heart."

I'm about to say something flippant, about bankers not having hearts, but instead I say, "He really admires you; he owns two of your paintings."

"I thought it was *you* we were talking about."

I make a goofy face to indicate that I'm just kidding around.

"Philippe's liking my paintings hardly constitutes a reason for falling in love with him," Jane says, ignoring my overture.

"You don't like him, do you?"

"Oh God, Constance, can't you see it doesn't matter whether or not I like him!"

"It matters to me," I say.

"All right, then," Jane says irritably, "I don't. He strikes me, frankly, as a ladies' man."

It's such a dumb and stilted expression that, for a second, I could swear it's Daphne, not Jane, speaking, which is no doubt why the smart-ass in me surges and I tartly retort, "Well, then I guess it's no surprise I fell for him."

"No," Jane says primly, "I daresay it isn't."

In the silence that ensues, several realizations hit me simultaneously: that Jane has grown closer to her mother over the years, that they share the cold eye of the aesthete, that being her least favorite daughter only made her love Daphne the more. But this is all off-limits, as Jane's expression makes clear, so I say, in yet another pathetic attempt at bridge-building, "We need to do something about that money in Zurich before Isabelle blows a gasket."

"I was wondering when you'd bring that up," she says.

"Yeah, well, I think the best thing to do would be to just divide it and get it over with."

"And how were you planning to divide it?"

I glance at her. The gates are still down. "Well, I think that's pretty straightforward: five ways."

Jane doesn't respond.

"Oh, come on, Jane," I say, annoyed. "Don't tell me you want to cut out Odette."

"The problem is not Odette," Jane says.

"I'm glad to hear you say that, because frankly, I think she deserves a break."

"Not from me she doesn't," Jane says, her eyes finally meeting mine. "But anyway, that's not the problem."

"Oh," I say. I guess my voice betrays my surprise because I catch a flicker of uncertainty in her eyes, which vanishes when she speaks again.

"You know how I went to see Mum before coming out here? She told me certain things I had had no idea about."

"Look," I say, "everyone knows Ross treated Daphne badly . . ." And then I stop because, well, so what? But I guess that was the opening she was looking for.

"Have you ever asked yourself why Ross adopted us?" she says.

"Well, it did seem a little strange at the time, but I think he honestly thought it was the right thing to do."

Jane smirks. "It certainly was—for Ross."

"I don't get it," I say.

"You, of all people, ought to. As you might recall, he adopted us in '84, which, if you go back and read the financial press, was not a good time for gold. He nearly went bankrupt, as you know; what you may not know is that he'd bought call options as a hedge. The margin calls started coming in and he asked Mum for a loan, then another—he was going to pay it all back when the market went back up. . . ." An unpleasantly sarcastic tone has crept into Jane's voice, though actually, what surprises me more is how much she seems to know about finance. "Eventually, Mum's money ran out. Lucy and I, however, had been left a bit in trust by our father. . . ."

More than a bit, I think.

"You can guess the rest. Not to put too fine a point on it, by adopting us, Ross hoped to put us in a position where we'd never question certain disastrous investments that were made with our inheritance. It was brilliant when you think about it: the combination of cheap sentimentalism and cold-blooded audacity. Quite the most spectacular con he ever pulled off."

I'm surprised to find that my mouth is hanging open. I shut it. "Look, I'm not saying Ross was a choirboy. I've always had a feeling that a lot of his ventures bordered the fringes of legality, but it's not that easy to rip off a trust fund. I mean, wasn't Daphne the trustee?"

"She was. Unfortunately, Mum was a bit of a twit about money."

"This is crazy, Jane. He couldn't have done anything without her signing off on it."

"That's the pathetic part: She did. Mum never paid any attention to forms. And she thought like everyone else that Ross was a brilliant financier, so after they got married, she left all the business decisions to him, and even more so after he adopted us. By the time she figured out that Lucy and I had become majority stockholders in a series of dubious South American prospecting firms, it was too late."

"That's not fraud," I point out, "just bad advice."

"Yes, so were the Angolan mining rights."

"Jane," I say, "it may have been sleazy and dishonest, but if Daphne approved it, it wasn't technically a crime. I mean, I'd be the last to try to whitewash Ross—"

"Would you? It seems to me that we are all perpetually engaged in doing precisely that. And yet, I, for one, have no obligation to perpetuate the myth of his greatness."

"Okay," I say. "So he ripped off your trust fund. You can't have just found out about this; didn't you ever look at the records?"

"I always suspected, but Mum never owned up to it until now.

She was too embarrassed, if you can believe it." Actually I can. Daphne, like a lot of upper-class English people I know, always pretended to be clueless about money.

We lapse into silence. Finally I say, "Well, this really sucks, but what am I supposed to do about it?"

"The money in Switzerland would be a beginning," Jane says.

I regard her with genuine consternation. "You've got to be kidding."

"I am not. Morally speaking, you owe it to Lucy and me."

I'm so bewildered that I blurt out, "But, Jane, you've got plenty of money—I mean, he can't have taken everything, and anyway, from your paintings alone—"

"You're making rather free with your assumptions about my wealth," she says coldly. "Yes, I am quite comfortable, but I'm about to embark on a venture that is going to require a large initial investment, and I'm afraid I don't want to eat into my capital. Surely you will understand."

I don't, but I say, "I guess Lucy's in on this, too, huh?"

"No, she's not. As you know, when given a choice, Lucy will usually opt for denial."

I'm surprised at how relieved I am. I can even feel a half-smile forming on my lips at the thought of poor, guileless Lucy, traipsing like Ophelia through the *maquis* in search of fragrant herbs. The sun is already starting to burn the morning freshness out of the air. Mr. Peretti comes out of his house in his blue worker's overalls and peers glumly at us before unlatching the wooden gate into his garden. He probably thinks we have designs on his tomatoes. I watch him bend down and tug at a weed before unwinding a garden hose that Yolande insists is illegally hooked up to her meter and turning it on so that the water rushes out with a spurting sound.

"Fucking suspicious peasant," Jane says, startling me.

"Jane," I say, "you can have my share if you want, but I don't think Isabelle is going to go along with it. She has plans for that money."

"Don't we all," Jane says.

CHAPTER *thirty-eight*

As it turns out, even if I'd wanted to relay my conversation with Jane to Isabelle, I couldn't, since she's nowhere to be found. More perplexingly, Richard hasn't been seen since yesterday, before the countess's party, when Yves ran into him at the café.

"Maybe he's been kidnapped," Marge says.

"I doubt anyone would want to kidnap Richard," Lucy says, slathering butter on toast for the girls. "Maybe he just took a room for the night." Odette eyes her with amazement, though it's hard to say whether over her cavalier attitude toward her husband—I'm not sure that Odette is entirely aware of Richard's existence—or because she is actually feeding her daughter butter.

"Jam too," Agnes says gloomily. The child may be making progress, but she's not about to win any charm contests.

"Oh, all right. . . . I do think she's lost a bit of weight," she whispers conspiratorially after the girls have run off.

"It is the glands," Odette says. "You should take her to a *homéopathe.*"

"Really, Odette! I'm not going to take the child to some witch doctor—a sensible diet and exercise are what she needs."

Odette shrugs. Jim looks uncomfortable.

"Jeem, don't you think it's time to light the grill?" Odette says.

"What's eating *you?*" I ask, catching up with him on the patio.

"Hey," he says. He darts his eyes around as if to make sure no one is listening. "I'm not sure I should be doing this, but I think I know where Richard is."

"You'd better tell Lucy; the suspense is killing her."

"He's with Albertine," Jim blurts out. I burst out laughing. Odette comes clicking out on her little heels.

"What is so funny?" she says, a bit sharply. Jim tells her.

"Ah, well, what can she expect?"

"What do you mean by that?" Jim says. God, he's such a butthead sometimes. Odette smiles at me.

"What Odette means," I say, "is that if you don't keep an eye on your man, he'll run off with the kitchen help. It's an old French saying."

"Mais non . . ." Odette says disingenuously.

Lucy comes out with the sausages, humming to herself and practically skipping on the pavement. Maybe Richard should stay away all the time

"We'll just throw them all on, don't you think? Whoever's not around can have a cold one later." She lines up the sausages on the grill, perfectly symmetrically, and surrounds them like little prisoners with halved onions and slices of green pepper. Under the fig tree, the girls are playing a modified version of jacks with their pebble collection. Agnes is winning, as usual. I thought at first that Sophie was letting her, but now I'm not so sure.

"That kid's gonna be a card shark," Jim says.

"A very silent card shark," Lucy says.

"Hey, that's the best kind."

Jane emerges from behind the house with her drawing pad. She gives me a look and I make a little shrug as if to say, *Why don't we just drop it for now?* Marge glances at her inquiringly. At least they've stopped making out all the time in front of Odette, who's getting used to it anyway. A door bangs up the road and Yolande comes out of the Perettis' house. She hastens over to us.

"I must tell you that the countess is *very* upset," she says to Odette.

"She's *not* a countess," Lucy says heatedly. "Her name is Lupa Romesco and I think we should turn her in to the police!"

"Really, this is too much! Madame Fatulescu is a distinguished poet. I—"

"Ask her to show you one of her books!"

"I shall do no such thing," Yolande says with dignity. Just then she notices the girls crouching in the dust. "Well, now, and what nice game are *we* playing?" she whines in the dulcet tones some adults feel obliged to adopt with children.

"None of your business," Sophie says churlishly.

"*Sophie!*"

Yolande dismisses this with a wave of her hand, a motion that causes her many rings to flash dazzlingly in the sun. "It is nothing. Children will be children, no?"

"*Vraiment,* there is no excuse for rudeness."

"Well," Yolande says meaningfully, "when the mother does not teach them . . ."

"What's *that* supposed to mean?" I say, but Yolande ignores me, her eyes fixed on the girls.

"What pretty pebbles," she simpers. "Did you find them on the beach?"

"Oh, they're always picking up things," Odette says. "It's quite impossible to keep the house tidy. . . . Which reminds me, has anyone seen the big blue pot?"

"We stuck it in the attic," I remind her.

"Oh, of course—could you run up and fetch it?"

I head upstairs. At the top of the house, across from the room where we store all the junk we no longer use but can't bring ourselves to throw out, is the garret that Yves has been occupying. As I pass the closed door, I hear a soughing sound. I think at first that Yves must be taking a nap, until I remember that I just saw him in the kitchen peeling potatoes. I pause and listen. The soughing turns in to a gasp, followed by a low moan, then a silence broken abruptly by Isabelle's voice.

"I hate you."

"I know," Jiri says.

I creep away. The attic light doesn't work, but in the penumbra, I can make out Ross's diving equipment, the oxygen tanks and masks and the speargun with which he famously never caught anything. A vanquished inflatable raft lies in a corner, in a jumble of mismatched flippers, broken nets, and the Chinese paper lanterns Lucy bought for Ross's seventieth birthday party, which caught fire because she insisted on putting votive candles inside them. Odette's pot is on a makeshift shelf along the far wall. When I bend down to lift it, I notice an old postcard lying on the floor, its face obscured with grime. I pick it up and wipe off the dust. It's a view of the old town square in Antwerp, with the Brabo Fountain in the foreground. I turn the card over. It's addressed to Ross, the handwriting bleached and smudgy but still legible. There's a scrawled note in the message space—*Greetings from Antwerp!*—and a loopy, European-looking signature, *Jacques Van* Something, which, on closer inspection, turns out to be Langendonck, the same name as Yolande's. Something at the back of my mind is nagging me: a trip we took when I was little to a northern city with spires and canals, chocolate shops, a tall blond man meeting with Ross in a café, huge ice creams that reeked of bribery.

I slip the postcard into my pocket, pick up the pot, and let myself out, closing the door softly behind me. In the little room, Isabelle and Jiri are still at it. Maybe it's my imagination, but there's a sort of desperate intensity to the noises they're making, an animal pitch, or is that what everyone sounds like? I slink back down the stairs. On the second-floor landing, Jim is waiting for me.

"I was just going up to look for you."

Maybe it's what I just heard upstairs, or something about the way he's standing, or the tone of his voice, but I am suddenly overwhelmed by the desire to rip my clothes off and throw myself at him. I blink.

Jim gazes at me solicitously. "Hey, Connie, what's up? You look like you just saw a ghost."

I hand him the pot and steady myself against the banister.

"What's that noise?" he asks.

"Just the eaves creaking," I say. "Is it really true, about Richard and Albertine?"

He turns serious. "You know, I wouldn't have said anything, but I think they might be taking advantage of him—she and that brother of hers."

"Why would anyone want to take advantage of Richard?"

"I don't know, it's just a hunch I have."

"Maybe it's just what he needs," I say lightly, my wanton thoughts now dispelled. "A little rest and recreation."

"She just doesn't seem like his type of girl," Jim says with a worried look. "I mean, Lucy is so beautiful, and Albertine—well, she's kind of coarse . . . and they kept pouring him free drinks."

"Free drinks at the Marmite? Something is definitely up."

"I think we should go look for him," Jim says doggedly.

"Oh, come on."

"I mean it."

Since he sounds like he does, I decide to humor him. "Okay, I'll tell you what: If he hasn't turned up by morning, we'll send out a search party."

"By midnight. If he hasn't turned up by midnight."

"Honestly, his own wife isn't even worried about him. Doesn't that tell you something?"

"Hey, us guys have to stick together," Jim says with a goofy smile, though in fact I don't think he's entirely kidding.

CHAPTER *thirty-nine*

Naturally Richard doesn't show up by midnight.

"I'm going out to look for him," Jim says. Odette makes a clucking sound and, with a sigh, puts down her knitting needles. Ever since I've known her, she's always been knitting something, though I've never actually seen a scarf or sweater. Maybe she unravels her work every night like Penelope.

"You stay here," I say. "I'll go with Isabelle." From the couch where she's been sunk for the past hour in a sated stupor, engrossed in an *Astérix* comic, my sister gives me a befuddled look.

"*Ah non!*" Odette protests. "You must take the men."

"We're in a French village," I snap, "not downtown Detroit."

"She's right,"—Isabelle yawns, dropping her book on the floor—"you'll just make a scene, Jim. I can handle Eddie and Fabrice. Come on, Constance, let's go."

We step out into the darkness. At this time of night you can pick out the vacation houses by their lights, the bright yellow squares spilling their patchy illumination onto the path. I glance up at Philippe's window.

"Aren't you going over?" Isabelle asks, a solicitous tone in her voice.

"In case you hadn't noticed," I say irritably, "I've been trying to catch your attention all evening."

"It's better that way, you know," she says kindly. "You should always keep them guessing."

"Spare me the philosophizing."

"Men only fall in love with you if you treat them badly," she imperturbably continues.

"Yeah, and tall, good-looking people get paid more than fat, short ones."

"Is that true?"

"Yup. They've done research."

"I thought it was different in business," Isabelle says. "I thought it was about how smart you are."

I turn to her. In the ghostly light cast out by the Perettis' TV, my sister looks like a priestess, the guardian of some ancient rite. My leg brushes against a bush and a dry scent wafts up: rosemary? Lucy would know. I will my mind to clarity. "Don't waste your time sucking up to me. I spoke to Jane, she wants her share of the money."

"Yeah, I figured she would. . . . How do the rich stay rich, huh?"

"I'm not sure she's all that rich. She's got a project and I have a feeling it involves Marge."

"They're starting a foundation," Isabelle says.

"What?"

"I heard them talking about it: It's some kind of eco-feminist thing in Oxford. Marge is going to be the president."

I hoot. "Really? No wonder she doesn't want to use her own money. Anyway, if I were you, I wouldn't press the issue."

She peers at me with the disarming intensity she has always been able to summon at the drop of a hat, brushing my arm softly with the tips of her fingers. For someone who's been betrayed by her body, my sister has a puzzling faith in physical contact. "Constance, I know you're mad at me, but you have no idea what it's like. . . . I know exactly how prostitutes feel."

"Isabelle, just because you had sex with your husband doesn't make you a prostitute."

"I don't love him."

"I don't love most of the guys I sleep with."

"I hate myself for being so weak," she bursts out. "He pushes my buttons and I roll over like a dog; it's like I have no control over myself!"

I could tell her that I know how she feels, but something within me recoils at this cheap kinship. I touch her shoulder. "Come on," I say.

We step out onto the road. From the tables outside Frédé's snack bar, the uneasy summer mix of local kids and vacationing teenagers watch us glumly.

"*Salut,*" Isabelle calls out. Twenty years ago she would have been one of them, a forgotten glass of that beer-and-lemonade concoction they all drink beading up before her, stealing glances at soft lips and cruel eyes. The Parisian girls, like the summer houses, glow with a careless effulgence. A slim-hipped boy glances at us.

"*Salut,*" Frédé calls back. A couple of the kids wave halfheartedly. They all know her: She comes up here when she's drunk to bum cigarettes.

"We're looking for the Englishman," she says.

Frédé shrugs. "Try the café."

We cross the deserted *place,* our steps soft in our espadrilles. I used to think they were an affectation, but now I wear them like everyone else, buying them for twenty francs from the wire baskets outside the Perettis' shop. Ross had to special-order his in the States because they never had his size. All of a sudden I remember the postcard.

"Did Dad ever take us to Belgium?" I ask.

"Sure, a couple times. We went to Bruges, remember? There was this shop where they sold breast-shaped chocolates and we brought some back for Daphne. She totally didn't get it." Isabelle sniggers.

"You mean we went without her?"

"Yeah. Don't you remember?"

"How old was I?" I ask.

"I don't know, four or five. , . ."

"I thought Mom died when I was four."

"Yeah," Isabelle says vaguely.

"And she was sick for a year?"

"I guess so. . . ."

"So what was Dad doing in Bruges, buying chocolate breasts for Daphne?"

"I might have the dates mixed up," Isabelle says uncomfortably.

"I don't believe you. Dad was cheating on Vera with Daphne, wasn't he?"

"Look, it was complicated—"

"For Christ's sake, she was dying of cancer!"

Isabelle whirls around. "You have no idea what our mother was like—she never had any time for him *before* she got sick!" she says angrily. "She was busy with her stupid ballet school, and she was crazy and anorexic and if you want to know the truth, she wasn't even that great a dancer: Why do you think she was *teaching?*"

"What about the Kirov?" I ask.

"Oh, she danced at the Kirov, all right, but she wasn't a principal; she was in the chorus."

"I kind of figured," I say. "Why did you go along with it, though? All those posters on your walls—or was that just to piss Daphne off?"

Isabelle shrugs in her inimitable French way. "I don't know. I guess I was jealous because Daphne so obviously adored Lucy; Vera always acted like she never knew I existed. After she died, though, I could make her into anything I wanted." She grins. "You know me, I always liked fairy tales."

"Like someone else I know," I say.

She scrutinizes me with a mysterious expression. "You're a lot more like Dad than you realize."

I know. It's not something I think about a lot, but the consciousness is there, in the back of my mind, that I, too, am my father's daughter. Not until this moment has it ever occurred to me, however, that I may also be my mother's child.

"So much for our moral debt to Jane and Lucy," I say. "I wonder if *they* know."

"Lucy does. I'm not sure about Jane—she was too little. If you really think about it, though, they kind of owe us," she adds hopefully. "I mean, their mother did seduce our father. . . ."

"You're just not going to let go, are you?"

"Sshhh! Isn't that Eddie?"

I follow her gaze to the Marmite's doorway where a figure stands in the shadows, the tip of his cigarette glowing.

"*Eh, les filles!*"

"He saw us; we'd better go over."

We cross the *place.* Eddie sucks on his cigarette again, tosses it to the ground, and grinds it down with the heel of his boot as we approach. "You're out late."

"We're looking for Richard," Isabelle says.

Eddie smirks. "He's busy."

I peer beyond him into the empty bar. "Looks like you had quite a party," Isabelle says. Eddie should shower more often: His cologne doesn't quite succeed in masking his body odor.

"She's funny, your sister," Eddie says, addressing himself to me. "The English guy is funny, too—he told us some good stories."

"Yeah, we find him pretty entertaining too," Isabelle says. "Now, if you'll get out of the way, we'll take him home."

"Don't be such a wiseass," I whisper.

"I know what I'm doing." She turns back to Eddie.

"*Arrête de faire le con . . .*" Great, now she's calling him names. There's a rustling sound as someone parts the beaded curtain in the back of the bar, only to withdraw at the sight of us.

"Hey," I say, because I could swear it was the countess, or Lupa Romesco, or whatever her name is.

Eddie shrugs and motions behind him with his thumb. "Go right ahead."

"Come on, Constance, don't just stand there!" Isabelle snaps as Eddie steps aside to let us through. The room has that desolate late-night look, dirty glasses lined up on the counter, full ashtrays. The curtain clicks back into place as we enter the kitchen, where there is no sign of the countess or anyone else. There's a back exit though that leads through a courtyard to the annex the Simonettis built a couple years ago to house paying guests. I've never been back there, but Isabelle seems to know her way around. I follow her through the cheap glass-and-aluminum door into a corridor lit by a naked bulb hanging on a cord. "Third on the left," Eddie calls from behind us.

Isabelle turns the latch and pushes the door open. The room smells like sex and toilets, the latter from the bathroom en suite that is separated from the sleeping quarters by a plastic accordion door. Under the window, our brother-in-law and Albertine are slumped on the bed, naked except for Richard's socks. Albertine gasps when she sees us. Richard lets out a bubbly snore.

"Who knew he had it in him?" Eddie cracks.

"Get out of here!" Albertine says, grabbing at the sheet. She sounds like she's about to cry. Softly, Isabelle closes the door.

"I told you he was busy," Eddie says.

Isabelle whips around to face him. "Why did you do it?"

"You know why."

"It was you who broke into our house, wasn't it?"

"He never paid us for the last job."

"And you blew up Yolande's cabin."

"Why don't we get out of here?" I say in English.

Eddie winks. "She doesn't know anything, *hein?*" He turns to me. "We had a little business arrangement, me and your father. Cigarette?" He takes his time lighting it, the flare of the match illuminating his jaw, before drawing the smoke in hungrily in that addict's way. "What was I saying? Ah yes, the money—your sister can tell you about that; I'm not going to interfere in family matters." He smiles discreetly. "I thought at first, what with Monsieur Wright dying so suddenly, you might need some time to get his affairs in order, *je suis un type raisonable*. . . . But, like you say in America, business is business: Weeks are going by and I'm not hearing from anybody, and I'm starting to think, *What's going on here?*"

Funny he should say that: That's just what I'm thinking. Isabelle is avoiding my gaze, which for some reason pisses me off even more than Eddie's snide sarcasm. Not that I require an explanation of the overall picture: It's more the details that are bugging me, such as just what racket was Ross involved in, and how much did my sister know? Eddie must have noticed my expression, because he raises his hand in a conciliatory gesture, as if to signify that it's all water under the bridge.

"But no matter. We spoke with your brother-in-law, what's his name—ah yes, *Richard.*" He says it the French way. "And he told us about a certain discovery your little girls made—well, he told us some other things, too, but that was between boys. . . ." He winks jocosely. "Anyway, it's all clear now. You pay us our share, and we forget all about it. . . ."

"Oh, shit," Isabelle cries. "The doll!"

"What are you talking about?"

"In the box, with the account number! I let the girls have it!"

Eddie gives us an encouraging smile. "*Et voilà!* Now you understand: We'll take cash or a check." He winks again.

"Excuse me," I say, "am I missing something?"

"I'll explain later," Isabelle snaps, then turns to Eddie. "I can't believe you used Albertine like that; don't you have *any* scruples?"

That's a good one, I observe to myself.

"No," Eddie says, his eyes turning cold.

"Hey, guys!" a voice calls out—Jim, ambling across the courtyard toward us, his mouth stretched in a loopy grin.

"Merde! What's he doing here?"

"Hey!" I call back enthusiastically.

"Just thought I'd check on you. Eddie, what's up, dude?" Jim raises his hand in a high five, which Eddie reflexively returns, though with a somewhat puzzled expression.

"Wow," I exclaim, looking at my watch. "I didn't realize it was this late!"

"Yeah, well, Odette was worried, you know how she gets. . . . Did you find Richard?"

"He had a few too many," Isabelle says. "They're letting him spend the night."

"Oh, that's cool. So, you girls ready to come home?"

"Yes!" Isabelle cries.

Jim looks hesitant. "Shouldn't we check on Richard?"

"He's fine," Isabelle says briskly, lacing her arm through his and tugging at him. "Come on, let's go." Without really thinking about it, I take his other arm.

"Be seeing you around, Eddie," Jim says.

But Eddie ignores him.

CHAPTER *forty*

Albertine made me think of Emma Bovary. Clutching the sheet to her chest, she had a kind of furious dignity, an expression in her eyes that seemed to say, *You can't take this from me.* Maybe in her fantasies she'd turned Richard into someone worth making a fool of herself over. Or so I told myself last night when I finally got to bed and, unable to banish the image from my mind, picked up the book to try to put myself to sleep. Maybe I'm surprised I feel sorry for her, though my Christian charity doesn't extend to Richard, who as far as I'm concerned just got what he deserved. It's only as I drifted off that it occurred to me to wonder why neither Jiri nor Philippe came looking for us.

As you might expect, the first thing I do in the morning is corner my sister for a little heart-to-heart. I find her in the bathroom, applying gel to the dark circles under her eyes.

"Bad night?" I say sarcastically.

She dabs away. "What do you think?"

"Maybe your conscience was bothering you. Here's your chance to unload: I'll be out back."

When Isabelle joins me a few minutes later, she looks serene and refreshed. It's amazing what you can do with makeup: Those high-tech wrinkle creams and toners and glow lotions, the fruit acids and plankton extracts and, of course, Botox—they all work. If I were a stockbroker, I'd tell everyone to invest in cosmetics.

"I'm going to tell you everything," she announces.

"Oh, good."

She sits down next to me on the bench and assumes a serious expression. "Remember how you were asking me about Belgium? Dad used to go there all the time. He'd started a business with a man called Jacques Van Langendonck—yes, Yolande's husband. He had all these contacts in what used to be the Belgian Congo and he was selling mining rights or something; I'm not really sure of the details. Anyway, they were doing really well for a while— that was when Dad bought the East Hampton house—and then the market slumped and they had to start scrambling. Well, Yolande's husband knew people in the diamond business, and next thing you know, he'd got Dad into it, bringing diamonds out of Africa to Antwerp, which is where the cutters are. I think it might have been legitimate at first, but the way Dad put it to me, it was Africa. . . . All these countries were going to war with each other, and they needed weapons. Nobody in their right mind was going to sell arms to Sierra Leone or Angola, or at least own up to it, but the Bulgarians and Romanians, and the Czechs, were more than happy to—it was still communism back then, not that things changed that much afterwards—so they came up with this thing called arms-for-diamonds, smuggling the guns out of Eastern

Europe and the gems out of Africa, and running the money through phony bank accounts in places like Switzerland and Belgium. They've got all these embargoes now, but they didn't back then, and Dad knew his way around the Eastern Bloc from his days in Russia. . . .

"Right around the same time, I met Jiri. He came to Bennington as a visiting poet, which was kind of a joke, because all he did was smoke dope and sleep with his students, including me, but it made the college look good to have a real Eastern European dissident on staff. . . . Anyway, I did wonder at the time why Dad was so thrilled—I mean, about my going to live in a Marxist country with a penniless poet—but I guess it all sort of makes sense now. Not that he didn't like Jiri—they really hit it off, but you know, I think he was really in over his head. He'd just married Daphne, and he owed money to a lot of people—"

"And he had to pay for Bennington."

"Yeah, very funny, it's all my fault. Let's just say he wasn't really himself. You know Dad, he'd always been kind of reckless, but . . . anyway, he started coming to Prague all the time, then he'd disappear for a few days. He said he was looking into turning one of those old Bohemian castles into a hotel. I didn't really believe him—Dad, in the hotel business?—but I didn't think about it all that much, either. You know how he was: He would bring crazy presents for the girls, and he'd invite twenty people for dinner. . . . Jiri thought he was great—he used to call him The Big American. What he was really doing, of course, was setting up these arms deals with Lupa Romesco, who was basically a broker, and other people who'd either come over to Prague or he'd go off to meet them at some Party resort in the Tatras. . . . I know what you're going to ask: No I never met her, but I'd seen stories about her in the paper and kind of started figuring things out when she turned up here." She draws a breath.

"You must be wondering what any of this has to do with Santerre. Well, all of a sudden communism ended and the corrupt officials Dad was dealing with got thrown out, and even if he could've made new connections, nobody wanted to mess around with shady deals anymore, they all wanted to get in to the European Union. Well, Odette—she and Dad were together by then—had always wanted a house in Santerre, and guess who was here already: Yolande. Of course, Odette didn't know anything—she really thought Dad was indulging her. . . . This is where Eddie comes in. Yolande's husband had done some smuggling deals with him— hash from Morocco, mostly, in his fishing boat—and he wanted to get into the bigger stuff. Meanwhile, the Belgian police had caught wind of Jacques and Dad's operation. They'd been using a little airport near Ostend as a hub, flying the diamonds in from Africa and the arms from Eastern Europe; it was all organized by some Bulgarian pilot Lupa knew. Something happened, though—I guess they confiscated a shipment, and Yolande's husband was almost arrested. You'd think he would've gotten scared, but instead he decided to move the operation here: He figured it was perfect, right between Europe and Africa, surrounded by water, and full of thugs for hire. They would smuggle the stones in and then use Belgian tourists as couriers—the tourists had no idea; Yolande would ask them to take a little package to her aunt in Antwerp. The arms came from Yugoslavia through Albania and Italy and then were relabeled as crates of Santerran produce and loaded on the car ferries. That was the part that Eddie handled. I'm not sure how much the mayor knew—I think quite a bit, but he was willing to look the other way as long as it was good for tourism.

"I had no idea of any of this for a long time, but then Yolande's husband was killed in Angola. That really freaked Dad out. He was staying with us in Prague, and he did something I'd never see him do: He got drunk. We were sitting at my kitchen table at three o'clock in the morning and he started telling me things, like he needed to get them off his chest. I couldn't believe it; I mean, I always wondered about some of the stuff he was involved in, how legal it was—but guns? But he was in so deep by then, he was afraid he was going to get murdered too. They never really figured out what happened to Yolande's husband, by the way, if it was the secret police or just some angry warlords. . . . Anyway, there was Dad, left with the whole mess and a couple deals still pending."

"So you decided to help him out."

"What else could I do? He was desperate."

"Yeah, and he must've made it worth your while too."

"You don't have to get up on your high horse, Constance, it's not like the business you're in is any nicer. . . ."

"You mean equity analysis?" I say incredulously.

"*No,* I mean emerging markets. You just walk into countries and privatize their factories and fire the workers and—"

"Been talking to Marge much?"

"And you don't even take an interest in the local culture, you don't go to the theater, or the movies . . . You're just like Odette! You've been all over the world and nothing has made an impression on you!"

I'm so taken aback by this statement that I pause to consider it. She's right, I'm really not all that interested in other cultures. I get on the plane, go to my meetings, fly home. After a while, every place starts to look the same, especially if you stay in big hotels, and people are pretty much alike the world over: greedy, scared, confused. . . . "It doesn't matter where you go," I say, "you have to take yourself with you. Look at Dad."

"Dad was always interested in everything around him, he was open to new ideas, he—"

"He smuggled diamonds. Have you ever read about this stuff? Have you seen those pictures of kids in Sierra Leone with their arms lopped off? For Christ's sake, it's worse than drug dealing!"

"I don't see it that way," Isabelle says stubbornly.

"No, you wouldn't. Did Jiri know?"

"Of course not, he would've freaked out."

"I see your point: He may be a bum but he does have a conscience."

"I don't mean *that*. Dad knew a lot of people in the government . . . Oh," she says exasperatedly, "don't you *get* it? When was the last time Jiri was in jail? Right—ages ago. Dad pulled some strings and the authorities left him alone. If he knew, it would kill him."

"Yeah," I have to agree, "it would. There's one thing I don't get though: How come you never had any money?"

"Only in the past couple years. We were doing really well for a while."

"I see, and now that you're no longer being subsidized, you're going to fly the coop. It was never about Jiri cheating on you, was it?"

"I have to get out of Prague—you have no idea what it's like! They think Kafka's having being born there makes them sophisticated, but it's like living in a village: horrible, petty, and provincial! Everyone knows your business, and when they don't, they make up stories about you. And Czech women are the nastiest bitches on earth—stealing husbands is like the national sport!"

"Really? It seems to me you once had a thing about married professors. . . ."

"That was a long time ago. I know you refuse to see this, but I've evolved."

"Into a criminal."

"It wasn't like that! I was just bringing messages to Eddie at first, I didn't know all the details—and by the time I did, it was too late!"

"You knew about that bank account, didn't you?"

She hesitates. "Well, I knew the money had to be somewhere."

"Yeah, you just didn't know you'd need my signature too. Maybe Dad knew you better than you thought. . . ." *And counted on me,* I mentally add, *to sort out the mess.*

"What a mean thing to say!" she cries, but she averts her eyes from my gaze.

"What were you thinking, anyway? That you'd abscond with the funds and leave us all here to deal with Eddie and friends? What if he'd tried to kidnap the girls or something?"

"Eddie would never think of that, he's much too stupid."

"You are unbelievable!"

"I guess I panicked," she concedes.

"And I'm supposed to believe Odette didn't know any of this?"

"I know it sounds crazy, but she really didn't." She hesitates. "To tell you the truth, I'm pretty sure Dad was using her as a courier, back when she was a stewardess."

"You mean he was planting stuff on her?"

"Well, you know Odette, she never would have agreed. . . . I think she must have suspected something, though, later. I mean, you know how it is when you're in love: There's stuff you don't *want* to see. But now . . ." Her voice trails off.

"Well, I hope you realize we're going to have to tell her everything."

She gives me a horrified look. "We can't do that!"

"What are you worried about," I say coldly, "that she'll think less of you?"

She stares at her nails. "I don't want Jiri to know."

"You think he hasn't figured it out? Didn't you just say something about willfully not seeing?"

"He might try to divorce me, and take the girls away."

"I doubt it." We sit in silence. "What are we going to do?" I finally say.

"I guess what Eddie said: pay him whatever Dad owed him. It can't be that much—he was just a courier." Isabelle brightens up. "Look, maybe we can still fix this—I mean, without everyone having to know."

I stare at her incredulously. "You really thinks that's going to be the end of it?"

Her hopeful look fades. "I guess not."

We find the girls crouching in the dirt behind the house. It's been a while since anyone's thought of taking them to the beach or giving them a shower. They look seedy and unkempt. Olga has a festering scab on her leg, probably from a mosquito bite she keeps scratching, and a rivulet of snot is seeping out her nose. Isabelle squats down and puts on that conniving face parents get when they're about to screw their kids over.

"What are you doing?"

"Building a castle," Sophie says, as if this should be obvious to any moron. She lays a stick across a pile of rocks and studies it.

"Sweethearts," Isabelle simpers, "remember the dolly Mommy let you have?"

Sophie eyes her with indifference. Olga wipes at her nose, spreading snot across her cheek. Agnes blinks, slowly, like a lizard.

"Well, Mommy needs it back, but she'll buy you an ice cream to make up for it." Isabelle grins engagingly.

"We operated it," Sophie says.

"Excuse me?"

"She had stones in her stomach so Agnes cut her open."

Isabelle's smile looks like it's about to split her face in half. "Wasn't that clever of you! What did you do with them?"

"We gave them to Yolande," Sophie says, turning back to her sticks. "She paid us."

"I see," Isabelle says, straightening up.

"We already got ice cream," Sophie adds, but Isabelle can't hear her. Rage doesn't become her: The blood seems to have drained from her face, and her hands, I notice, are shaking. I look away, at the castle. It reminds me of an installation I saw once at the Whitney, a huge structure made out of twigs and little Christmas lights that was somehow both monstrous and whimsical. Not unlike our family.

CHAPTER *forty-one*

Jane doesn't say a word as I recount the whole sordid tale to her—just raises her eyebrows and darts an occasional glance at Marge. I wanted to include Lucy in the conversation—kill two birds with one stone, as it were—but nobody could find her. I've decided to let Isabelle break it to Odette; I'm getting a little tired of these family conferences.

"A lot of it doesn't make sense," Jane says.

"Well!" Marge huffs. "If that's the only thing that's bothering you!"

"Frankly, I don't know what to think."

"It's fucking horrendous, that's what!" Marge explodes. "We should turn your sister over to Interpol!"

"Hey," I say.

"Hey *what?* She's got blood on her hands!"

"I find it hard to believe that neither Odette nor Jiri had any idea of what was going on," Jane says.

"I don't," I say. "I think they both saw what they wanted to see."

Marge snorts loudly. "Talk about raping the third world—"

"Don't be so tiresome, darling," Jane snaps. "It's not going to solve anything. In a way we're just as guilty: We've all known for years that Ross was a crook."

Speak for yourself, I think, though I'm really not so sure. I was the executor of his will. How could I have not noticed anything?

"So we're just going to hush it all up, then?"

"Where *is* Isabelle?" Jane asks.

"She ran off like a bat out of hell to Yolande's, who probably has some Antwerp dealer holding a knife to her throat—it's the only explanation for her grabbing the diamonds like that," I reason.

"You mean somebody who'd already bought them?"

"That would be my guess, and who's been waiting ever since. Either way you slice it, that two million dollars won't even begin to cover everything. Lupa Romesco hasn't been paid for the arms, either, or so she claims. I guess there's no way to find out."

"There must be other accounts," Jane says.

Marge looks at me, horrified. "You don't actually intend to make good on these supposed obligations!"

"That's beside the point," I say. "The fact is, if we don't hand the goods over pretty soon, we're going to get to know Lupa Romesco a lot better—or the goons she hires to break our kneecaps."

"But surely you're not planning to give in to her?" Marge now says with an expression of total outrage.

"Got any better ideas?"

"I certainly do! I say we hand them all over to the police and use the money to do some good."

Jane and I stare at her, perplexed.

"Of course, we can't possibly return it to its rightful owners," Marge continues, "but we can certainly put it to use indirectly for their benefit."

"Through this nonprofit organization you're starting, for instance," I suggest.

"Well," Marge allows, "that would be one way."

"She's out of her mind," I observe to Jane.

"I am *not*. The only way to deal with this mess is to assume responsibility. That money could purchase vaccines, or AIDS drugs, for entire towns and villages. I think it's entirely appropriate."

"Except that we'll get killed," I point out. "How are you planning to get all these people arrested? We don't have any proof."

"We have Isabelle's testimony."

"Right, she's going to incriminate herself."

"She will if you threaten her," Marge says placidly.

"I'm not entirely comfortable with this," I say.

"Hullo!" Lucy cries, bursting in with her arms full of wildflowers. "Why does everyone look so grim?"

"You'd better sit down," Jane says.

"In a sec, I have to find a vase. . . . Yves picked these—aren't they lovely?"

"Great, the discreet fucking charm of the bourgeoisie. . . ."

"Please stop swearing, Marge, it's so unnecessary."

"Would somebody please tell her?" Marge says, rising heavily from her chair. "I don't think I can take much more of this."

"You tell her, Jane," I say, getting up myself. "I'm going to look for Isabelle."

"I hope it's not bad news," Lucy says, arranging her flowers. "We've had quite enough of that lately."

It's not until I step outside that I see the woman walking toward Philippe's house, though I remember at that moment that I heard a car door slamming. She has the chic Parisian gauntness you get from eating small portions and smoking, dark hair cut briskly to her collarbone. She looks exactly as I'd imagined.

"Bonjour," she calls out.

"Hi," I say in English, because it seems like my only defense.

Philippe appears in the doorway. He kisses her cheek. I think he makes a little shrug in my direction, as if to apologize, but maybe not. You can tell from the way they touch that they never hated each other.

"This is Constance," he says, "our American neighbor."

She extends her hand. Her skin is dry and pleasant and smells faintly of eucalyptus. "You have the better house," she remarks, taking off her sunglasses to reveal gold-flecked green eyes.

"We've been here longer," I say.

She smiles in that perfunctory French way, then glances a bit impatiently at Philippe. "Well, aren't you going to invite me in?"

He stoops to lift her bag. Only when she's inside does he glance back, but I look right through him.

"Isn't she a bit old for you?" I hear her say through the open window.

CHAPTER *forty-two*

Isabelle found Yolande at home, giving herself a manicure and looking for all the world as if nothing had happened. She came back with her willingly enough, but it's clear from the set of her frosted pink lips that she's not going to cooperate.

"You are foolish girls," she says contemptuously. "And you, Odette . . ." She doesn't bother finishing her sentence, though I'm sure we all get the idea: At least Yolande was a partner in crime; what kind of woman lets her husband keep her in the dark?

"Leave her out of it," Jim says, putting his arm around her and setting his eyes into a steely glare. Odette looks almost pathetically grateful.

"The stones are on their way to Antwerp." Yolande says. "You will have to deal with the countess—I suggest you pay her what she is owed; it is not wise to anger these people."

"What exactly do you suggest we pay her *with?*" I ask, just for the record.

"*Ah ça . . .* it was your father who handled the money. Undoubtedly he has left instructions."

"We'll have the lot of you arrested, is what we'll do," Lucy says.

"This would not be a good idea. The rules are different here, as you know," Yolande says mildly.

"Are you *threatening* us?" Lucy cries. My eyes fall on Yves' flowers, which she's arranged in a vaguely bridal-looking bouquet on the mantelpiece, the petals already beginning to drift down onto the stained marble. It's funny how it suddenly hits you that two people are perfect for each other. Yves, as if fortified by his new-found status, rises from the sofa and announces, "Madame, we are not going to take this lying down."

"It's not about the money," Lucy says. "We couldn't bear to take it, knowing where it comes from, but I don't see why that dreadful woman should have it, either."

"If you do not give it to her, she will take it. I remind you that she has already blown up my property. . . ."

"That's the part I don't get," I say.

"They thought I had the diamonds. They had already searched your house. I am trying to make you understand that these people will stop at nothing."

"I can see now why you were trying so hard to suck up to her," Isabelle says sourly.

"You are hardly in an irreproachable position yourself," Yolande retorts.

"There's one thing I don't understand," I cut in. "If the countess wanted to lie low, why did she have a cocktail party?"

"To get you out of the house," Yolande says, as if this were the most obvious thing in the world.

"You mean they searched it again?" I suddenly remember the open window.

Yolande shrugs. "If your father had not made such a mess of things, none of this would have happened. It is really all most unfortunate, and with young children involved, too. . . ."

Odette's hand flies to her mouth. "The girls! Where are they?"

"Aren't they with Jiri?" Isabelle says, a bit hesitantly.

"I don't think so," Marge says. "He went in to Flore."

We all gape at each other, until Lucy breaks the spell by rushing out of the room and charging upstairs two steps at a time; the rest of us run outside. There is no sign of the girls either in front or in back of the house. A sick feeling grips the pit of my stomach.

"I found Electra!" Lucy shouts from the third-floor window, her voice hysterical with relief. "Do you have Olga and Sophie?"

"The water!" Isabelle cries. "Maybe they went down to the cove!" We rush down the path, Jim and Odette in the lead. We're all panting by the time we emerge above Yolande's cabin, the top of which, I notice, has been boarded up. There's no one around except a couple of Parisian girls sunning themselves on the rocks, their breasts splayed like fried eggs on their thin chests. They sit up with a start when Isabelle bears down on them. No, they haven't seen any little girls.

"What were they wearing?" the older one asks. Isabelle hesitates, but her reddening face betrays her: She has no idea. She lets out a wail.

"Now, now," Odette murmurs, only to be shoved away. I think at first that Isabelle is going to hit her. Instead she crumples to the ground like a rag doll.

"I'm going to the police," Jim says. "Constance, come with me; you can translate."

We sprint back up the path, leaving Odette to deal with Isabelle. A torpid midday hush has descended on the *maquis*. It's turned dry as tinder over the past month, as the sun beat inexorably down and the little springs that seep out of the rocks earlier in the season shrank to a trickle and then dried up. I suddenly realize it's almost August.

"You don't have to tell me the whole story," Jim says as we pause to catch our breath halfway up. "I've figured out some of it, but you know, maybe I can help."

"There's nothing you can do," I say. "There's some money in an account in Zurich. As soon as we've found the girls, we're going to get it. I don't care *who* we hand it over to, as long as it's out of our hands."

"Do you really think that's going to be the end of it?" Jim says.

As our luck would have it, the *gendarmerie* and the mayor's office next door are both deserted for the lunch hour. A fried-fish smell wafts over from the Marmite, where a busload of day-trippers has just been disgorged onto the terrace. We're seeing more and more of them—people on package tours in the South up to view the rugged charms of the *cap*. Maybe all this skullduggery *has* been good for tourism. Albertine comes bustling out, sharply dressed in a tight skirt and blouse and looking rather more chipper than usual. The reason why instantly becomes clear: Richard, seated at a table off to the side with a Pernod and a little dish of peanuts before him.

"Looks like someone's come back for more," I observe to Jim.

"Jesus," Jim says.

"I've never seen anyone get peanuts at the Marmite."

Albertine is momentarily disconcerted when she sees us, but quickly regains her composure. She's really quite attractive, in the broody, vaguely menacing way of Santerran women—or at least Richard seems to think so, something I bet Eddie hadn't planned on. His brow corrugates as we come closer.

"I don't want to hear any sermons," he says. "As you are perfectly well aware, my wife has deserted me."

"Eddie's made off with the kids," I say, adding hastily, "not yours: Olga and Sophie."

"Why should I care?" Richard says.

"You really are a jerk, aren't you?" Jim says.

"Not at all. They're wretched brats, just like their mother. I very much doubt they've been abducted, though, at least not by Eddie. He's in the bar with that half-witted sidekick of his; been there all morning, right, sweetheart?"

Albertine nods in agreement. She won't look at us, but then, I guess we did catch her in an awkward situation the other night.

"The countess!" I say.

Albertine shrugs. *"Elle est partie."*

"What?" Jim says.

"She's gone," I translate. "Are you sure?"

"Go ask Eddie; he's all bent out of shape about it for some reason," Richard says. "Seems she made off like a bandit in the middle of the night. Amazing what goes on in this village after dark . . . ," he adds sarcastically.

A volley of imprecations erupts from the tourist table, from under which a scrofulous mutt has just shot out. The dog skids past us, a hunk of *charcuterie maison* clamped in its jaws.

"Pilou!" a shrill little voice squawks. Sophie comes tearing around the corner, followed by a gleeful and disheveled Olga shouting, "Come here, you dumb dog!"

"See?" Richard says. "Safe and sound, and as odious as ever. . . ." Albertine's expression leaves no doubt as to *her* opinion of ill-mannered children whose parents can't even keep track of them.

"Hey, girls," Jim calls after them. Sophie turns reluctantly around.

"What?"

"Where were you? Everyone was looking for you."

She glares sullenly at us. I guess she figures if she tells, it'll be another fun thing they won't get to do anymore.

"You can't just disappear like that, you know," I say lamely, just as Jojo comes ambling round the bend, his hands stuck in his pockets and a beret perched jauntily on his head, giving him the appearance of a demented *boulevardier*. Now I remember the dog.

"Bon appétit!" he calls to the tourists, before strolling over to us. I'll say this for the guy: He's got unfailingly good manners.

"Ah, my American friend," he exclaims happily. "Is this your fiancé?"

"No," I say.

"Yes, he is," Sophie squeals.

"What do *you* know about anything?" I snap.

"More than you think." She sticks her tongue out at me. Richard has a point: It's hard to imagine why anyone would want to abduct these brats.

"Lovely girls," Jojo says, ruffling Olga's hair. "They came to visit me."

"He gave us a dog," Olga pipes in.

"It gets lonely on top of the mountain," Jojo says wistfully.

"Why didn't you take Agnes with you?" I ask Sophie.

"She's afraid of dogs. And she doesn't like Jojo; she thinks he smells bad."

"Sshhh!"

"He doesn't understand English," Sophie says.

"Well, then," Richard says, "now that we've sorted *that* out, would anyone care for a drink?" Jojo brightens right up. Before he can pull up a chair, though, Eddie emerges from the bar, followed by a doleful Toto—who, one can't help but notice, is sporting a magnificent black eye. Albertine inches closer to Richard.

"Going to open your shop, are you?" Richard calls out with a smirk. Eddie shoots him a sour look.

"You should stay away from him, you know," Jojo says. "He's a bad sort."

"All right," Richard says, "what's everyone having? It's on me."

"A little whisky, perhaps," Jojo says, leaning back in his plastic chair. "Ah, this is what I call the good life: sitting at the café terrace with friends. . . ." His eyes start to well up. Blinking back tears, he fishes around in his pocket.

"Here," Richard says sympathetically, "have a napkin."

Jojo takes it and dabs at his eyes. "Thank you, my friend—it's the solitude: You know what it does to a man. . . ."

"Yes, I do," Richard says. Albertine smiles at him in a maternal way.

"We should go back and tell Isabelle the kids are safe," Jim says, his voice suddenly drowned out by the roar of an engine as a red Škoda comes tearing up the road and screeches to a halt before us. Jiri leaps out, followed by a still-sobbing Isabelle.

"*Where are my girls?*" he roars.

"Calm down," I say. "They're fine—they're playing in the back."

Isabelle moans with relief and dashes to the courtyard. "Are you hurt? Did anyone touch you?" we hear her babbling under the irritated yips of the dog.

"Would someone please tell me what the fuck is going on?" Jiri demands.

"I'd be glad to," Richard says, "but, as I suspect is the case with most of us around this table, I have only a partial picture. Perhaps your wife could enlighten us."

A big beribboned package in the back of the car catches my eye. "What's that?" I ask.

"Her birthday present," Jiri says glumly. "She turns forty today."

"Well," Richard exclaims, "I'd say this calls for champagne!"

"Let's get out of here," Jim says.

"Yeah," I say.

Albertine returns with the drinks. I guess she's not giving up her day job just yet. "I'm staying right here," Richard says, swatting her rear end as she passes—a gesture she finds so inexplicably delightful that she bursts into giggles, causing the glasses and bottles to rattle on the metal tray.

CHAPTER *forty-three*

The countess is indeed gone, as Yolande hastens over the next morning to inform us, interrupting our breakfast and provoking Isabelle to mutter under her breath that some people have a lot of nerve. Yolande is obviously trying to put a good face on things, but the state of her makeup betrays her, as does the fact that she's seeking solace in our company—a plan that is swiftly derailed when it becomes apparent that there's a hitch.

"You mean she just took off—like that?" Marge says.

"Well . . ." Yolande demurs.

Isabelle jumps. "She took the diamonds, didn't she? You never sent them to Antwerp—you had them all along!"

"I think we've had quite enough obfuscation, Yolande," Jane says firmly. "Why don't you just tell us what happened?"

Yolande girlishly lowers her eyes. I'll bet that used to work for her once upon a time, but all it nets her now is a chilly silence. With a sigh, she raises them again and adopts a businesslike tone. "*Eh bien,* yes, I kept them, though I fully intended to send them on. This is now immaterial, however, as I no longer have them. My house was broken into yesterday."

"Oh, right," Isabelle says scornfully. "We're going to believe that."

"I don't think you have much choice. As I told your father many times, this is what happens when you deal with this class of person: I suspect Madame Romesco wanted to cut her losses—I understand the mayor told her that it would be better if she left Borgolano—and she must have known that the diamonds were worth more than whatever she was owed."

"You mean the two million dollars?" Jane says.

"That is what Mr. Woland in Antwerp paid for the diamonds. I do not know exactly how much was to go to Madame Romesco. As I have said to you, your father handled the money. The point is that she was never paid for the last shipment. Nor were the inter-mediaries . . . ,"she adds delicately.

"Such as yourself."

"I really don't think—"

"Well, that's what you were, isn't it?" Isabelle says.

"Let us say," Yolande replies with an air of aggrieved dignity, "that that is what I was reduced to."

"But what about the manor?" Lucy asks. We all turn to her, perplexed.

She flushes. "I mean, just out of curiosity, what will happen to the countess's house?"

"I expect she will sell it." Lucy's eyes light up at this. "Though frankly," Yolande continues, "I am not sure she even bought it properly in the first place. I really know very little: Since the death of my husband, I am not as privy to information as I once was."

"Well," Marge says, "good riddance, either way."

"It doesn't really solve anything," Jane points out.

"Yes it does," Isabelle says. "The countess is gone. We keep the money. Everybody is happy."

Yolande clears her throat. "Everyone except Mr. Woland in Antwerp, who has still not received the diamonds he purchased."

"That's your problem, isn't it?" Isabelle retorts.

Jiri, who has been sitting with Odette on the couch, rises.

"I've had enough," he announces. "I'm taking the girls back to Prague. When you've cleared up this mess, you can join us, or not."

Isabelle's eyes flash. "Oh, really? Is this too sordid for you? Let me ask you something, Mr. Sensitive Poet: What do you think we've been living on all these years?"

Jiri looks surprised. "What living? The big apartment? The vacations? I don't need all that stuff. . . ."

"That's right, be superior!" she spits.

Jiri shrugs and starts to head for the door. "You can call it what you want."

"You can't take the girls, you—you philandering toad!"

He stops and turns around. "And what are you going to do with them?"

"I'm their mother!"

"You're no mother," Jiri says. I think it's something all men know: that there's nothing worse you can do to a woman than leave the room. Isabelle looks like someone just took food out of her mouth.

"Go with him," Odette says. "Go," she repeats. "Don't be foolish."

But Isabelle just stands in the middle of the floor, arms limp at her sides, a puzzled expression on her face. Maybe she thinks it's a trick.

"We'll take care of everything," Odette coaxes, and all of a sudden, as if she'd uttered a magic word, Isabelle blinks.

"I don't want to lose my children," she says.

"Of course you don't. Go with him. Everything will be fine."

"It's not good for a woman, all this stress," Yolande pipes in, but Odette silences her with a gesture.

"Go ahead," I say. "You can trust us."

"Yes, I can, can't I?" Isabelle says, already making for the door. Her footsteps sound on the stairs and, presently, muffled voices reach us from her bedroom above. They'll probably just have sex again; it's the way they've always worked things out. From outside we hear laughter and the sound of little feet running. The girls burst in all sandy and sticky, followed by Jim and Yves laden with towels and buckets and, Sophie announces excitedly, a whole netful of SEA URCHINS!

"Aren't you clever!" Lucy exclaims. "We'll have them for lunch."

"YUCK!" the girls scream. Yves whispers something in Agnes's ear. She scowls and moves forward, her hand balled into a fist. When she reaches Lucy, she opens it. Lying in her palm is a smooth green pebble.

"For you," she says in her odd, toneless voice.

Lucy's eyes widen. "Oh, sweetheart, it's beautiful. . . ." She reaches out her hand, gingerly, as if she were afraid to scare her away. Agnes squints with concentration, then, with a slow, precise movement, picks the stone up and gives it to Lucy.

"Oh, Yves," Lucy murmurs, her eyes filling with tears.

"*Non,*" he says. "It was her idea."

Yolande clears her throat. "About our little business . . ."

"You can have the money," I say.

"Now, wait a minute—" Jane objects.

"You've got to be kidding!" Marge expostulates, half rising from her seat.

I turn to them. "Look, the only thing that strikes me as clear in this whole mess is that it isn't ours."

Yolande presses her lips into a smile. "I always knew you were a sensible girl, Constance."

"I believe we ought to have a voice in this too," Jane says.

"Okay," I say, "let's say we keep the money. Do you think this Mr. Woland, if he exists, is just going to throw up his hands and take a loss? And what about the countess, and Eddie?"

"Frankly, I don't see why we should trust her," Jane says. Yolande looks like she's going to take exception to this, but evidently decides it would be more productive to keep her mouth shut. She rearranges her expression into one of wounded dignity. Marge rolls her eyes.

"I don't trust her, either," I say, "but I feel even less like dealing with Lupa Romesco and whatever other characters she's in bed with. Let Yolande duke it out with her."

"I still think we could put the money to better use," Jane insists with a glance at Marge, who makes a noncommittal snorting sound.

"Well," I say, "I'm out. And keep in mind: Whatever you decide, you need both my signature and Isabelle's."

"Do you mean that Daddy only put *your* names on the account?" Lucy blurts out.

"Yes."

"Lucy," Jane snaps, "it's time you took your head out of the sand. Ross was a shit. He lied and stole and cheated. He took advantage of us and anybody else who ever crossed his path. Frankly, he's better off dead."

Yolande's mouth opens and shuts like a fish. Lucy weighs the little green stone in her palm. "I know," she says, "but that doesn't mean he wasn't a good father."

"How little you understand him, Jane," Odette says quietly. I'd forgotten she was in the room. Jim, who took the place vacated by Jiri, squeezes her hand, but she brushes him off. "Ross was like most people: He had good and bad sides. One does not cancel the other."

"Typically French attitude," Marge remarks. "That's how they got off the hook for Vichy."

"Save it Marge, will you?" I say.

She shrugs. "Sorry, Odette, cheap shot."

"It's nothing," Odette says wearily.

"Why can't we just pretend we never found the money," Lucy cries. "It's not like any of us need it!"

"Speak for yourself," Yolande says.

"I'm serious, it's like the tree falling in the woods—"

"She's right, you know," Marge says.

"Let Yolande have it if she wants it so badly!" Lucy continues, heated up now.

Yolande raises her hand as if to object, then catches herself. "*Quand même . . .*"

"I vote with Lucy," Odette says.

"So do I," I say.

"Well," Jane allows after a pause, "I suppose you're right. I still don't trust her, but—"

"And what about your sister?" Yolande asks, a bit too hastily.

"I'll deal with Isabelle," I say—though, judging from the sounds that are coming through the ceiling, Isabelle right now has other things on her mind.

CHAPTER *forty-four*

I was bound to run into Philippe eventually; what I didn't expect was that he would seek me out. He's lying in wait when I head out for a run the next morning, the thrum of heat already in the air. *Of course,* I think, *he gets up early.* Now he stands before me and I'm having the dumbest thoughts, such as *Did they have sex last night?*

"It's not what you think," he says.

"Come on, you can do better than that," I say harshly.

"It's complicated," he says.

"I know, you never actually said *divorced.*"

He holds his hand out, an honest man trying his best. "Will you at least believe that I was not expecting her?"

"What's her name?" I ask.

"Fabienne."

"Fabienne." It sounds so sweet and old-fashioned.

"It doesn't suit her, does it?" he says with a smile, but I won't be bought so cheap.

"She's very beautiful." I say. "I can see why you married her."

"Oh, Constance . . ." He reaches for my arm and I step back, banging my head into the Perettis' wall. "Are you all right?"

I laugh. "I'm fine."

"I thought you of all people would understand," he says in a sad voice.

"Sure, your wife showed up: That really sucks."

He reaches for me again and, backed up as I am against the wall, I can't really shrug him off. "Look at me," he wheedles.

All of a sudden I understand: It doesn't have to end! Of course it's complicated, but life is complicated, and we're all adults, aren't we? I am momentarily so seduced by the elegance of this logic that I almost let myself step forward, until he says, "She'll only be here for a week," and I see that it's not the first time he's done this.

"We have an arrangement," he adds.

I laugh out loud. His eyes cloud with hurt.

"Is that what you used to say to your students?"

He gazes at me with disappointment. "Perhaps it was too much to expect you to understand."

"Do you think I'm a moron?"

His eyes grow cold now. "I am sorry if I have hurt you."

He turns to leave and I think, *Sure, I'll let you have that.* It's funny how you're afraid you might cry and instead you just feel empty. I watch him walk away with a sort of detached curiosity, like a figure in a movie, and I ask myself once again if there's something wrong with me, some genetic crimp that makes me unable to feel the way I ought to. I'm still pondering this when I feel a light tap on my arm. Lucy.

"I thought he might not be very nice," she says.

"He's not," I say.

"Best to find out now, you know. You might have married him."

"Not likely: His wife turned up."

"Oh, is that who that woman was. . . . Terribly smart, isn't she? I wonder how French women do it—you know, look intimidating in jeans."

"Lucy, has anyone ever told you how peculiar you are?"

She grins. "Oh yes, Richard was always going on about it. Yves, on the other hand, finds me quite normal—isn't that interesting?"

"I didn't mean it that way."

"That's all right; it can actually work to one's advantage, being perceived as a mental case. Poor Richard . . . Do you know he's run off with Albertine?"

"I heard."

"You don't need to look embarrassed: I really don't care. In a way they're perfect for each other: grim and ghoulish and desperate for attention. . . ." She laughs. "I don't really mean that—she's a sad sack, but so's Richard. Maybe he'll be nicer to her. She won't intimidate him the way I did."

"I'm surprised you realize that," I say.

She shrugs. "I'm not stupid, it's just that you can't see as well from the inside, know what I mean?"

"Totally."

"For instance, you're sad, but you'll get over it."

"I'm not sure I can take all this wisdom right now, Lucy," I say wearily.

"Oh, sorry. Anyway, I think you did the right thing, about the money. That's what I really wanted to tell you. Let Yolande deal with it, the nasty old trout. . . ." She makes a mock shudder.

"It's not quite in the bag yet: I haven't talked to Isabelle. Last time I checked, they still hadn't come out of the bedroom."

Lucy giggles. "I always thought Jiri would be sort of fabulous in bed, didn't you?"

I stare at her. "Lucy, are you sure someone didn't put something in your orange juice?"

"Oh, Constance, don't be such a prude," she says airily. "You know, it's awful to say this, but I feel so happy—I feel like everything is going to work out. Are you going to take Jim back?"

I look at her with amazement. "In case you hadn't noticed, he's moved on."

"Oh, Odette doesn't want him. . . . I think he amused her at first, but now she's wondering how to get out of it. It's one thing to have a fling on vacation, but what on earth would she do with him in Paris?"

"Oh, well, no problem, I guess I'll just take him back, then."

"Think of it as his sentimental education," Lucy says, "like Julien Sorel."

"Doesn't he get decapitated?"

"Only at the end—the French are so bloody-minded, aren't they?"

"I guess you'd know," I tease. She blushes a rosy pink. I never noticed she had freckles, a little pale dusting of them across her nose. Is it possible that Lucy has been out in the sun unprotected?

"Isn't it awful? I actually caught myself thinking the other day that it's a good thing Agnes is a bit slow: Maybe she won't notice what a slut I'm being. . . ." She titters a bit uncertainly.

"Lucy, you are not a slut. You and Richard were a disaster together."

"I know, but he's such a good father. . . ."

"Where have I heard that before?"

She giggles again. "It sounds silly, but Yves just makes me so happy. He's sweet, and thoughtful, and considerate—"

"And he restores furniture."

"Yes, he does." Her brow clouds. "Don't think I haven't wondered, if I'm pathetic enough to fall for the first person who's nice to me . . ." She brightens up. "But we really do have so much in common: We like the same things. Everything was always such a struggle with Richard; he was so *angry* all the time, and I was too. I'm afraid we brought out the absolute worst in each other." She fixes her big blue eyes intently on me. "But you see, I've always been good at ignoring things that don't suit me. It's how I cope."

"I think I understand."

"Or how I used to cope, anyway. This is going to sound crazy, but I've come to realize that I've spent huge swaths of my life as a spectator of myself. You know, you're standing there wondering, *Oh, who's that dreadful person freaking out?*—and it's you, but it doesn't altogether register because you're just watching. It's like when Elec—Agnes was a baby, I knew that something was wrong, but it didn't really matter because she wasn't *my* daughter, she was the child of this curious out-of-control woman I was observing. . . . When Mum sees her, she gets this *Oh dear, she can't possibly be related to us* look—which she covers up immediately, of course, but it's there, always, that tinge of dismay, and the scary thing is that I understand, I don't despise her for it: Mother love isn't automatic, it's not like someone flips a switch inside you. You have to work at it just like anything else, and Elec—oh hell, Agnes,

I mean—doesn't exactly make it easy. She's not pretty like Sophie and Olga, and she can be quite rude. And she's fat, and there's something wrong with her brain—nobody really knows what, I've been to every specialist in England; the best they can come up with is that she's somewhere along the autistic continuum—isn't that a stupid expression? And yet, I do love her—it hasn't come easily, but perhaps it's the stronger for that. Do you know how I was dreading this vacation? I was terrified the girls would be mean to her—they're not babies anymore, and nothing escapes them. But look how they've accepted her: They think she's the most fab thing they've ever met! So if she really wants to be called Agnes, well, so be it—it probably does suit her better. I find that I quite respect her spunk actually. . . . Oh, Constance, don't look so sad."

"I *am* sad," I say helplessly.

She rushes forward and folds her arms around me. It's such an unfamiliar sensation that we sort of butt against each other, like storks, and then all the parts lock together and I realize with a shock that I'm crying, which I don't think I've done since I was five years old. Lucy makes a clucking sound: "Sshhhh, just let go. . . ."

When I look up, Madame Peretti is standing there, hose in hand, watching us—not in an unfriendly way, just perplexed, as if for a second she couldn't quite place us. The water comes on, and with a brisk nod she turns and aims the jet at her patio. A tingling chlorine smell rises, wiping out the scent of Robusta that had just begun to insinuate itself into the air.

"Bleach and coffee," Lucy says dreamily. "The smell of a Santerran morning." And all of a sudden something clears inside me, or maybe I just feel dizzy, and I believe that it's true, that love can change you.

CHAPTER *forty-five*

The summer I turned twelve, we went to Mallorca. Ross's divorce from Daphne was just about to go through, and I think it was his way of making amends. Lucy was already at Harvard, but Jane, who was only fourteen, would be going back to London with Daphne. She was miserable about it. She'd gotten used to New York and American schools, and she felt like her whole life was being turned upside down. I didn't care about Daphne leaving—I never could quite shake the feeling that she couldn't remember my name—but I hated her for taking Jane away, which seemed all the more cruel since Lucy was her favorite. The only consolation was that we would spend the summers together, beginning with this one, family togetherness being something Ross set deep store by, as strange as that may seem in one who changed wives so often. Isabelle was even going to fly in from Prague, minus Jiri, who was afraid they wouldn't let him back into the country.

When Ross did things, he did them with flair. Our hotel, a sixteenth-century palace that had once belonged to an Austrian archduke, sat high up in the Tramontana Mountains north of Palma, far from the beachfront high rises of Lucy's nightmares but equipped with a limpid swimming pool that overlooked the sea. Years later, when we first came to Borgolano, I was reminded of Mallorca, not only because of the rugged topography—though Santerre is even more forbidding—but by the resinous scent of the air that I breathed the first night from the balcony of the room I shared with Jane. She'd just found out that she'd be going to boarding school in the fall, another incomprehensible twist in Daphne's logic, and was apprehensive about it—though, as she confessed to me, she thought it would be more fun than living with Daphne in London. I never really understood the loyalty that caused Jane to feel guilty about not liking her mother. Maybe, having only known a stepmother, I was just incapable of that kind of attachment.

Jane had been assigned a load of books to read over the summer—I guess they were afraid her brain had been addled by American education—one of which was the *Odyssey*. It sounded boring as hell but, out of sympathy, I offered to read it to her out loud, which I thought would make it go faster. In the end we decided to take turns. Every night, as we lay on our beds waiting for dinner, one of us would pick it up and tackle a few pages. At first the corny verbosity made us giggle, the way Homer couldn't just say *The sun rose* but always went on about young dawn with her rose-red fingers, and never introduced a character without listing all his relatives and ancestors, but after a while, I found myself looking forward to it. Perched on our rocky crag, it was easy to picture Odysseus and his men plying the very waters that fanned out blue and endless from our window, longing for home even as they kept ruining their chances of ever getting there by bringing upon themselves the wrath of the gods.

If Jane and I ever felt buffeted on the whims of higher powers, it was that summer, and yet, we didn't pity Odysseus. It was Polyphemus we felt sorry for, his home invaded, his flock and cheeses stolen. In my mind I saw him as I was sure he was meant to be: a monstrous but peaceful shepherd, no match for the wily Achaeans, who only got what they asked for when the blinded giant, crazed with pain from the stake they drove into his eye, ate them alive. Odysseus, it was clear to me, won his battles by guile and trickery, sneaking into Troy inside a wooden horse, creeping up on the unwitting brute Cyclops, sacking cities in the night and, as Jane grimly asserted, probably raping the women as well. Still, I couldn't help but admire his panache, even as I despised him. I, too, saw myself as someone who had to connive to get her way, though in my heart, just as Calypso and Circe took on the shape of Isabelle, I dreamt that I was Nausicaa, pure, bright, and untouchable.

It was a magical month. Unencumbered by wives or mistresses, Ross devoted his full attention to us, strutting around like a peacock with his flock, supervising diving lessons for me and Jane and—late in the afternoon, when it got cooler—leading us in breakneck horseback rides up and down the mountain. In the evening we would all gather in the dining room. As men's hungry eyes followed Lucy and Isabelle, I remember thinking that I was glad I was still a child, safe from these troubling glances to which clung, like a caul, the dirty aura of furtive desire. I found myself wishing that we could stay like this forever, suspended in time on this enchanted island, like Odysseus on Ogygia, professing to long for Penelope, but returning every night to make love to Calypso in her cave, for, like my father, Odysseus never could resist a beautiful woman.

There was a ballroom on the ground floor of the hotel, where, after dinner, a ten-piece band played late into the night. Mostly it was old swing standards, like "In the Mood" and "Chattanooga Choo Choo," hilariously rendered in a Catalan accent by the short, plump, and suavely mellifluous Señor Emilio—who, like every other man in the room, was dying of love for Isabelle. Jane and I would lope happily along together, self-consciousness shed to the winds after the glass of wine we were allowed at dinner, as our sisters glided by like dragonflies in the arms of German men with pink, sweating foreheads. Every now and then Ross would appear and gamely take turns with all of us before retiring again to the casino, where he vanished like an avuncular genie in a cloud of cigar smoke. Strangely enough, there was no woman that summer, though many were interested, and I think now that this, too, was meant as a gift.

Before we left, Ross had taken us shopping in New York, letting us pick out two party dresses each. Even Jane, impressed by his sense of occasion, had caved in, selecting a pearly gray silk sheath that, I assured her, brought out the color of her eyes. I, in a moment of madness, had picked out a sugary pink folly of a dress, all bows and ruches and gossamer flounces, an outlandish and completely inappropriate creation that Lucy declared made me look like a wedding cake—which, as I realized the moment I tried it on again at home, it indeed did. Still, I was determined to wear it at least once, if only to prove that I didn't care what she thought.

It wasn't until our last night that I got up the nerve to put it on. After all the others had gone down, I slunk in through a side door, profoundly regretting the ice cream sundaes I'd been having every night for dessert. Cringing with shame, I crept along the wall, feeling like a monstrous bridesmaid, until Lucy caught sight of me and winced, and in that moment I lost all my nerve and just prayed for the earth to swallow me up. Which was when, to my dismay, the band struck up "The Blue Danube." As the syrupy strains swelled in the overheated ballroom air, Ross appeared. Without missing a beat, he made straight for me across the parquet floor and, bowing, extended his hand and said solemnly, "May I have this dance?" And before I could protest, he swept me away, twirling me across the room so that my gauzy pink dress lifted and floated like the petals I had imagined, and as my sisters looked on and Ross inclined his head to tell me how beautiful I looked, I felt, for the first time in my life, like a princess.

CHAPTER *forty-six*

I'm not surprised when Odette announces the next morning that she's going back to Paris. "Watch out where you sit," she says to me, folding a pile of her neat little blouses and stacking them just so on the bed with a pat. She'll have everything organized before it goes into the suitcase, T-shirts color-coded, tiny pastel bras stacked like egg cartons, sandals tucked away in felt bags. As she has often pointed out, being a stewardess is great training for life.

"He loved you," I say.

She looks at me wryly, and we fall silent. "You can manage the rest," she says, glancing at the urn with his ashes on the shelf.

It's as if we had both acknowledged the bond between us, and agreed not to discuss it, and yet, I want her benediction.

"Tell me something," I say.

She laughs, her eyes suddenly merry. "I will tell you something,

Constance"—she pronounces it the French way—"sometimes you remind me of myself."

Well, I'm tempted to say, *we did share the same boyfriend.*

"Let's see, what wisdom can I pass on? Ah yes: Never tell the truth; no one wants to hear it."

"That's grim."

"All right, then, never be ashamed. *Le coeur a ses raisons, que la raison ne connaît pas.*"

"The heart has its reasons."

"Yes, and perhaps God watches over us."

"And makes lists of all the bad things we do."

"Isn't that funny? I used to believe that too."

"But now?"

"Now I think . . ." She clicks the suitcase shut. "Now I think life is complicated. Take Jim back," she says, not looking at me. "He is a good man."

"Yeah," I snigger, "I bet he's a way better lover now too." I can't help it, it just comes out.

She shakes her head. "Why do you Americans always have to spell everything out?"

"Wasn't that one of the things you liked about Ross?'

She smiles, as if at a fond memory. "Whatever he may have done, you must remember, he knew how to make a woman feel cherished."

"Is it that important?"

"I think you know the answer," Odette says, turning back to her packing.

This is only the second or third time I've been in her room—not that I've felt unwelcome, she was just always more private than the rest of us. There's none of Jim's stuff around; maybe she gave him his own drawer, or told him to move out. On the dresser a few photographs stand in silver frames: Odette and Ross on honeymoon in Venice; on safari in Kenya; Ross alone in front of his airplane; and, to my surprise, one of all of us, at Isabelle's graduation from Bennington, that I'm sure was taken by Daphne. As I'm standing there wondering why she picked that one—she wasn't even in the picture yet—she says, "That was his favorite; he always kept it with him." She hands it to me. "Here, take it."

"No," I say, "you don't have to—" though I've already reached for it.

"I want you to have it," she says with a sly smile.

"You already knew him, didn't you?" I blurt out.

"What does it matter? It's all in the past."

A dull rumbling reverberates in the distance as a gust swells the net curtains, causing them to billow and flutter back into place like veils. During the night, a cool front dispersed the last traces of the sirocco. Apparently these weather swings are common in August—something to do with conflicting winds, atmospheric masses rushing at each other.

"Storm," I say.

"Maybe," Odette says. "Will you drive me to the airport?"

"Sure."

"We should hurry if it's going to rain."

"It's okay, I don't mind."

"Good." She closes her suitcase and looks around the room, in a way that tells me she won't be back.

"What are we going to do about the house?" I ask.

"I expect we'll have to sell it."

"But he bought it for you," I say. "It's your home."

She smiles. "Home is not a place, you know. It's in here." She points to her heart, and there's something about that gesture that opens up a hole inside me.

"Please don't leave," I say.

She enfolds me, even though I'm twice as big as she is. "Sshhhh," she whispers. "Everything will be fine," and, as stupid as it sounds, I believe her.

CHAPTER *forty-seven*

"I can't believe she just *left,*" Jim says miserably.

"She didn't want to make a fuss." I pat him on the shoulder. "Look, it wouldn't have worked anyway. There's no way you could have moved to Paris; you don't even speak French."

"I could have learned!" he protests, but I can tell by his eyes that he knows I'm right. Jiri comes in, bleary-eyed, unshaven, and exuding the odoriferous animal magnetism that keeps getting him in trouble with actresses.

"Hey, kids," he says, thwacking Jim on the back.

"I thought you were going back to Prague," I say.

He yawns and scratches his head. "Any coffee?"

"I'll make it," Jim says resignedly.

"What's wrong with *him?*"

"Don't ask."

"Aha, heart troubles. Don't worry, my boy," Jiri says cheerfully. "There's plenty more fish in the sea!"

"I'm supposed to believe this guy is a poet?" Jim says.

A fresh blast of rain pelts the window, causing it to rattle ominously. Sheets of water obscure the view of the ruin across the street. With the window shut, the kitchen feels close and steamy.

"Shit weather," Jiri remarks. "We should all go back to bed."

"Where's Odette?" Isabelle asks groggily, entering the kitchen. She plops herself down in Jiri's lap, where he proceeds to clasp his furry mitts around her breasts. "Hi, honey," she coos.

Jim and I exchange sidelong glances. "She left," I say.

"Oh," Isabelle says, reaching for one of the *biscottes* Lucy buys under the conviction that they're a staple of the authentic French breakfast. No one's gone out for croissants because of the weather, and it didn't occur to me to stop for some on the way back from Canonica. "Gosh, these are horrible," she exclaims, putting it back down. "How come your hair is wet?"

"I drove her to the airport." The storm hit on the way back, after Orzo, unleashing such a torrential downpour that I had to stop on the side of the road.

"Just like Odette to jump ship and leave us with all the mess," Isabelle says peevishly. Her eyes wander to the greasy black smudge on the wall above the fireplace, its origin a mystery, though we think it might have something to do with the asbestos miners who used to board here. "This place is turning into a dump," she observes.

"Odette thinks we should sell it," I say.

"What do you mean?" Isabelle bleats. Even Jiri is aroused out of his postcoital bonhomie.

"You can't sell Ross's house!" he exclaims.

"We should have long ago," I say. "We can't afford it. It needs a new roof, for starters. Go up to the third floor if you don't believe me; the rain is pouring right in."

"Duh, what do you think got us out of bed?" Isabelle says with ill grace, intimating, I guess, that only a cold shower could have roused her from her erotic trance.

"And the stairs are falling down," I continue, "and Mr. Peretti has put in a complaint about the toilet; he says the pipe is running directly into his garden, which is total bullshit, but anyway. . . ."

"That's the first *I've* ever heard of that," Isabelle says.

"The mayor told Odette. Because the house is a historical landmark, we'd have to get a permit for renovations, and guess who's going to make sure it's never approved?"

"But the mayor loves us!"

"Right, the family of the man who brought organized crime to Borgolano."

"That's not fair!" my sister cries, so incensed that she jumps up from Jiri's lap. "What about Yolande?"

"She's been here longer," I say. "Plus, she owns half the village and she's paying to have the church restored. They can't afford to get rid of her."

"But the mayor was Dad's *friend!*"

"Some friend," Jim says.

"Golly, what's gotten into *you* all of a sudden?" Isabelle's hand flies to her mouth. "Oops, sorry. . . ."

"Don't mention it," Jim says. "Coffee?"

"I'll have some, thanks," Marge barks from the doorway, striding in and grabbing the last chair. "Crap weather; someone should complain to management."

"We need the rain," Isabelle says, just to be contrary.

Marge picks a piece of dry skin off her sole and examines it. "The hell we do. Last thing I heard, people don't come to the Med to get poured on. A bloody disgrace, is what it is."

"Where's Jane?" I ask.

"Sleeping in."

Jiri grins. "Wore her out, eh?"

"Fuck off, you old goat," Marge says amiably. "What's with the long faces? Did I interrupt another family conclave?"

"Constance wants to sell the house," Isabelle says accusingly.

"Great idea, place is a tip. Pick up a nice condo on the Costa Brava for the money; much nicer for the kids."

"Well it may be a tip to *you*, but *we* think it has character," Isabelle says.

Marge shrugs and stuffs a *biscotte* into her mouth. "Character! Bunch of yuppie artistes roughing it in digs your average Guatemalan peasant would consider too squalid for human habitation. Ugh, what is this, a diet biscuit?"

Jiri raises his fist in the air. "Comrade Marge! I was afraid you'd gone soft on us!"

"I shouldn't think you'd care either way," Marge retorts. "Don't you have some kind of dacha on the Polish border?"

"To which I heartily invite you, my lesbian friend! Sadly, the peasants next door are no longer collectivized: They were recently purchased by a German agribusiness concern."

"Is that so?" Marge says with interest.

"I'm sure she'd much rather go to Guatemala," Isabelle snaps.

"We're thinking of moving there, actually," Marge says.

"What, with Jane?"

"No, with Nicole Kidman. Jane is very excited about it—it's

about time she stopped painting soft-core porn for the bourgeoisie."

Jiri whistles the first bars of the *Internationale,* and, as we all roll our eyes, reaches for Isabelle and grabs her butt with both hands. "Look at this ass! Like bread dough!" he growls.

"Oh, honey, don't be such a pig."

"Thank God I'm a dyke," Marge says.

I can't entirely explain why Jim ends up in my room that night. Maybe it's all the pheromones flying around the house. Or maybe we're both just lonely. Odette has definitely taught him some new tricks; what I don't expect is his remark to the effect that I, too, seem to have picked up some technique.

"What do you mean by that?" I say, piqued.

"Well, you know, you used to be kind of brusque."

"It never seemed to bother you."

"It didn't," he says, suppressing a grin. "I guess I'm only noticing now, in comparison."

"I think people make a lot of unnecessary fuss about sex," I say huffily.

"Well, you know, it kind of seemed to me, when we were together, that it was the only thing you were interested in."

"Look," I say, "that's the way I am: businesslike and to the point."

"You don't have to get mad," Jim says. "I still liked you."

"Yeah, but you like me even better now that I got screwed by the neighbor, right?"

"Could I hold your hand?" Jim asks.

"Okay," I say, taken aback. I extend it across the mattress and he clasps it, our palms fitting moistly together. It seems a strangely intimate gesture.

"Is this what you did with Odette?" I ask.

"Look, there's some stuff we're not going to talk about, okay?"

"Okay," I say. I peer out the window at the black sky, listening for the moan of the sea. I want to pull my hand away—even as a child I never liked to hold hands—but I leave it in his, sensing that if I don't, I will have done something irrevocable, even as I'm beginning to realize that there's nothing, really, that you can't take back.

CHAPTER *forty-eight*

On the day of Ross's memorial, the sun rises high and bright, flooding the water's surface with the pellucid light that turns it the fake-looking turquoise featured so prominently on every post-card in Flore. Ross would have been pleased. He used to say, "I'm not a complicated guy," and I never knew what he meant until now. The fact is, most people are a lot less interesting than we make them out to be, though every now and then they will surprise you.

As Jim and I set up the folding table on the patio, spreading it with a cloth as per Lucy's instructions, Yolande waves to us from Philippe's bedroom window, which, judging by the tape measure in her hand, she is fitting for curtains. She bought the house shortly after we gave her the money, which makes you wonder about this Mr. Woland in Antwerp—though, as she made haste to point out, Philippe gave her a *very* good price, adding, "so sad, these divorce cases," with a little glance at me.

294

I have to say I find it pretty amusing to be cast in the role of the home-wrecker, even as I know perfectly well that Philippe's wife dumping him, and demanding half their assets, had very little to do with me; I was just the last in a long string of tawdry seductions. Jim and I have booked our flights. We're going to give Solomon Pierson Webb a try after all. Jim may grill a mean steak, but he's no Alain Ducasse, and I can't even finish *Madame Bovary*, let alone embark on a new career as an international woman of mystery. They must have worried we were getting cold feet though because Al Blacker, one of the managing directors, called us from New York to remind us how badly they wanted us and what a fun and *exciting* time we were going to have helping them build up their emerging-markets division. He kept repeating, "The sky's the limit!" which I'd forgotten is the way people talk on Wall Street. They are particularly interested in Latin American markets. I don't know much about them—it's more Jim's thing—but I did goofily point out that I know a woman who's an expert on Guatemala. I'd forgotten that you can't joke around with these guys: The next thing I knew, Al wanted me to fax him Marge's CV. When I mentioned it to Marge, she hooted, then she asked me how much money it would involve. I gave her a rough idea.

"You know," she pondered, "there's something to be said for blasting the system from within. . . ."

"Marge!" Jane exclaimed, horrified, "you can't possibly be thinking of becoming an investment banker!"

Marge settled herself more comfortably in her armchair. "Why not? When you think about it, it's just another crumbling bastion of the phallocracy—put in a few good women and watch 'em shake things up. . . . If these places were properly run, we'd have the third world on its feet in no time. I just read somewhere that if the top financial firms contributed a hundredth of a percent of their profits to a development fund, we could put running water in every village in Africa."

The funny thing is, I can totally see Marge on Wall Street.

We've never stayed on Santerre this late into the season. The Parisians and the Marseillais are already packing up, their laden Renaults snaking their way up the road like weary mastodons. There's not exactly an autumn chill in the air, but the heat has mellowed into a lambent glow that I can feel on my shoulders as I line up the champagne flutes on a tray. Beyond wanting his ashes scattered over the sea at dusk, Ross didn't go into a whole lot of detail as to the final disposal of his remains; in fact, he never actually used the word *memorial,* which has left us a bit stumped as to the form the ceremony should take, especially now that the mayor is coming after all. It was Lucy who suggested that we serve champagne. "He would have wanted something festive," she asserted, drawing the line at hors d'oeuvres, which she thought the mayor might have found undignified. Jim thought maybe we could have some music, but a survey of our collection yielded only a dusty Claude François tape ("Where did *that* come from?" Isabelle wondered) and *The Beach Boys Greatest Hits.*

We decide to skip the music.

"I wonder if the mayor will really show up," Lucy now frets as we wait for everyone to show up.

"He said he would," I say. "Yolande's coming too. . . . I keep meaning to ask, what are you going to do about the fishing hut?"

Lucy's face grows pink. "I sold it back to her."

I whistle. "Boy, she's really cleaning up, isn't she?"

She reddens some more. "I know you think I'm rich, but there's hardly anything left, really, and now, with the divorce . . . Oh, I might as well tell you: Yves and I want to get married. His family's from the Auvergne, you know, and you can still get fabulous stone houses there, completely untouched, for pennies." Lucy's eyes light up at this prospect, but she sounds a bit troubled as she adds, "It *is* uncanny, though: It's almost as if Yolande *knew* that she had me in a tight spot. . . . I actually sold the cabin back to her for less than I paid for it."

"You know what I can't figure out? Why, if she's so eager to buy up more properties, she sold it to you in the first place."

"Yes, I've thought the same. It doesn't make sense, does it?"

"Unless she arranged to have it blown up."

"Why would she do that?"

"I don't know, maybe there was something wrong with it—you said it needed a lot of work. Or maybe it was an insurance scam, or maybe she was trying to scare us. . . . Either way, she obviously ended up making a profit."

"I never did trust her," Lucy says.

"It's a bit late for that," I remark.

"I wish Jane and Marge would get back with the flowers," Lucy says. "It looks so bare. . . ."

Jiri comes out of the house, followed by the girls in full dress-up. He himself has shaved and put on a tie. Sneaking up behind Lucy, he swats her on the butt.

"Jiri! I wish you wouldn't do that!" Her eyes fall on Agnes, who, her eyes rimmed with blue and her mouth painted red, has the rather unsettling appearance of an Indian totem. "Goodness, darling, what have they done to you?"

"We curled her hair too!" Sophie crows. "Doesn't she look great?"

"She looks," Lucy says, searching for the right word, "amazing."

Agnes silently picks her nose.

Lucy sighs, "Oh, darling, I wish you wouldn't . . . ," but the girls have already run off. "She *has* lost a bit of weight, hasn't she?" she says to me.

"Definitely."

Isabelle comes tripping across the patio, unsteady in her high-heeled sandals. She's wearing a red dress with a slit up the thigh that, Lucy observes to me, doesn't look very funereal. A gust of perfume envelops us as she draws closer.

"What *is* that scent?" Lucy says, wrinkling her nose.

"Don't be such a snob, Lucy, it's French—I bought it on the airplane. Doesn't Agnes look fabulous? The girls dressed her up."

"*You* look fabulous," Jiri growls, bearing down on her and making as if to suck on her neck. Lucy rolls her eyes. "Look at those tits!"

"*Jiri!*"

"Forty years old and as firm as a schoolgirl!"

"Honey, don't be such a pervert. . . ."

"Tell me honestly," Lucy whispers, "what do you *really* think of his poetry?"

"It's kind of heavy-handed," I say.

"Remember that collection he wrote for Isabelle: *Goddess?*"

"Talk about soft-core porn for the bourgeoisie."

"I'm not so sure about the *soft*. . . ." Lucy giggles and then frowns as if an unpleasant thought had just struck her. "Oh dear, I hope Richard doesn't show up."

"Do you really think he would?"

"You never know; he might feel he ought to. Poor Richard, he so hated Daddy for not liking him. Do you know that he never even made a toast at our wedding?"

"Yeah, I remember. It was a crummy thing to do."

"Yes, it was, wasn't it, especially after the way he carried on when Isabelle got married, clasping Jiri to his breast and calling him son. He might at least have pretended. . . . I wonder sometimes if it would have changed anything," she muses, "if Ross had thought more of Richard."

"Do you really think it would have?"

She smiles. "No, not really. . . . Oh God, the mayor is going to be here any second and Jane and Marge still aren't back—I'll go see if the champagne is cold." Watching her hurry off, it strikes me that Ross wouldn't have thought much of Yves, either. In fact, of the present company, Jiri having gone off to find his camera, the person who comes closest to Ross's ideal of a guy's guy is Marge, just now coming down the path with a huge beribboned arrangement in her arms. We were all a bit surprised when she offered to drive into Flore for the flowers, but as Jane once observed to me, Marge is a conventional middle-class English girl at heart.

"Simplest thing they had in the shop," she says. "Had to pull half the ribbons out as it was—I'd hate to see what they do for weddings."

"Oh dear," says Lucy, who had initially planned on gathering a bouquet of wildflowers in the *maquis,* until it was pointed out to her that whatever decorative vegetation it once contained had long been fried to a crisp by the heat. "The lilies are quite pretty— maybe we could take it apart and the children could throw them in the water. . . ."

"Not on your life! D'you have any idea how much these cost!"

"Darling," Jane says soothingly, "she doesn't really mean it."

"Like hell she doesn't; if she'd had her way, we would've tossed a bunch of weeds in after him. Isabelle," she barks, "as long as you're just standing around in your underwear, why don't you make yourself useful and go find a vase?"

"Feast your eyes," Isabelle says saucily.

"A good spanking is what *you* need," says Marge, leering.

"You *wish.* . . ."

"Why," Jane sighs, "do the conversations in this house always have to degenerate into sexual innuendo?"

"I suppose you'd rather discuss the Great Authors," Marge says.

"You guys . . . ," Jim sighs. The chug of an approaching Renault makes us all turn our heads. "Well, blow me," Marge exclaims as the mayor and his deputy come into view, the deputy obscured by a gigantic wreath with a black sash across it. "Looks like we rated the works after all."

"I should hope so," Lucy says. "All those *pétanque* tournaments Daddy sponsored—they should erect one of those roadside mausoleums to him."

"With weeping angels and a cherry on top," Jane says.

"Sshhhhhhh!"

Now that he's got our attention, the mayor picks up his pace, hastening toward us with his arms extended. "My friends, I hope I am not late!"

"Not at all," I say. "We're still waiting for Yolande."

"A sad occasion," the mayor intones, his eyes sliding from the table with the champagne glasses to Isabelle, advancing precariously in her tarty outfit with Marge's bouquet in a vase clasped to her breasts. "Ah. Mademoiselle Wright, you look charming as always—allow me to help you!" He rushes forward, but Isabelle, laughing, has already plonked the flowers down on the table, where they look strangely festive—more, indeed, like a wedding bouquet.

"It's Madame Orlik, really, you know," she says with a coy glance at Jiri, whose rumored revolutionary past has always made the mayor a little nervous, though he looks quite relaxed now as he accepts a glass of champagne from Yves. With a little cough he adjusts his glasses on his nose, as if the better to take in the scenery, until he notices his deputy still standing there with the wreath.

"*Eh bien,* aren't you going to put it down?" he snaps. The deputy—whose name no one ever seems to remember—looks helplessly about until Jiri, taking pity on him, strides over and relieves him of his burden. He props it on the low wall against the fig tree so that we can all make out the gold inscription on the sash:

À un ami

"Very nice," Yolande murmurs, for she has finally made her appearance, robed and turbaned like a fakir, her wrists loaded down with gold bracelets, a pear-shaped amulet dangling between her breasts on a beaded leather thong. As if repressing a strong emotion, she dabs at her eyes, prompting Isabelle to elbow me and mutter under her breath, "Cow!"

"Is she going to perform a rain dance?" Jane whispers.

"It feels so final," Yolande says in a choked voice.

"It's been a year, actually," Isabelle says.

The garden gate crashes open and the girls come racing out, the state of their dresses suggesting that they've spent the past half hour rolling in the dirt. "Mommy!" Sophie whines, tugging at her skirt. "Can *we* throw the ashes, *please?*"

Isabelle turns to me. "I hadn't even thought about it—I always thought Odette would do it. . . ."

"*Please,* Mommy!"

I shrug. "I don't see why not."

"A charming idea," the mayor says uncertainly. He falls silent and we all look expectantly at each other. "Well," I say, "we might as well get started," which is when I remember that the ashes are still on the shelf in Odette's room. "I'll get them!" Sophie shouts. Before anyone can stop her, she's galloped up the stairs, charging back down with the box clutched tight in her hands, so excited that she forgets about the step in front of the house, which she trips on. We let out a collective gasp, but the box has already flown into the air and opened, releasing a cloud of grayish powder that rises and then, slowly, drifts to the ground.

"Oh," Lucy says.

"Shit," Marge says.

Yolande crosses herself.

Sophie just stands there, her mouth open.

CHAPTER *forty-nine*

Yolande bought the house. I thought there was a certain poetic justice to this, since she always felt it was rightly hers, but Isabelle was outraged. It turned out, however, that the suddenly miraculously valid deed was in Odette's name, and she needed the money. By now Yolande must own half the village. She's moved into the countess's mansion and rents out the rest of her empire to assorted Belgians and Germans. Our house, which has a new kitchen and two bathrooms, is particularly popular with big families. All this I hear from Jojo, who writes devotedly. He would love to visit New York and, to this end, has offered to sell me his share of the *hameau*, Lucy having lost interest now that she's renovating Yves's ancestral home in the Auvergne. The Auvergne, she reports enthusiastically, has just as many abandoned hilltop villages as Santerre, and the *charcuterie* is far superior.

If you were thinking that Jim and I were going to get married, think again, though I probably shouldn't have burst out laughing when he proposed. As wounded as he was, he had to admit in the end that it was a pretty dumb idea, and that he was only doing it for sentimental reasons. In his heart of hearts it's Odette he wants to marry, but that's not going to happen, either. He went to see her in Paris, only to find her cold and distant, though I suspect what he came up against was just French formality. He's dating a woman at work now—Karen Rothbaum, in Mergers and Acquisitions— and while I don't think she'd mind merging with him eventually, she looks decidedly askance at what she's described to Jim as our "weird relationship." Poor Jim, he wants to do the right thing, but deep down, he's as much of a reprobate as I am.

Isabelle and Jiri went back to Prague, where Jiri resumed his philandering, though more discreetly. Isabelle has adopted the philosophical stance that as long as he stays out of the tabloids, she can live with it. She's come to agree with his mother: In the end he will get bored. He's already showing signs of flagging, which she attributes to his advancing age. Now that Prague is over-run with Americans, she and Maria are thinking of opening an art gallery or a boutique. She laments that it's getting as expensive as Paris, and someone's going to have to pay for the girls' education. They're going to spend the whole summer this year at Krasna Hora, and Jim and I are both invited. Jim eagerly accepted, but I persuaded him that going off on vacation with me just on the off chance that my stepmother might turn up was exactly the kind of thing Karen was bound to misinterpret.

I just saw Odette in Paris. We had lunch at Lipp, right around the corner from the new apartment she bought with the proceeds from the house. The way she smiled when I asked if she got a decent price leads me to believe that she drove Yolande a hard bargain. I think there might be a new man in her life, but she kept mum on that, too, except to say mysteriously that she's been spending a lot of time in Nice. "It's much more civilized," she said, tucking a strand of hair back under her headband. There truly is something ageless about her, and it's not all surgery. With a malicious twinkle in her eye, she told me she ran into Philippe on the subway. He looked right though her but she's sure he recognized her. There was a young woman with him. "But then, of course," she added, "there will always be."

Afterward we went shopping on the Rue de Buci. I've gotten quite chic under her guidance; women at work are always asking me where I buy my clothes. As Odette explained to me, it's the little things that count, like the cut of a skirt, or a certain way of knotting a scarf. Why do I bother? I've just been promoted to vice president. The higher you get on Wall Street, the more important it is how you look, and I plan to go high. The money is only secondary, though that's nice too. It's the power that I like. I'm still senior to Jim, which he's always teasing me about. The truth is, his heart's never been in it, and I fully expect him to drop out one of these days and open a restaurant, which is what he really wants to do.

With seed money bullied out of the World Bank, Marge started a micro-lending fund for rural women in Quetzaltepec, Guatemala. They have a 98 percent repayment rate so far, which Marge attributes to no men being involved and, according to the annual report I just received, have financed such diverse projects as a tortilla factory, a dairy, and a herd of goats. All right, I sent a donation. Jane teaches drawing to girls in the attached school— definitely a case of art for art's sake, as it's hard to imagine what Guatemalan peasants are going to do with a mastery of chiaroscuro technique. She's working on a series of paintings for an exhibit in New York next fall that she says are a total departure from her former style. Whatever money it makes will go into the fund. Now that she's no longer a bourgeois parasite, Marge has officially proposed marriage to her, though they're not going to have the reception in Quetzaltepec as they think the locals might not yet be ready for alternative lifestyles. They'll have it at Daphne's place in Surrey instead. Jane has asked me and Lucy and Isabelle to be bridesmaids. The theme is going to be fair trade, apparently the latest thing in hippie lesbian weddings, and we all get to wear matching saris.

Richard isn't invited but he's too busy anyway. Shortly after they got married, he and Albertine engineered a *coup* at the Marmite, unseating Marcelle and Fabrice and taking over the management. Lucy, who went over to sort out some custody issues, says that both Richard and the food are much improved. It seems he's come into his own as a small town *hotelier*. Since taking the helm, he has overseen the renovation of the annex, put a dishwasher in the kitchen, and even convinced old Mr. Simonetti to start fishing again, the effects of which are much appreciated by patrons of the restaurant. Lucy chalks it all down to his finally feeling appreciated. They've become friends again, which is probably all they should have been in the first place, and Lucy is going to send Agnes for the summer.

Agnes is making improvements at her new school. Nothing earth-shattering, but she's more communicative and less surly, which I was able to see for myself when they came to visit over Christmas. I took her to FAO Schwarz. Being the weird kid that she is, she wasn't impressed at all by the holiday displays, but Yves thought they were fantastic. Lucy and Yves are getting married, too, next fall, in the early-Romanesque chapel in his family's village, where Lucy has just made an offer on a *fabulous* four-hundred-year-old house that just needs the tiniest bit of work. She's three months pregnant; if you look closely, you can just make out a little bulge. We went shopping at Baby Gap because London is sooooooo expensive, and she bought twenty color-coordinated outfits in ascending sizes. Lucy will always be Lucy. Watching her select the tiny pajama-sleepers, I couldn't help but feel bad for Agnes. The new baby will probably be perfect. Will Lucy love it more? As we made our way down Fifth Avenue toward the tree at Rockefeller Center, Lucy and Yves got ahead of us in the throng, and I found myself alone with her. I asked. "Are you excited about the new baby?"

She shrugged and stared at the sidewalk, and I felt a little tug as she slipped her hand in mine. I gripped it tight.

UP CLOSE and PERSONAL
with the Author

WHY DID YOU CHOOSE TO WRITE A NOVEL ABOUT A FAMILY THAT COMPRISES THREE DIFFERENT NATIONALITIES—AMERICAN, ENGLISH, AND FRENCH?

I grew up all over Europe and had many friends who came from mixed marriages. It's a territory well-mined by Henry James and, more recently, Diane Johnson, and with good reason. Americans and Europeans have always been fascinated with each other, even as they've disagreed on just about everything. I wanted to explore these themes within the context of one family.

ALL FOUR SISTERS SPENT MOST OF THEIR FORMATIVE YEARS IN NEW YORK CITY, YET THREE OF THEM CHOSE AS ADULTS TO LIVE OUTSIDE THE U.S. WHAT DO YOU THINK DREW THEM TO THE EXPATRIATE LIFE?

America seems to be the only country on earth that has such a powerful romance with expatriation, beginning with the junior year abroad. Try to find a French equivalent to Hemingway or Fitzgerald! There is something within our culture that fuels a fantasy of exile, an idea that we have to leave to be free. None of the European characters in my novel have really left home: Lucy and Jane have both returned to the country of their birth; and Odette, though she has traveled all over the world, remains immutably French. Isabelle is the true expatriate: She can never go home because she is rootless, and she has no desire to go home because she knows that her fantasy of herself as a free-spirited bohemian can only survive in a void.

WHY DID YOU SET THE STORY ON AN ISLAND?

Islands are places of metamorphosis and enchantment, from Ogygia and Circe's island in *The Odyssey* to Ibiza and Capri. They evoke a loosening of bonds, erotic possibility, and of course, death. I wanted to place my characters in a setting where they would be unmoored and, to a degree, disoriented, and where they would be forced to act on instinct rather than convention.

WHICH SISTER IN *GOING TOPLESS* DO YOU IDENTIFY WITH THE MOST?

I don't generally identify with my characters (some of them I find quite horrifying at times!) but, as an obsessive cook, I do feel a certain kinship to Lucy. While I certainly don't share her obsession with thinness—in fact, the mere thought of dieting makes me cringe—I have been known to spend an entire afternoon simmering fish heads for bouillabaisse, and I would *never* eat asparagus out of season.

WHAT'S SO SPECIAL ABOUT THE BOND BETWEEN SISTERS? AND IS THE BOND BETWEEN BIOLOGICAL SISTERS NECESSARILY STRONGER THAN THAT OF STEPSISTERS?

This is one of the things I was thinking about when I wrote the novel. The definition of family has undergone so many transformations in the past fifty years that the idea of a biological bond seems almost quaint—and yet, when it comes to sex, money, and death, those atavistic blood ties seem to come back to haunt us. By setting the story in the Mediterranean, I wanted to evoke these primordial instincts, which the Santerrans still abide by, and confront them with the sisters' more modern sensibilities.

YOUR VIVID DESCRIPTIONS AND THE ALMOST PALPABLE ATMOSPHERE YOU CREATE MAKE ME WONDER IF SANTERRE IS BASED ON A REAL ISLAND. IS IT?'

I've spent time on many islands, from Mallorca to Corsica to D'Jerba in Tunisia, and Santerre is a composite of those places. I wanted to capture that elusive Mediterranean flavor—the food, the smells, the sound of the sea, the torpor that sets in at midday, and also the sense of a very old civilization.

WHAT LESSONS OF ROMANTIC ATTRACTION CAN WE DRAW FROM LUCY'S ENDING UP WITH YVES AND ISABELLE'S STAYING WITH JIRI?

That's an interesting question. I hadn't originally planned on Lucy ending up with Yves, and yet as the characters developed, it began to make perfect sense. Everyone thinks that Lucy wants to be worshiped, but in fact she just wants to be liked, and Yves is the one who figures that out. Lucy and Richard never liked each other, a problem I think exists in many marriages. Isabelle and Jiri, on the other hand, are a prime example of what we've come to think of as *chemistry*, but it's those restless pheromones that are constantly getting them in trouble. I think that what keeps them together in the end, besides habit, is the fact that they understand each other—rather too well, perhaps.

WHY DOES CONSTANCE FORSAKE JIM FOR PHILIPPE? ARE FRENCH MEN REALLY BETTER LOVERS THAN AMERICAN MEN?

Constance finds in Philippe the mystery that she doesn't see in Jim. I do think that mystery is a component of attraction, though it doesn't necessarily make for lasting relationships. . . . What's interesting to me is that, while it's assumed that all women are looking for a fairy-tale romance, we all in fact have startlingly different scenarios in our head. To a large degree, love is theater, and I do think that French men understand this better than Americans.

IS THE TITLE *GOING TOPLESS* A METAPHOR FOR A KIND OF FREEDOM PEOPLE HOPE TO ATTAIN DURING THEIR SUMMER VACATIONS?

I do find it fascinating how Europeans and Americans have such different attitudes toward breasts! Odette thinks nothing of sunbathing topless, but to Isabelle and Lucy, the gesture is fraught with implications. I'm not sure that freedom is one of them, though it's undoubtedly what Isabelle would like to believe. Isabelle, though she prides herself on her European sensibilities, bares her breasts in an act of very American exhibitionism. Lucy, on the other hand, feels painfully obligated to conform to local customs.

HAVE *YOU* EVER GONE TOPLESS ON A BEACH?

Yes, but I stopped after childbirth!

Then don't miss these other great books from Downtown Press!

Scottish Girls About Town
Jenny Colgan, Isla Dewar, Muriel Gray, et al.

Calling Romeo
Alexandra Potter

Game Over
Adele Parks

Pink Slip Party
Cara Lockwood

Shout Down the Moon
Lisa Tucker

Maneater
Gigi Levangie Grazer

Clearing the Aisle
Karen Schwartz

Liner Notes
Emily Franklin

My Lurid Past
Lauren Henderson

Dress You Up in My Love
Diane Stingley

He's Got to Go
Sheila O'Flanagan

Irish Girls About Town
Maeve Binchy, Marian Keyes, Cathy Kelly, et al.

The Man I Should Have Married
Pamela Redmond Satran

Getting Over Jack Wagner
Elise Juska

The Song Reader
Lisa Tucker

The Heat Seekers
Zane

I Do (But I Don't)
Cara Lockwood

Why Girls Are Weird
Pamela Ribon

Larger Than Life
Adele Parks

Eliot's Banana
Heather Swain

How to Pee Standing Up
Anna Skinner

Look for them wherever books are sold or visit us online at www.downtownpress.com.

dоWn
tОwn
press

Great storytelling just got a new address.

PUBLISHED BY POCKET BOOKS

10403